Sue Watson was a journalist on women's magazines and national newspapers before having a career in TV working as a producer with the BBC. She has published six novels, her most well-known being *Love, Lies and Lemon Cake*. Originally from Manchester, Sue now lives in the Midlands and writes full time.

For more information visit the author's website at www.suewatsonbooks.com or follow her on Twitter @suewatsonwriter

D1165992

DISCARDED
Bruce County Public Library
1243 Mackenzie Rd.
Port Elgin ON N0H 2C6

Also by Sue Watson

Fat Girls and Fairy Cakes
Love, Lies and Lemon Cake
Younger, Thinner, Blonder
Snow Angels, Secrets and Christmas Cake
Summer Flings and Dancing Dreams
Bella's Christmas Bake-off

We'll Always Have Paris

Sue Watson

sphere

SPHERE

First published in Great Britain in 2017 by Sphere
as a paperback original

3 5 7 9 10 8 6 4 2

Copyright © Sue Watson 2017

The moral right of the author has been asserted.

*All characters and events in this publication, other than those
clearly in the public domain, are fictitious and any resemblance
to real persons, living or dead, is purely coincidental.*

All rights reserved.
No part of this publication may be reproduced, stored in a
retrieval system, or transmitted, in any form or by any means, without
the prior permission in writing of the publisher, nor be otherwise circulated
in any form of binding or cover other than that in which it is published
and without a similar condition including this condition being
imposed on the subsequent purchaser.

A CIP catalogue record for this book
is available from the British Library.

ISBN 978-0-7515-6457-0

Typeset in Bembo by M Rules
Printed and bound in Great Britain by
Clays Ltd, St Ives plc

Papers used by Sphere are from well-managed forests
and other responsible sources.

MIX
Paper from
responsible sources
FSC   FSC® C104740
www.fsc.org

Sphere
An imprint of
Little, Brown Book Group
Carmelite House
50 Victoria Embankment
London EC4Y 0DZ

An Hachette UK Company
www.hachette.co.uk

www.littlebrown.co.uk

For Nick, who showed me Paris.

Acknowledgements

This book has been a joy to write, and I wasn't alone on this journey, sharing it with a whole team of wonderful people.

Thanks to everyone at Sphere, especially Lucy Malagoni, who started it all, bringing inspiration, enthusiasm, amazing insight and a strong guiding hand throughout. And to Emily Ruston a big thank you for her editorial wisdom, humour and patience. Huge thanks also to my wonderful agent, Hannah Ferguson, who believed in me and held my hand along the way.

Thanks to my lovely friends, fellow writers and bloggers online and in the flesh, who support me daily, make me laugh and give me cake (virtual or real) whenever I need it – which is quite a lot.

Big kisses to Nick and Eve Watson, who often take second place to my characters when I'm writing a book, thank you both for understanding. And thanks to my mum, Patricia Engert, for making me believe anything is possible.

Prologue

All he wants is pineapple yoghurt. It might be his dying wish and I can't find a pot anywhere. It's the least I can do for my husband, now lying in bed at home with nothing left of his life, just a tube in his arm and a vague desire for pineapple in fermented milk.

I've trawled all local supermarkets and convenience stores and am now screeching into a parking space at a Tesco too far away. I stop for three seconds, calm myself and check my watch. I've been gone fifty-three minutes. I miss him already.

Almost falling out of the car I run through the car park, winding round shopping trolleys and kids and harassed parents, my hair unbrushed, my face without make-up, but it doesn't matter. In the great scheme of things lipstick is nothing. Once through the doors, I land somewhere near the chilled cabinets. It's strange being here on a Friday night when everyone is buying burgers and beer for weekend barbecues and family get-togethers.

I haven't been anywhere or done anything for weeks, just moved between the window and the bed in the sitting room around which my life has revolved, watching and waiting, torn between needing to leave and needing to stay. For two days now Mike's lain still, emerging only now and then from a deep drug-induced sleep to have a water-soaked sponge pressed against his lips, his forehead. I stopped the visitors a week ago, trooping to his bed in a convoy of sympathy, long faces filled with posed pity. 'It's like having an audience with the queen,' I said to him when the last of the gawkers had gone. I was trying to make him laugh, my default position in times of upset, but he'd gazed ahead, beyond laughter, beyond me – his shiny scalp ravaged by chemo, charcoal grey etched under faded eyes.

Earlier today, when his eyelids flickered open for the first time in two days, I had leapt at the chance to make him happy, to make him smile one more time and asked if there was anything he wanted. When he whispered, 'Pineapple yoghurt,' I dropped everything. Anna took my place by the bed and I ran as fast as I could, away from

2

the dreadfulness, knowing as soon as I shut the front door I would feel the need to go back.

It had all happened so quickly after the diagnosis. 'I think we're looking at weeks rather than months,' the doctor had said.

I'd stared at his glasses sitting on the bridge of his nose, unable to turn and look at Mike; I didn't want to see his reaction, that would make it too real. 'But what about treatment?' I said. 'You can't just say that ... surely there's something we can ...'

The doctor shifted uneasily in his seat and Mike's hand covered mine.

'It's too far gone,' he said gently. 'You heard what the doctor said.'

On the way home we talked and by the time we pulled up outside we'd convinced each other things weren't as bad as we'd thought.

'We'll sell the business, remortgage the house and get you treatment in America,' I was still saying stupidly, refusing to accept what was happening.

'No. Let's spend that money on us, take some time off, or pass the business down to the girls and travel. It's not like we haven't thought about it ... we'll just do it sooner,' he'd said. I'd been swept along by Mike's enthusiasm, his desperate need to live – okay, so the doctor had given him only six weeks, but what did he know?

The following day I discovered Mike in the bathroom coughing up blood and I knew it was too late.

The girls sobbed as we told them the news, the tableau of him sitting on the sofa, his arms round both of them, reassuring, comforting, will stay with me for ever.

Six weeks later he's still here and I've tried to make every moment special. Even now, with this pot of bloody yoghurt, I'm trying to show him how much I love him. Stupid really, but I want him to take my love with him wherever he's going, like a packed lunch of all his favourite things. I want to send him off feeling loved. That's all any of us want in the end, isn't it? I try and keep up a brave front for him and the girls, but I can barely comprehend what's happening. After forty-six years, Mike, the man who held me in the night, built garden walls, put the bins out and slayed life's dragons, is now frail and scared. Now he wants me to hold *his* hand and tell him it's all going to be okay. Each day I tell him I love him, and I do – but it makes me incredibly sad, because we both know my husband hasn't been the love of my life.

It occurs to me while running blindly round this alien Tesco, looking through the chilled cabinets, that it may be a ruse. Perhaps Mike knows his time is imminent and he can't bear to watch my pain so he's sent me on an impossible quest? Perhaps he knows how futile the pursuit of pineapple yoghurt will be and in a final and typical act of selflessness he's planned it all so he can slip off his mortal coil without me being there?

This puts me in a further state of panic and seeing a young shelf stacker I demand to know the fate of the yoghurts. 'Do they even *make* pineapple ones any more?' I ask the bemused young man. He shrugs. He doesn't care because pineapple yoghurt isn't something one gives any consideration to until it becomes perhaps the last wish of a dying man. So I continue on alone, rifling frantically through the strange-sounding names – Nestlé, Yoplait and Müller Light – hoping that one, just one, might contain the Holy Grail.

Mike and I will laugh about this one day, I think, instantly realising that we won't.

I move on, restraining myself from pushing other shoppers out of the way and emptying the shelves with one sweeping arm movement. It's now eleven minutes past seven on a Friday evening, but I don't care – time and place have lost all meaning. We are existing in a state of limbo – waiting for the end, the agony of loss, tinged with the guilt of relief when it's finally over – he is finally over.

'I couldn't get the pineapple, they had mandarin … with chocolate chips … can you believe?' I start, as I open the front door and run into the living room holding my breath that he's still here.

'Ssshh, Dad's asleep,' Anna hisses, whipping her head round accusingly. I feel stupid and selfish and thoughtless – like my announcement about mandarin yoghurt might just be the final blow that convinces him to let go.

I immediately shed the panic and Friday night bustle and sink into the churchlike atmosphere, silently pulling up a chair to Mike's bed. I'm now sitting next to Isobel, my younger daughter, who looks at me through redrimmed eyes; the crease in her smile causes tears to run down her cheeks and I gently stroke her arm. Isobel is like me – during difficult times she reaches for others to lean on, and Mike has always been that person for me. Anna, my eldest, is just like him, and in the bleakest of times she finds comfort in 'managing' situations and people, channelling her distress into tidying up and organising, for which I have always been deeply grateful. We all need an Anna and a Mike in our lives.

I reach out and touch Mike's hand, continuing to stroke Isobel's arm with my other, and looking at Anna for signs of stress, stretching myself and my love as far and wide as I can.

'You okay, Mum?' Isobel mumbles.

I nod, trying to hide the catch in my breath, and she looks at me questioningly, like I have all the answers. I'm reminded of a rainy day, the squeal of tyres and our dog Willow dying by the side of the road, the rain beating down as I cradle her and a sobbing, five-year-old Isobel. I am rocking them both, my hair plastered to my face, the tears and the rain washing together, I'm trying to hide my despair: 'It's okay, Willow's in heaven now, she's playing ball.'

'But she doesn't want to stay ... she's scared without me, she wants to come home. Bring her back, Mummy.' The lisping baby voice, the trembling chin.

'I'm sorry, darling, I can't do that,' I say through my tears, the blood now mixing with rainwater and running away together along the gutter.

Now, as her father's life ebbs away, Isobel is looking at me in the same way – but I still can't take her pain away.

We continue to sit in silence round the bed while Mike sleeps; he stirs occasionally and groans when the pain pushes on through the morphine. The cancer came quickly, a small lump in February, a routine visit to the doctor, followed by an inconvenient trip to the hospital, then tests. Each appointment more serious, more scary, until results day. Hard to imagine now, but I recall feeling slightly disgruntled that the hospital appointment for Mike's test results was on a Friday, the day before a big wedding, and a busy time for our small florists.

'Can you change the appointment?' I'd sighed, stressed with the workload before us.

'No,' he said. 'I could do with you there, Rosie.' I

looked up from the carnation buttonholes and saw his face and in that instant everything changed for me. If Mike was worried, I was worried.

I couldn't let the girls see my fear and kept telling myself and everyone else that it was 'probably nothing'. Yet somehow I knew.

When it finally happened and his life ended, I felt like mine had too.

Chapter One

A year after Mike's death

Since losing Mike, life's been strange for me. He'd been so unreachable in those last few weeks I'd almost wanted him to go. I longed for his release from the pain and the limbo he and the rest of the family existed in. At sixty-four, Mike was a year older than me, and though neither of us were spring chickens, we had our plans. Before the diagnosis I'd finally convinced Mike to retire and together we were going to tick a few things off our to-do list. This wasn't an easy ask for my practical, dependable hubby, but when I thought we still had a life ahead of us I had researched the possibility of a holiday in New Zealand. My idea was to visit the Aoraki Mackenzie International Dark Sky Reserve, because there was nothing he loved more than stargazing. It was ironic that Mike, a factory worker who'd never left his hometown, enjoyed gazing at the stars millions of miles away. But even when looking up into that vast velvet night, his feet stayed firmly on the ground. As I marvelled at the 'diamonds in the sky', he'd say, 'Rosie, that's not diamonds, love, it's distant nuclear fusion.'

Neither of us were religious. I'd had it thrust down my throat from an early age and my atheism was rebellion against everything my mother had held dear. Mike had lost his father in a road accident when he was just nine and found it hard to believe in God, but he seemed to find solace in the stars – he said they gave meaning to his life. The ability to see something that existed millions of years ago provided a surreal concept of time and the past, and put life into perspective for him. He said he found it comforting to think life goes on, that we are all just part of the cycle, and it helped him come some way to dealing with the loss of his father.

Becoming a dad was also a revelation for him, discovering the joy of children and family life. When the children were tiny some of our happiest times were when we'd all head off in the car to nearby fields on summer nights and spot constellations, meteor showers or misty clusters of 'exciting' young stars. 'They're hundreds of light years away,' he'd say, adding that they were young at 'only' a hundred million years or so, which always made the girls giggle.

The stars retained their significance in our family and when Mike had known his time was short he said, 'I'm not leaving. Look up into the sky and I'll be there, swinging through the Plough.'

The girls were comforted by this, a perfectly rational concept for two women who had both been able to say aurora borealis by the time they were three years old.

In the few months after he died, living in my starless universe without him, I felt lost, like my future had been taken away. I lived in the past, wandering around directionless, waiting for him to come home. I would listen for the key in the door, his voice in the hall, the sound of the kettle going on, then I'd remember that it was just me and thick, thick silence.

Recently, the old me has reappeared, a forgotten figure waving from a distant shore, a shimmering sea between us. She's been gone a while, but yesterday I breathed her scent on a bunch of freesias, sweet with spring promise. I feel a frisson of hope glimpsing sunshine in muddy puddles, stars glowing in a black sky, her voice a rustle of leaves whispering to me like a ghost. Life is slowly thawing, and I'm reassured by the way my heart lifts again at a faint glimmering on the horizon . . . I don't know what it is, but I'm finally feeling warm again.

'Mum, you've put make-up on,' says Anna with a smile when we meet for coffee. I'm sitting in her sunny kitchen, it's Saturday morning and the house is filled with the noise of arguments and hairdryers upstairs. Anna has two girls and I'm constantly surprised that despite laptops and iPhones the arguments about lipstick and boys still dominate as they did when my girls were young. We all think we're the start of something new and that our generation has all the answers, but we're just a mash-up of every other generation. Even my sixties' youth of miniskirts and free love wasn't as liberated as we're now led to believe; we were still conflicted and shaped by the morals and values of our parents. We were a reaction to their repression, I think, as Anna pours boiling water into a cafetière of ground coffee.

'If you put boiling water in, it kills the taste,' I say absently, now immersed in the sixties and that wonderful summer.

'So would you like to come over later? James is cooking,' Anna asks, dragging me back into the twenty-first century.

'Will the girls be here?' I take a proffered cup.

'No, they're with their dad tonight.'

'In that case I won't. Thank you, darling, but I doubt James would appreciate three at the table.' I smile.

'Oh, he'd be happy to have you around, you make him laugh.'

'Mmm, well I doubt it's laughter he's planning on tonight, my love. No, I'm going to phone Corrine – I haven't seen or spoken to her for weeks.'

'You two were so close once, you need to go out with her again, it will be good for you ... Mind you, she's a bit wild. Didn't you say she ended up in bed with someone within ten minutes of meeting him?'

I laugh. 'Corrine certainly gives a new meaning to the art of "speed dating".' I love my friend, but she can sometimes be a bit full on. I'm not sure I'll get to speak to her on the phone tonight as she's got a new man. Everyone's busy with something or someone.

'Well, we don't want you "doing a Corrine".'

'That's never going to happen, love, I'm not the type. I'm not interested in meeting new men, not at my time in life. Besides, I'd never meet another one like your dad.'

Anna smiles wistfully. 'I miss him so much, Mum.'

'I know, love.'

'He was just always there, wasn't he? Last night a fuse went in one of the plugs as I turned a lamp off and my first thought was, "I must get Dad to look at that."'

'Yes, I'm the same. I changed a tyre on the car the other day. I wouldn't ever have considered doing that when Dad was here.'

'Wow, I wouldn't know where to start, well done!'

'Ah yes, but who knows, it could fall off at any time,' I laugh.

'Mum, you shouldn't be struggling with tyres at your age. James would have done that for you.'

'I'm perfectly capable. And it's actually quite nice to look at the tyre on the car and think, "I did that." It's time I became more independent— And what do you mean "at your age"?' I said, just realising the implication of what she'd said. 'If Mick Jagger's still tearing up stadiums at seventy-two I can change a tyre at sixty-four.'

She laughs. 'And pout?'

'Yes, I can pout,' I say, pursing my lips.

'No, I mean like Mick Jagger,' she laughs.

I pout even more now and she reaches out across the table, touches my arm. 'You are funny. It's good to see you smiling again.'

'I think you'll find that was more of a trout pout than a smile.'

We laugh, then I say, 'Yes, after my tyre success I'm feeling rather confident – I don't need a man to do stuff. I was thinking, I might decorate ... some fresh wallpaper and a lick of paint, you know?'

She nods. 'Okay, but don't take on too much, it looks fine.'

'I just fancy making it a bit more modern, more me.'

Decorating is something Mike always did and though the house is looking a bit shabby, I put off doing any decorating after he died. I know it's silly, but I didn't want to paint him out of our lives, cover the past up with new wallpaper, but as I gazed at the stars through the back bedroom window last night I realised I must. I need to respect the past, but embrace the future. 'Yes, I'm feeling very positive, I'm going to do a spring clean,' I say. Then I take a breath. 'I thought I might sort through the wardrobe and give some of your dad's clothes to charity. Some of his shirts are still in good nick. I'm sure he'd like to know they were being worn again, what do you think?'

Anna is silent as she pours herself a strong, dark coffee and holds the steaming mug with both hands in a comforting gesture. 'I suppose so,' she says eventually. 'I mean, we can't hang onto his stuff for ever.' She says this doubtfully, taking a cautious sip.

I nod and take a drink. Neither of us want to say any more, but both of us know it's another closed chapter in our story. It's about more than suits and shirts and ties, it's a step further down the line, away from Mike, and it won't be easy letting go of the past. The feel of his shirts, the memories in each tie, the weddings, the parties, the funerals when he wore his best suit … Our lives are stitched into the fabric, holding everything together. But

I must be strong and try to move forward if I want to make the best of what's left for me.

Grief isn't a linear journey, it's not a wound that heals, feeling better each day until one day you wake up and it's gone away; the process is jagged and unpredictable, two steps forward, three back.

Just thinking of his suits waiting in the wardrobe takes me back to his grey wedding suit from Moss Bros. Our wedding day, his happiness, my relief and my mother's anger. As if things weren't difficult enough given the circumstances, she'd come shuffling over in her new shoes to inform me that, 'Mike's mother is wearing the same bloody hat as me!'

I don't know what she expected me to do: run into the registry office and wrestle it from the poor woman's head?

'The cheek of it,' she'd spat. That was my mother, she ruled the bloody world. Dad just winked at me, took my arm and we slowly walked in. I thanked my lucky stars for sweet escape as I was delivered to Mike, waiting calmly for me with a big smile.

I think about the look in his eyes during the ceremony and later the gentle way he held me. I felt like a precious jewel; someone finally loved me enough to treasure me. Mike was a thoughtful, reliable, loving husband and he was always there for me, which is why it's such a shock he isn't any more. Thinking about our wedding and all the hopes and dreams we had, I wonder now if I could have loved him more.

Some days I still wake up and feel the loss as I did the day he died, like a huge weight on my chest, pinning me down. But those days are ebbing now, a new tide is slowly coming in and now most days I wake, see the sun and think, Okay, I can do this. I can take on the world ... or more realistically clean the windows or return one of Corrine's many phone calls – things I did before without even thinking.

Tonight Anna has called round after work with yet another toy for Lily, my lovely new dog.

'Katie saw this in the supermarket and said to bring it for her,' she says, handing me a pink ball.

I thank her and give it to Lily who grabs it gratefully and stows it away under her floral bed.

Anna has also brought with her a takeaway and a bottle of wine and we call Isobel to see if she wants to join us. She says she can't as she's helping Richard with some DIY project. His latest obsession is their loft conversion, but you'd think it was a penthouse apartment with all the fuss he's making.

I tell Isobel we'll miss her but to have a lovely evening in the roof. She giggles and we say goodnight.

'Richard needs someone to hold his ladder,' I tell Anna as I put down the phone. I'm trying to sound impartial, Richard is lovely but he can be such a bore when it comes to DIY.

'Oh, not that sodding loft conversion? I'd pull the bloody ladder from under him,' Anna laughs.

'Well, they've been married ten years and she's been through all his DIY "projects" ... give her time.' I wink. 'The joy of holding a man's ladder can only last so long.'

'Well, I'm never going to hold another man's ladder again. Apart from James, they're all pigs,' she announces, sounding like my mother while lining up foil cartons on the kitchen worktops and uncorking the bottle of chilled white.

'Some of them are okay.' I breathe in the aromatic hit of chicken bhuna, the air spicy with curry and anticipation. I haven't felt this for a long time and it feels good. While Anna enjoys huge forkfuls of curry and rice, I take small bites, savouring the tingly flavour and my daughter's warming presence. 'So how's the lovely James?' I say, trying to be interested without seeming to pry.

After fourteen years of marriage and two children Anna's husband Paul walked out on her for someone much younger. It's been a difficult time for her and the kids but after three years they are now settling into a different routine and she's recently started seeing James, a local lad she met when he came to do some building work on our florist shop. They've been together now for about six months and I'm happy for her.

'He's good, thanks. I really like him, Mum. And it's nice to have someone in my life again ... someone just for me, you know?'

'Yes, I do. I think when you're married you take it for granted, but afterwards you miss the company of someone who knows you really well. The shared memories ...'

She nods. I was remembering how Mike and I ... But this is about her relationship, not mine, so I move quickly on. 'Emma and Katie will soon be living their own lives, and you mustn't neglect yours. I'm glad you've found James, I like him, so easygoing. Why don't you bring him and the girls over for Sunday lunch? I'd love to see him again ... it's about time I put my apron on.'

'That would be lovely, we'll come over next Sunday if you're asking?' she says, leaping in before I change my mind. I've been all over the place since Mike died. I know she and Isobel both want their old mum back and Sunday lunch is a good place to start.

I nod enthusiastically. I enjoy cooking but as soon as Mike lost his appetite so did I. 'I'll look forward to it.' I smile, finishing the last of my curry and taking a sip of wine.

'Anna, I've been thinking – that big wedding is only a few months away, isn't it?'

'Yes, Mrs Parker's paying for all the flowers for her granddaughter Poppy's wedding, no expense spared. It's in Cheshire at this big hotel . . .'

'I remember you telling me. She came in when I was off work with Dad, didn't she? Everything was a bit of a blur back then.' I smile sadly.

I haven't retained much from that time, I think my brain has anaesthetised itself. The only phrases I've held on to are those with numbers – 'Grade four cancer,' and 'Six weeks at best'.

I look up and thankfully Anna hasn't noticed me drift off, she's still talking. ' . . . the bridesmaids are in blush pink, lots of roses and lilies. Hundreds of button-holes and corsages . . . huge floral decorations and table arrangements for the reception.' Her words stressing the enormity of this booking.

'That's a hell of a lot of work,' is all I can say, 'which is one of the reasons I've decided it's time to come back to the shop.'

She puts down her glass. 'Oh, Mum, really? That's good news; no, that's great news. But are you ready?'

I nod. 'Yes I am.'

'Mrs Jackson is lovely but she hasn't a clue and I don't have your patience with her. She cocked up a wedding and a funeral last week.'

'Oh dear, did she? What happened?'

'You don't want to know – but suffice to say the funeral felt like a party and the wedding looked like a wake.'

I have to laugh. 'Oh, she's fine, she just needs to be managed,' I say.

'Yes, I would like to "manage" her out of the shop, but we've been so short staffed. Isobel's offered to muck in if her supply teaching's still dried up, but she can only do buttonholes at best. If we're going to do this we definitely need you back at work doing your magic on that bride's bouquet.'

'Well, count me in,' I say. I'm flushed with wine, and smiling, but inside I suddenly feel quite petrified.

I've only just mastered a visit to the corner shop. Am I ready for a complete return to life – especially a big summer wedding and all the slogging and smiling that will entail?

'I didn't want to put you under any pressure so I never said, but I can't tell you how relieved I am that you're coming back. This wedding is a huge deal for Rosie's; the profit from this alone will mean a great year for us. And you always say for one good wedding we can get at least three more bookings.'

'Absolutely!' I smile, pleased my daughter feels so passionate about our small business. I remember going home to Mike in floods of tears the day Mrs Cooper told me she was retiring and I'd have to find another job. He thought someone had upset me and was all ready to go out there and sort them out, but when I told him what had happened he said, 'Okay, let's think about this. You want to stay working there and Mrs Cooper wants to sell – so let's kill one bird with two stones, and buy it.' I'd laughed when he said that, we were only in our twenties, and people like us didn't buy businesses. But Mike said he'd be by my side and though never ambitious for himself he believed in me and gently pushed us all to achieve our own small dreams. A flower shop for me, a marriage and babies for Anna – and for Isobel, a degree in French that almost defeated her. He was always there supporting us, urging us on in the wings.

'Dad would have done anything for you, wouldn't he?' Anna says, finishing her wine.

It was true, Mike wanted to give me everything and we had nothing. To buy the shop we took a huge risk, remortgaged the house, and a week later began the process of becoming shop owners. I enrolled in a floristry course at night school and after a great deal of hard work we eventually had a thriving business. I was going to

22

keep the Cooper's name, but Mike came up with the idea of Rosie's Roses, and that was it.

'Dad worked so hard on the shop,' I said, remembering him toiling late into the night to redecorate and get everything ready. 'It really was a labour of love for him,' I said fondly. 'He spent our holiday money painting the walls rose pink and paying to have the shop sign with my name on. I felt like a celebrity: "There you are, Rosie – up in lights," he said, "where you belong."'

'Do you remember our late-night picnic?' Anna was smiling at the memory.

'Oh yes, gosh I'd almost forgotten about that. I felt so bad that your dad was there all on his own fitting shelves on a Friday night ... and as you didn't have school the next day we all went over to the shop to keep him company.'

'We made sandwiches and I carried the flask of tea. Me and Isobel thought we'd died and gone to heaven.' Anna's eyes are shining at the memory. 'I'll never forget that night, putting the blanket down in the middle of the shop floor and us all sitting round eating KitKats. People were peering in on their way back from the pub, it must have been very late, but we thought we were very important picnicking in our new shop.'

'I remember telling you not to mention it to Nan. I doubt Margaret would have approved of me taking you out for late-night picnics.' I giggle at the thought of my strait-laced mother ever doing anything after nine p.m., let alone putting two little girls in pyjamas in the back of the car and taking them out into the night.

'Are you sure you'll be okay, Mum? The last time you set foot in that shop it was to do the flowers for his funeral.'

I sit back in the chair. 'The funeral was only one day – and it isn't going to overshadow the hundreds and thousands of days Dad was in there, drinking tea, chatting to the customers, alive, full of life and helping out. It'll be good to get back there.'

'Yeah.' Her eyes fill with tears and my heart breaks. I wanted to make her feel better remembering her dad, not upset her.

'This sounds selfish, but when Dad died my first thought was "Who's going to lift all the boxes for us when we have a delivery? Who's going to drive us to the flower market when it's icy in winter?" Do you remember he'd get up before his own work and insist on driving . . . He couldn't bear to let us go out there on our own in the freezing cold.'

'Yes, and I keep looking out at those stars and I'm sure he's telling me to stop being a lazy sod and get back to work,' I laugh.

Anna discreetly wipes an eye. Neither of us want the other one to see we're upset, always trying to protect each other from hurt.

'I'm so grateful, love. I appreciate you've been grieving too and I know it's not been easy. It's hard to explain, but I've just been scared to go back into the world again alone – it sounds so stupid, doesn't it?' I am a terrible mother leaving her to do all that by herself.

'No, I get it, and you mustn't throw yourself at it like you always do. Why don't you just focus on the Parker wedding? I can deal with the day-to-day stuff.'

'Okay, it's a deal. Let's start by making some notes; I have to work out what exactly needs doing,' I say, getting up from my seat at the kitchen table to delve in what we call 'the messy cupboard' for my work notepad. The drawers are still full of nondescript bits of wire and screws that Mike dumped in there, along with grand-daughters' flavoured lip balms and cola-scented erasers. I know my notepad is in here somewhere but as I haven't used it for a while I have to go deep, and end up at the back of the cupboard, a place no one has ventured in for some time.

'I wondered where this was,' I say, pulling out an old shortbread tin decorated with Scottie dogs in bow ties.

'Oh, the photograph tin. We got that out for Dad, do you remember he wanted to look at all the old photos?' Anna's smiling, taking it from me. I recall Mike sitting up in bed, a frail old man smiling at a picture of the kids on the beach at Blackpool with my mother. Mike

25

had said something funny and when my mother was unable to get out of her deckchair for laughing he took her picture, which made her laugh more, capturing her for ever with his Kodak, legs splayed, her head back, in stitches. Margaret had always liked Mike – if it hadn't been for her I probably wouldn't have married him.

Before long we are knee-deep in faded photos and grainy memories.

'Remember this?' I hold up a picture of Isobel and Anna on holiday.

She takes it, smiling at her six-year-old self in Cornwall holding her bucket and spade in one hand and her two-year-old sister's hand in the other.

'Dad taught you to swim on that holiday,' I say, rummaging for the photo of Mike holding her up in the sea like a trophy, her arms waving around in triumph.

She gazes at the photo. 'He was always there for me. I'll never forget the night I found out about Paul and that woman. He'd stormed off and I called Dad in tears – within minutes he was at the door, bundling us all into the car and bringing us home here.'

'Yes. You were so upset and trying to tell me what had happened and in the middle of all the madness the girls wanted Granddad to play Monopoly with them like he always did.' I giggle.

'He just got the box, set it all out and by two a.m. they

26

were buying up Mayfair and Park Lane.' Her eyes filled with tears again and my heart twisted.

'The girls miss him so much. Their own dad's such a waste of space I always thought Dad would be there for them . . . teach them to drive and tell them they're beautiful when boys upset them, like he did with us. He always knew the right thing to say or do . . .'

'Yeah, a broken fence or a broken heart and he was straight to it – always fixing something,' I say, using my napkin to discreetly wipe my eyes.

'I wonder what he'd want for us all, Mum?' She's looking at me, waiting for the 'right' answer.

'He'd want us all to be happy, but mostly he'd want me back there behind that counter making bloody bridesmaid's posies,' I laugh.

'Yes he would, and you seem ready, better, brighter,' she says. 'A few weeks ago you wouldn't have been able to look at these photos without collapsing in tears.'

'I'm only just holding it together now,' I say. 'Now, where's that wine?' I grab the bottle, pour us both another and send up a little thank you to whoever is up there for sending me such wonderful daughters.

'I can't believe you were ever so young, or so trendy.' Anna's now rummaging around in the tin, producing random photos from down the years, and I tell myself I must make some albums, the photos are all mixed up.

She sighs, lifting up a photo of me taken at art college – I was seventeen and wearing a black polo neck and tight jeans.

'Look at you, all Kate Moss with your long hair and skinny legs,' she laughs.

'I thought I was more Marianne Faithfull. Kate Moss hadn't even been born then, that's how old I am.'

'I can't imagine you being so young . . . you look just like Emma.'

'I can't believe I was that young either! And yes, I can see Emma – I never realised how pretty I was. I wish I had, I'd have made so much more of myself,' I say, studying the serious girl with the straight blonde hair and the skinny legs. 'I thought I was so cool, very existentialist in my black polo neck . . . I never really understood what "existential" meant, and I still don't. I remember a boy I knew trying to explain it to me: "I exist therefore I am," he said, and I just nodded. Between you and me I also wore polo necks so your nan wouldn't see my "disgusting" love bites.'

'Love bites! You were quite a goer then?' Anna laughs and waves another photo at me. 'Was this one your boyfriend before Dad? You've told me about him. He broke your heart, didn't he? Did he give you the love bites?'

'Yes,' I laugh, 'he was a dangerous boy.' I gaze at his picture, thinking of his blue eyes, dark, wavy hair, and

Salford carnival on a muggy day in August. It was in 1968 ... a year etched deep in my memory.

'He was very good-looking.' Anna nods, apparently impressed, admiring it as she puts the picture back in the tin.

As the photo mixes back in with all the other memories there, I glimpse the smile that once made my heart beat faster. I see those blue, blue eyes that twinkled and it feels like yesterday – I also feel the ocean of pain that came after. I want to tell Anna all about the boy, but she isn't up for an evening of 'all our yesterdays', and she's now closing the shortbread tin on my past. I take my cue, and keen to push it to the back of the cupboard and the back of my mind, I offer to put the kettle on.

'Come on then,' I say, closing the cupboard door on the past and brandishing the rediscovered notebook. 'I'll make the coffee and we'll sit in the other room and talk about this wedding. Did you say the bridesmaids are wearing blush pink?'

After Anna leaves I go to bed and try to relax, but I feel like I'm caught between the past and the present, both pulling me in different directions, vying for my attention. Unable to sleep I go downstairs in the dark. It's so quiet, except for Lily's paws clicking behind me on the wooden floor. I'm still not used to being alone in the house in the middle of the night so I put all the lights on downstairs. 'I know, Lily, I'm daft, aren't I?' I say, half-smiling at my own silliness. My head is filled with blush-pink gerberas and black and white memories and I soon find myself opening the cupboard, taking out the tin again and sitting at the kitchen table nursing a mug of hot tea.

I look at the unopened tin. Is this my personal Pandora's box? Dare I open it and release the butterflies from my past? Can I bear to see the vivid colours flooding back to life after all these years? Recalling splashes of love and pain like paint on canvas, I run my fingers along the embossed edges and wonder if I dare open it again. My impetuous side (the one that took me down slides with my grandchildren, raced them to the ice cream van and joined in all their party games) wants to lift the lid, but the seventeen-year-old scared Rosie wants to keep the tin firmly closed on the past.

Finally, by the second cup of tea, the ice-cream-van-racing granny has won and I open it – and even after all these years I'm afraid of what's waiting for me. I pluck a few photos out from the middle: a sad bride, no white lace and promises, just a cream suit and blind hope; my mother's tight lips and a finger buffet at the local working men's club – not the stuff little girls' dreams are made of. The groom was young and handsome though, and he was so in love – how I envied him, how I wished I could match his love. Back then it didn't matter how hard I tried, I just couldn't feel it, and wished someone else was waiting for me on the registry office steps. I hate myself still for those feelings. Mike knew I didn't love him, but he married me anyway and over the years our love grew, but it was a slow burn, nothing like the fireworks of passion I'd felt with Peter.

I find the postcard Peter sent me from Italy and my heart dips a little.

Having a great time, the pasta is amazing, the galleries are wonderful.

See you soon, all my love,

Peter xxxx

I smile to myself – how could he write about pasta when my heart was breaking? Reading his teenage words my eyes fill with tears and my mind screams 'What if?' After a while I pick up the old black and white photos of us at college – there are only a few, it wasn't like the selfie age we're living through today – and in those few snaps I'm transported back to my youth and a world filled with possibilities. And I return, as I have so many times, to the summer of 1968; students were rioting in Paris, the Vietnam War was raging and I, Rosie Draper, was in love for the very first time.

*

I remember it like it was yesterday, that crisp, September morning when I arrived for the first time at Salford College of Art. The sun was low in the sky as I walked briskly along the pavement, the air veiled with autumn mist and expectation. I was sixteen years old, so young, so vulnerable and so easily impressed entering the art room and seeing the riches before me. Easels everywhere, enough paintbrushes for everyone, soft B pencils and pots of paint in every colour from ochre to aquamarine. I was in heaven as I gazed around me – art all over the walls, stacks of thick white paper and ... Oh God, a naked woman standing in the middle of the room.

I was alarmed – we didn't do that sort of thing where I came from and I barely knew where to look. Averting my eyes from the nonchalant unclothed form in front of me, I realised this was our life model and not only would I have to look at her pert breasts, I was expected to study them in detail, along with the dark intimate shading of her upper thighs. I'd read about such things in my mother's *Reader's Digest* but didn't think real people actually posed like this for a living. Everyone else seemed to be taking this in their stride, gliding to their seats chatting and laughing like there wasn't a completely naked woman now lying across a chaise longue right in front of us.

Then, amid all this madness, I saw him.

Even now I remember him in Technicolor. He was sitting back in his seat, one foot up on the chair in front, surveying the rest of the room, like he owned the bloody world. It was clear from that first glance that here was someone who was sure of himself, of his place in the world, and this was heady stuff to a gauche, scared young girl taking her first steps. I was a working-class teenager, thrashing around, not knowing where I fitted in, desperate to make something of my talent but unable to visualise a future for myself in a middle-class world of art and easels. But here was someone who knew what he was doing, where he was going, and to me that was special, different. Everyone else was new and nervous but he had this laid-back air and a lazy, sexy smile that began in those blue eyes, slowly sending a spark to his lips, and lighting his face up. I remember watching his laughing eyes gaze idly around the room looking for mischief and excitement and I was immediately taken. I settled at my easel looking discreetly under my fringe at the gorgeous boy while averting my eyes from the bare woman Mum would no doubt consider 'a hussy'. I could almost hear her voice: 'It's like Sodom and Gomorrah,' she'd say. 'Get your coat, you're leaving.'

My mother had shaken her head in despair when I'd told her I was going to art college. 'I don't know why you don't get a nice job as a shorthand typist – you've got your head in the clouds. An artist? It's not for the likes of us.'

I was the first in my family to do something different, to want something more. My two brothers, both older than me, worked in jobs my mother and father approved of – David was a car mechanic and Mark had gone into what Dad laughingly referred to as 'the family business', at the local factory. But I was considered a rebel because typing or a job making tea at the local bus depot hadn't appealed to me. No, sixteen-year-old Rosie had big dreams, she wasn't going to end up in a little terraced house in Salford like the rest of them, she was going to see the world, paint the world and then go round all over again.

Chapter Two

After my solitary reminiscing over photographs from the past I was ready to get back to real life again, and a week later I turned up at the shop. It was slightly daunting after a year away, but I needn't have worried; old customers seemed genuinely pleased to see me, and there were a few tears, but so much laughter.

'It's so good to have you back, Mum,' Anna said, bringing me a mug of tea while I grappled with an anniversary bouquet of red roses, secretly jealous of the recipients reaching fifty years of marriage without dying.

But being back here and busy is the best thing for me. I'm amazed at how quickly I've slipped back into my old life. It's good to be in the shop doing what I love, my daughter at my side, chatting again to customers

I've known for over thirty years. I love the bustle and the way, as a florist, I've played a small part in people's lives over those years. From births to funerals there are always flowers. Yes, it's good to be back, yet I can't help but wonder, now I'm alone, is this it? Is the rest of my life going to be devoted to making floral tributes celebrating other people's weddings and watersheds? Do I have any watersheds to look forward to apart from a seventieth, an eightieth and if I'm lucky a ninetieth birthday? What's left for me now? It's a fleeting feeling, an intangible yearning for something, yet I don't know what it is. Of course I miss Mike and that may have something to do with these sudden dips, these overwhelming feelings of 'Where am I going?' But there's something else: I need to know what will be the next page in *my* story ... are there any pages left?

'Mum, you're doing great. I can't believe how much you got through, we'll be able to leave early tonight at this rate.' Anna smiles at me as we wrestle with the last of the flowers for a big funeral tomorrow.

'Great, but I see from a note in the book that Mrs Parker's coming in at four – do you mind dealing with her?' I ask. 'I don't know I'm quite ready for the Wedding of the Year. The Bridezillas are bad enough, but the mothers and grandmothers can be positively venomous.'

I still have my moments of fragility, but being back at

work has helped to dilute my loss and I'm starting to smile again. I think about the past a lot these days and remembering him helps, but I'm also readjusting to the idea of a tomorrow without Mike. It isn't a future I'd envisaged, and I don't know what it holds any more. There are no certainties now, no anchor to secure me. Sometimes I wake in the night, alone, petrified afresh at the prospect of never seeing my husband again. We'd been together for over forty years, knew everything there was to know, shared every wonderful and every awful moment of our lives – this wasn't meant to happen. Where do I go from here? I can't share my fear with Anna or Isobel, it would upset them and they'd worry about me. I'm supposed to be the one supporting my children, not the other way round. And they are grieving too – losing Mike was the hardest thing any of us have had to deal with, and though the girls are adults with their own lives there were times when they cried like little girls. For my grown-up children to sob in my arms was probably the most painful part of Mike's dying. And like a layer cake of grief, my own loss was laid on top of it all, over and over again, until sometimes I really couldn't see the light.

I'm the first of my friends to be widowed, which makes life even more difficult because I am now the 'odd' woman. Before Mike was ill we'd often spend an evening with the small group of friends we'd known for years. We'd met when the kids were young and spent many summer barbecues and family bonfires together, then the kids all left to live their own lives and we were all about being grown-ups again. We'd returned to our 'couples' status, the evenings went on later and louder and more alcohol was drunk. Our social lives morphed into something slightly different, as did our friendships; secrets were shared, sex discussed without sign language and we now laughed with each other about getting old. There's something comforting in having friends the same age, your aches and pains, worries and disappointments similar, if not the same. Most of all you learn to laugh together about the difficulties in life and I valued those friendships.

Looking from the outside I can see we were all quite smug in our M&S dinner party lives. Untouched by any major tragedy, we were always moving forward, another child's wedding, a birthday, a wedding anniversary. Our families kept safe, with nothing to disturb our cosy, sub-urban social lives.

They didn't totally abandon me after Mike's death, but I felt the fraying of those friendships early on. They sent cards, made the odd call, and tried in their way to bring me back into the fold; I was invited to Stella and Dave's dinner party just a few months back, but everyone sat round the table with long faces, talking in serious voices.

I know it was because they wanted to respect my loss but I felt like the spectre at the feast. I should have said something, but the way they behaved around me made me feel self-conscious and brought it home to me how together Mike and I had been, and I didn't feel strong enough to say anything without bursting into tears. I realised that evening, as Stella served up the fruit salad and Dave poured the wine and made corny jokes, that this wasn't what I needed any more. We've all moved on, this was my life with Mike and now I can't do that, and to them I am a reminder of loss and what's still to come. It will never be the same for them – or for me.

Despite many aspects of my life with Mike now closed off to me, I still have my flowers. Almost instantly, I fall in love again with the exotic blooms, stunning colours and delicate shades of my craft. I wander through the flower market in the cold darkness before dawn, breathing in the full, rounded scent of roses and the almost sickly sweetness of lilies. The fragrance of flowers brings with it memories of happier times and reminds me that buds are still growing, life is continuing, moving forward. I choose my blooms, running my fingers along the satin of petals, the waxy whiteness of camellias, imagining the celebration they are destined for.

It's a month before the big Parker wedding and I

discover a cloud of pastel hydrangeas at the market. There was a time when I couldn't bear to look at hydrangeas, but now I hold a bunch in my arms, gazing into the tiny, heartbreakingly pretty faces. Each bud jostles for attention, no two the same with their own unique hue, from deepest blue to lavender pink to pistachio – I suddenly want to paint them. I haven't picked up a pencil or paintbrush for years, since the girls were little and we'd sometimes draw together, when I'd remember how good I was. With the girls we'd draw houses, dogs and stick people, but now I want to get back to 'real' sketching and capture the subtlety of changing shades, the delicacy of tiny starry petals. And thinking about sketching takes me right back there again.

I loved being immersed daily in the business of drawing and painting at art college; I also enjoyed gazing at the gorgeous boy with the blue eyes. He didn't even know I existed, yet he filled my tummy with apple blossom. I didn't have anyone to share my ideas with and I longed to talk to someone like him, tell him my dreams of living in Paris, wandering through Monet's gardens at Giverny, sketching the places and people in 'the City of Light'. I knew he would understand because he was an artist too – and he seemed so open, so easy, and when I learned that he was called Pierre I wondered if he might actually be French. If so, I felt this might be a sign that we were meant to be friends. I hadn't yet been close enough to hear him speak, but I had enough imagination to conjure up his delicious French accent.

Recently the past has come to find me, whispering long-forgotten names and places and bringing with it vague sketches of what happened, of who I used to be – and I wonder where he is now. I imagine he's a great photographer, or a bohemian artist, living the life we once dreamed of together. I've been tempted to dabble, to find out where he is, who he became, and recently I went as far as to put his name into Google, but something stopped me pressing search. I can't explain it but to go there felt wrong, like opening up the Ouija board and disturbing something that's died and shouldn't be brought back. For all my yearning and wondering, the past wasn't always a pretty place to be and I'm not sure I want to return there. Along with the fun and freedom that comes with the package of youth there are always dark times, so why open up old wounds?

I loved my husband and I have a wonderful family, so there's no need to go meddling around in my past. And yet it seems the older we get the more we are drawn back to snippets of memory. Like magazine cuttings on a cork board they are pinned inside my brain and I find myself taking them down and looking at them.

I remember a girl with long dark hair and thick

eyeliner. Her name was Avril. She wore red lipstick, and looked like a model. I once watched her slowly take a Gitane cigarette from Pierre's lips and put it to her crimson mouth. Their eyes locked as she sucked in the smoke, never taking her eyes from his. And I had never been so jealous in my life.

I remember a mousy-haired girl called Anita. A fellow art student and the most colourless person I'd ever met. She talked of her boyfriend Brian the car mechanic pressuring her to 'do it', in his van. She would list Brian's scandalous demands over a lunchtime sandwich whilst I nodded in all the right places.

'Pierre and Avril are practically "doing it" over there at the table,' she once remarked, outraged over her mother's egg and cress. 'It's like something from one of those pornos!'

'Well he's French, isn't he?' I said, watching the beautiful couple kiss with tongues. I heard my mother's voice – and hated myself for my small-minded ignorance.

'Is he? He doesn't sound French.'

I didn't know, I still hadn't heard him speak.

'They say the French are quite wanton,' I remember saying. I was feigning knowledge of the French I didn't have and the 'they' I was referring to was of course my mother, who didn't trust anyone outside the British Isles. I look back now and see that mousy Anita wasn't good for me. She didn't challenge my views because she shared them. Her world was as small as mine and her sandwich wrappings were as tightly wrapped as she was. I can see now that in this new, exciting, but often scary environment I'd found comfort and safety in the familiar.

Perhaps I should have stayed safe and not ventured into the unknown territory that was Pierre, but when he dumped Avril and started making eyes at me I was lost.

After him, beautiful Avril was never the same. The light went from her eyes, her lipstick faded and she smoked a cigarette just like everyone else. It seemed she'd not only lost her lover – she'd lost herself. I still think of Avril and wonder if she ever got over him, and I'm reminded of my mother's warning: 'What goes around comes around.'

Chapter Three

Along with being back at work, my dog Lily has also given me a new lease of life. She's a small mutt with a slight limp and a tail that never stops wagging. Anna and Isobel decided to surprise me with Lily as a gift because they were worried I was lonely in the evenings.

'We wanted you to have some company, the house must seem empty without Dad,' Isobel said as she plonked down several cans of dog food. My granddaughters had chosen Lily's pink collar, her floral bed and various toys to play with and though I was a little surprised to receive this 'gift', when Katie placed her in my arms I knew it was love.

'We got her from the rescue centre,' Anna said. 'She's getting on and she's got a touch of arthritis, but all she needs is some TLC.'

'A bit like me then?' I said, cuddling her like a baby.

'She belonged to an old lady who died and the girl at the centre said she's been pining. Apparently she likes a walk but can't go for too long or you have to carry her home,' Isobel said.

'Again, she's just like me. And with a name like Lily it must be fate. Rosie and Lily, two flowers who've lost their bloom.' I smiled. 'But we'll get it back, won't we, Lily?'

Since then Lily has settled in very well, as though she's always lived here with me. I take her out for a short walk at least three times a day, which is good exercise for both of us, and as she spends a lot of time sleeping I can go shopping or pop round to see the girls without having to worry about her. And when I do the garden she likes to help, though I do worry what's going to come up this year as I suspect she simply follows me and digs up whatever I've just planted. In the evenings Lily sits on the sofa with me watching TV, her head in my lap and one eye open. But the best part about sharing my home with Lily is coming home from wherever I've been, knowing someone is waiting for me. I've never liked walking into the empty house since Mike went, but now I have an excited little mutt waiting eagerly to greet me. It doesn't matter where I've been or for how long, she's always delighted to see me, rushing around the kitchen, picking up toys to tease me, her little tail wagging so fast I fully expect her to lift off the ground like a helicopter one of these days.

The shop is always busy and though I only work four days I often come home exhausted, completely drained of every molecule of energy. I love flowers, but the unsettling feeling that I should be doing more with my life seems to be growing stronger every day. I can't help thinking I'm not perhaps being true to myself and living *my* life. It's strange, but Mike's death has made me think a lot about the things we meant to do but never did. One of those things was to travel; along with New Zealand we had a list of places we wanted to visit, food we wanted to taste, places to see, but with children and a business it wasn't something we'd had the time or the money to do.

I often think about what we'd be doing now if Mike was here, the life we'd live. When he died we were just about to enter that third stage; the kids were settled, I was going to retire soon, we'd pass the business to the girls and think about chasing some of those dreams. Now I'm unexpectedly alone I'm a little scared of the future. I never even considered a life without him. He wasn't the love of my life, yet I believe it was written in those stars that I would spend most of my life with him. Now, after many years and two children together, I know it was right – Mike was the only husband for me and I have few regrets. Yet his death has made me reach into the past and I can't help but sometimes wonder what if things with my first love had turned out differently?

If you'd told me at seventeen that I'd marry someone like Mike Carter I would have refused to believe you. He worked at the local factory, he had no wild dreams of ever living anywhere but here and his life was mapped out for him. Mike was a friend of my brothers and was often at our house but I didn't see him. There were a million boys like Mike – or so I thought – but Pierre, on the other hand, was a boy in a million.

One day after class Pierre asked if I liked his drawing.

'What do you think, Rosie?' he said, as I wandered over to his easel.

I was shocked to see a beautiful drawing of a girl with big eyes and long hair.

'Is that . . . me?'

He nodded, looking from me to the picture.

'It's good, but I'm not that pretty.'

'You are.' He leaned back with a half smile playing on his lips, his eyes never leaving mine.

'I . . . I thought we had to draw the model, I didn't know we were allowed to draw just anyone,' I said.

'Well, I'm not sure of the *exact* rules on these matters,' he said with a grin, at which point I could have kicked myself. I must have sounded like a seven-year-old who wouldn't dare defy the teacher, not a young and happening art student.

'Anyway I didn't draw "just anyone", I drew you,' he said, still looking at me, a smile twinkling in his eyes. He wasn't French, I thought, he was posh and must be from London. I'd never been to London.

I flushed, flattered to think he'd been looking at me for a whole two-hour session.

'Well, thanks. No one's ever drawn me before.'

'Look at the way your cheekbones stand out, beautiful,' he said softly, almost under his breath.

'Don't talk rubbish,' I said, my heart jumping as his fingers ran along the cheekbone in the sketch.

'It's not rubbish,' he laughed, mimicking my accent affectionately.

His lovely voice sounded clean and clear and made me even more aware that mine sounded like someone off *Coronation Street*. But the way he looked at me made me feel like a fashion model on a catwalk in Paris.

'You have a lovely face.' He lifted the canvas, holding it near me. 'In fact you're lovelier than my drawing . . . I'd like to photograph you.'

'Oh, you don't, I look awful in photos. My dad took some of me in Blackpool last summer and I've got a moon face.'

He laughed again and while looking at me he ran his forefinger slowly along the drawing of my face. 'You really can't see it, can you?'

I felt a frisson go through me. I didn't speak because I couldn't. I was tongue-tied.

Eventually I packed up my stuff and was just leaving through the door when I bumped into a teacher. 'Is Peter Moreton in there?' he asked.

I turned to gesture towards Pierre. 'No . . . just Pierre. I don't know a Peter Moreton.'

'Pierre?' he said, walking past me. 'When did you change your name?' He was smiling good-naturedly, and so was Pierre, but I also sensed some embarrassment.

Now I can smile at the gauche eighteen-year-old who smoked French cigarettes and called himself Pierre – but on hearing this I liked him even more. He wasn't quite as perfect as I'd feared, and he wished he was someone else too. Just like me.

'Don't you like your real name?' I asked him the next day.

'No, I don't, so I changed it.' He looked directly into my eyes challengingly; he wasn't asking anyone's permission, he was Pierre because he wanted to be. At almost seventeen I liked that he did as he wanted, but as an older, wiser woman I question the commitment of a man who can walk away from his own name.

'I thought I'd start being Pierre for when I live in Paris. They call it the City of Light, but until then I'll have to live in Salford – the city of grey factories and smoke . . . ' He rolled his eyes.

'It doesn't matter where or how you live, you can *imagine* another life in another place,' I said, taking out my pencils.

'And what about you, Rosie? Who will you be?'

'I'll be me, thank you very much. I don't have to be someone else to think about Paris, it can just be in my head,' I said, honestly. I was flattered by his interest and admired his ambition but for me, at that point, living in Paris was just a dream I slipped in and out of to get me through. And after that my dreams of Paris included a glimpse of Pierre, or should I say Peter?

He'd taken the time to sketch me, he made me feel like no one ever had before – I felt beautiful, special. I didn't know it then, but my fate was sealed; even if I'd wanted to, it was already too late to turn back, and I wonder now what might have happened if we'd played things differently.

Would I have lived a more adventurous, glittering, exciting life of parties and travel and artistic success? Would I be a different person living a bohemian life in Paris, my days spent painting in a studio in Montmartre – nights filled with absinthe and passion? I have often wondered if I'd have been happier, but who can ever say? There might also have been days when I gazed over Parisian rooftops from our artist's garret, longing for the comfort of a safe but happy life here in my home town with someone like Mike.

Going back to work means I don't have too much time to go over the past, which is probably as well. I need to think of the future now and concentrate on making sure the girls are okay and the business is doing well. When it's time to hand the flower shop to the girls I want it to still be a good little business, able to support them and their families.

The big Parker wedding is imminent and Anna is highly stressed. She almost resents my calm and complains bitterly that Isobel and I aren't wound-up balls of anxiety like she is.

'God, can you two please just hurry up with those bouquets?' she screams from the front of the shop, while Isobel and I work quietly in the back.

Disillusioned with teaching, Isobel has decided to join us and is now working full-time at the shop which is lovely. Along with Mrs Jackson, who, when managed, is very productive, we now have four members of staff and we work well together, each one's strengths complementing the others'. When Anna isn't stressing we have fun, chatting to customers, laughing at customers when they've left the shop and sharing hurried lunches while working on orders.

'I thought that was a salad leaf, but it was a flower one,' I laugh, taking a non-edible leaf from my mouth as we hunker down together over buttonhole detritus to eat pre-packed salads.

'I don't know why you're complaining about a flower leaf,' Isobel says. 'Our packed lunches at school always had oasis foam in them.'

'Oh yes, everyone knew our mother was a florist,' Anna adds, laughing at the memory. 'And while other kids had cheese and pickle, we had cheese and bits of spongy green stuff and even the odd petal!'

'Oh that's right, pile on the guilt. I am a terrible mother,' I giggle.

'It could have been worse – it could have been florist's wires,' Isobel says.

'Yeah, and I'd rather have her as our mum even though she did make rubbish sandwiches.' They smile at each other and I feel warm and wanted. It's good to be back with my girls in the shop – I'm beginning to feel a bit like me again.

As for the big wedding, I've yet to meet Mrs Parker, she only seems to come into the shop on days when I'm off, but apparently she's very glamorous and pops in to either add more to the order or share a picture of a celebrity wedding she wants us to reproduce.

'It's George Clooney and Amal this week. Apparently they said their vows under a white archway of imported roses . . . and Madam now wants one of those,' Anna says with frustration.

'Imported from where?'

'God only knows, but she's read about it and she wants it.'

'Then she shall have it,' I say. One of the reasons that the shop has done so well over the years is that I never say no, and though I laugh along with Anna about these outlandish requests, I'm actually enjoying the creative challenge.

'Who does she think she is?' Anna mutters. 'It's less than two weeks and now she wants "something fabulous" but she doesn't know what!'

'Suggest a field of red poppies as Poppy's the bride's name and because that would be "fabulous",' I joke, wrestling with a huge bunch of carnations.

'Don't laugh! I'll give her a *fabulous* kick up the backside and see if she likes that.'

'Charming,' Isobel giggles.

'It's okay for you two but I'm the one who has to smile politely while she gets all stroppy when I don't come up with something,' Anna sighs.

'Don't worry, darling, we can do it.' I smile, putting the kettle on, hoping a cup of camomile will calm her. 'I know she's annoying but it's her granddaughter so she wants something special. So what can we produce that's really stunning and will make her granddaughter's wedding stand out?'

Isobel shrugs, she's more academic than creative and any thoughts Anna might have are blinded by a red mist. 'It might be a big wedding, Mum, but she needs to understand it's not exactly Kim and Kanye's, is it?'

'Oooh, Kim Kardashian's wedding, that's given me an idea,' I say, reaching under the counter for a magazine and flicking through. 'Now, this is from a couple of years ago, but I recall seeing "something fabulous and floral" at that wedding. Look.' I point to a spectacular wall of white flowers.

'A floral wall?' Anna is saying doubtfully as I show them the beautiful photos. 'You have to be kidding . . . ?'

'Why not? Mrs Parker wants fabulous and this could be it. Especially if she's got Kim's money!' I smile, keen to take on this new challenge.

Chapter Four

On the day of the wedding not only have we spent almost a week making the rose archway, the bouquets, the buttonholes, corsages and table arrangements, we are also creating a seven foot square wall of spectacular white flowers.

Anna's never quite been on board with 'the bloody wall' as she refers to it. She's not good with change and this is certainly different from anything we've done before, but I'm really proud of it.

'I swear I've been having nightmares about this,' she's saying as we all lift the frame of the wall into the van. 'Mother, I blame you, Kim and Kanye – in that order,' she says to me. 'And as if making it hasn't been nightmarish enough, I just know it's not going to fit in the van – I *know* it won't,' she says, as the rest of us stay calm and haul together, lifting it in smoothly and easily. At this, even Anna has to laugh at herself.

'Okay, so it fits.' She puts her tongue out at me and Isobel who are standing with hands on hips and an 'I told you so' look on our faces.

'Oh no ... everything's going smoothly, what's our Anna going to complain about now?' Isobel calls after her. Anna's response is to stick up two fingers good-naturedly.

'I hope you won't be doing that at the society wedding venue?' I laugh. 'I doubt Mrs Parker would approve.' Mrs Parker's demands have now taken on mythical proportions with her enormous guest list, outlandish requests and endless budget.

'How the other half live,' Anna says as we drive through the Cheshire lanes, sweeping into the grounds, the van filled with the last of the flowers. The setting is magnificent, a beautiful Georgian house surrounded by acres of green, rose gardens in watercolours and a shimmering ornamental lake.

The weather is perfect too. 'Oh, just look at that sky,' Isobel says as we climb out of the van.

'Yes, when you're rich even the sun shines on your wedding day,' Anna sniffs. 'It rained on my wedding, must have been symbolic.'

I put my arm around her. 'Darling, I hate to break it to you, but it wasn't the weather – it was the groom. Dad and I married in the depths of winter, bloody freezing it was, and we were happy for over forty years.'

'Ahh. Dad would have loved it here. I bet at night you can see every single star,' adds Isobel, the romantic.

Before unloading the van, we decide to make our arrival known to Mrs Parker. We head for the reception where the manager leads us to the party room so we can bring in the table arrangements and add the final touches. The room is sparkly white with huge silk blossom trees dotted here and there. On their delicate white branches hang little favours wrapped in tulle and on the tables are our white lily and rose floral arrangements, made late last night and spritzed to within an inch of their lives so they will live through the big day. Each chair has a huge white chiffon bow tied perfectly around it and the tables are set with shiny white crockery and crystal glass. I wander around checking the oasis is damp and the flowers are in optimum condition and realise in this moment I am happier than I have been since before Mike died. I stop a moment and savour it, watching everyone bustling around and remembering a phrase Mike often used. 'Stop and smell the roses,' he'd say. 'Stop rushing around, Rosie, relax, take time to appreciate the world and the good things in it.'

Yes, I'm happy. I'm smelling the roses, Mike.

'Mrs Parker, this is Rosie Carter, head florist and my mother.' Anna's voice cuts into my reverie. She's walking towards me with a very sleek woman, shiny blonde bob, manicured nails and white shirt and jeans. Mrs Parker is about my age, perhaps a little younger, and is as elegant and classy as Anna has described her. She also matches the room perfectly. This woman leaves nothing to chance.

'Excuse me in these old things,' she says, referring to her designer casuals that probably cost more than some brides' wedding dresses. 'My "grandmother of the bride" blue satin Givenchy is hanging up in my room but as we have several hours I thought I'd make myself available to assist you before I dress. I love flowers, and daresay I have a talent – which is why I offered to manage the creative side of things.'

So, for the next few hours, accompanied by Mrs P, we cover the room in flowers and I send Isobel and Anna off outside to the rose garden to work on the flower wall. Anna is exhausted and on her last nerve – I know if she spends too long with Mrs Parker she is in danger of telling her where to put her corsage, and it won't be pretty. As she 'assists', I smile my way through Herr Parker's directions, requests and general all-round bossiness until we're finished and she says, 'I can't believe what we've achieved.' Despite the fact that the real donkey work has been done over the last four days and today is merely an extensive touch-up, I smile and thank her for all her help.

'Oh, it was a pleasure, Rosie, please call me Pamela,' she says, hugging me. 'Come on, let's go and take a breath of air and enjoy this beautiful sunshine while we can.'

So we wander the grounds arm in arm like two dowager duchesses, oohing and aahing at the loveliness of it all. The venue does look amazing, and I'm so proud of the white flower wall. 'It's a wonderful backdrop for photos and the bridal entrance,' Pamela is saying. 'I'm absolutely ecstatic!'

And I hear Mike's voice whispering in my ear, 'Well done, Rosie. I knew you could do it, love.'

I feel myself tearing up with tiredness, relief and pride.

'You okay, Mum?' Both my girls are soon fussing round me like mother hens. Daughters are good at role reversal, becoming mothers the minute you need them.

I smile. 'These are happy tears, I'm absolutely fine. Just pleased with how everything looks and proud of my two girls,' I say, putting both arms around them.

Anna nods towards Mrs P who's now instructing a waiter on how to set a table. 'Is your BFF happy?'

'My what?'

'Your Best Friend Forever?'

'Oh ... you're using Emma-speak,' I laugh, confused

59

as always by the initialisms my granddaughter uses which render simple phrases impossible for me to comprehend.

'Darling, she's AE,' I say in my Mrs Parker voice. The girls look puzzled.

'Absolutely Ecstatic, of course, you two need to get with the programme.'

'She's making it up, there's no such thing as AE,' Anna, ever the pedant, points out.

'Everyone will be saying it soon, just check out your Facebook pages ... and those Google ... thingies.' I smile.

They both laugh – and as it's now about an hour to go before the wedding we decide to clear off.

'Them posh folk don't wanna see the hired help,' Anna says in a funny accent, touching her forelock.

'Well, the bridal bouquet has been delivered to the bride's room, along with all the bridesmaids' posies, so our work here is done,' I sigh, getting ready to leave, happy with all we've done.

Just then Pamela appears at my side. 'Oh, Rosie, you're not leaving, are you?' She grabs my arm. 'I am so delighted with everything you've done I would adore it if the three of you would at least stay and have a glass of champagne with me in the bar. I called my friend who works on *Cheshire Love* – it's a local wedding magazine – and they are going to come and photograph the room and are absolutely ecstatic with the floral wall ... it's a triumph.'

'AE ...' I mutter to Isobel, as we all troop behind her into the bar. It would have been impolite to turn her down and we may be tired, but I'm buoyed up by the prospect of free advertising in a local magazine and ready for a glass of champagne. Anna asks for Buck's Fizz as she's driving, 'which leaves the coast clear for you and me to get plastered with Pamela,' Isobel jokes in my ear.

The bar is fresh and modern and we all sit at a round wooden table while Pamela orders a bottle of fizz. A few minutes later the waiter brings it over in an ice bucket with optional orange juice. I love champagne and am just about to take my first, cold, sparkly sip when my world topples on its axis.

Chapter Five

It's him. At least I think it's him. Of course it is, I'd know him anywhere, even after all this time. He is standing at the bar, his hair's greyer, his face more crinkled, but I'd know those eyes anywhere. He's still so tall, so handsome and my heart still leaps, almost landing in the ice bucket.

I'm momentarily distracted by Pamela fussing at my side. 'Oh, there he is ... Peter, Peter, come and say hello to the brilliant flower ladies,' she calls.

He turns away from the bar to look over at Pamela and in that moment my past crashes in like a huge wave, wiping away everything that's happened since. Everything stops and I can feel myself falling from a great height, tumbling backwards over and over, unable to see anything but him. I'm amazed at the physical shock I'm experiencing through my body – a fizzing sensation I haven't felt for decades. But why is he here now? What happened to him? Did he live his dream? And more worryingly, who is he to Mrs Parker? Her husband?

He slowly walks towards us, a bemused look on his face, his arms outstretched.

'Of all the bars, in all the world . . .' He starts with the old *Casablanca* line, and I smile. 'Rosie?'

'Pierre?'

We both laugh, sealing the devastating connection we once shared and the years fall away like petals blown in the wind. My heart is racing and I'm back in the art studio all those years ago looking into the bluest eyes, the warmest, sexiest smile. He's shaking his head slowly, he looks as incredulous as I feel that we should bump into each other here, now, after all these years.

I've thought about this boy, this man, for over forty years, imagined him then and now and my heart is filled with a delicious, delirious fear. In the few moments we stand facing each other all the love, the laughter and the pain run through me, like my whole life is playing on fast forward. I'm breathless and my head is spinning, my stomach churning. How? Why? What's he doing here? I try and assimilate all the information around me to explain his sudden presence after all this time, but it isn't making any sense.

I stand up on wobbly legs to greet him as he approaches the table, and we hug.

'I don't believe it,' I gasp.

It's like stepping back in time; he feels the same, his arms strong around me, his smell is sandalwood fused with musk – and like yesterday it fills me up and takes me there.

'Is it really you?' he says as we pull apart. He's holding me by the elbows and looking into my face and as my eyes meet his I see the seventeen-year-old boy smiling back at me.

I can't actually speak and am instantly reminded of the phrase my granddaughter uses when she's amazed/horrified/delighted – 'There are no words.' And in the absence of words, we both laugh and hug again. This time I rest my head for a brief moment on his shoulder, and greedily breathe him in again. It fills my lungs and cleaves open my heart. For over forty years I've kept my feelings airtight, safe in the Tupperware container of my heart and here it is, suddenly open, the contents tumbling out. I pull away, remembering where I am, and realising everyone is looking at me.

Peter and I can't take our eyes off each other – it's not just about attraction, it's like stepping into the past, all that was and all that might have been. Then I remember how old I am and feel a bit silly. I sit down and roll my eyes in self-deprecation, hoping to God he can't hear the thudding of my heart. Meanwhile my daughters are looking puzzled and staring from him to me and back again like they are watching tennis.

How could I ever begin to tell them this story and all that happened? I've imagined this for over forty years, the rational part of me never believing it would happen, yet for me there is an inevitability in this moment. Deep in the raggle-taggle of emotions still in my heart I've always known we'd meet again.

'So you know my brother! What a small world,' Pamela is saying. This, of course, is a relief, especially as we've been clinging to each other and hugging for the past few minutes.

I am trying to gather myself together. I hope my face isn't giving away too much as he sits down next to me. I turn to my daughters and say, 'This is ... my ... this is Peter ... Pamela's brother and my ... first boyfriend.'

Peter says hello and my daughters respond politely while regarding me like I'm in the early stages of a meltdown. As I haven't been back in the real world long they are currently on red alert concerning my emotional well-being, waiting to catch me if I fall. I love them so much but I wish they'd stop looking at me so warily, trying to work out what I'm thinking, and whether they need to take me away from all the excitement. I just want to be left alone with him. I have so many questions, so much to ask, so much to tell . . . and a strange urge to laugh hysterically. Now he's here, in front of me, I have to know where he's been, what he's done, and who he loved after me. Like my whole life has been leading to this.

'We met at art school. Your mum was the most amazing artist,' Peter says and the girls smile. They think he's being kind; I don't draw now and they've never seen my sketches or paintings, I didn't keep them after everything that happened. Anyway, on the plus side, the girls are calmed by this explanation and seem somewhat relieved that Peter and I do actually know each other and I haven't just accosted a strange man in a hotel bar. Given my recent wobbles they would be forgiven for thinking this, especially as I'm a little flushed and flustered. But in truth I'm keeping it all well hidden. No one here could possibly have any idea of the colossal emotions that are swooshing under my skin right now. I take a large glug of champagne and hear Pamela telling Peter how amazing 'Rosie and her girls' are.

'Like I say, Rosie always was a great talent,' he says, then gestures to the girls, 'and the fruit doesn't fall far from the tree.'

There's silence now and we all take a sip at the same time. The others are waiting for me or Peter to speak again, but apart from having an audience, it's impossible after all this time.

'Excuse me, ladies,' Peter says, and I think he's going to just leave the table, abandon me for another forty-odd years. But just as I brace myself for his departure, he puts his hand on top of mine and I feel a rush, both familiar and strange.

'I do hope you don't think me rude, but I wonder if I might borrow Rosie for a little while? I'm sure you young people don't want to be bored by our dusty old reminiscences . . .'

The girls smile and Pamela looks at her watch while giving me a wink and reminds him, 'Yes, you two go and catch up, but remember your great-niece's wedding is in one hour!'

I tell the girls I won't be long and Peter salutes Pamela which causes Isobel to snigger – our thoughts on Pamela obviously align with his. He then guides me through the bar towards the French windows overlooking the rose gardens and as we wind through the pre-wedding crowd now gathering, someone calls his name.

'Peter, where are you off to?'

'I'm . . . just going to see a lady about some flowers,' he says, and the owner of the voice, a very beautiful woman with a chic short haircut, rolls her eyes.

Over the noisy bar I hear the words, 'Camille' and

'my wife', and my stomach flops. But what did I expect? Of course he has a wife. I imagine he's had his choice of women over the years. As we reach the open doors leading to the gardens I manage to take a quick but thorough look behind me at the woman he married. I could have picked her out in a line-up: she's chic with great bone structure and very expensive clothes. I pick my heart up off the floor and follow him through the open doors into the brilliant sunshine. I take a deep breath.

Everything has suddenly changed in his presence, the air is fresher, clearer, colours are more intense – like a grey veil has been lifted and I can see again. The gardens before us are even more beautiful, fat-headed roses lie lazily around younger, perkier buds, all bathing in warmth, and exuding a delicious fragrance. I glance at him and a feeling flows through me, reaching out from the past like a ghost wafting through the gardens. I turn to him and his eyes are already on mine the way they used to be. It's been so very long and I know nothing about him or his life, he might as well be a virtual stranger – yet walking beside him feels like we are together again.

'I just had to talk to you and I didn't want my sister poking her nose in. She loves nothing more than to meddle in my life,' he says with some affection.

'Oh, of course – I remember now. Pamela your sister.'
I recall an open door in a big, beautiful house, a glimpse
of a young girl playing the cello.

'So what about you? I want to know everything,' he
says, still looking at me intensely.

I'm bewildered and delighted at his interest after all
this time. We both stop walking and look at each other.

'It feels like yesterday,' he says.

'I know … perhaps more like the day before yesterday?' I suggest and we instinctively start walking again.

'The day before yesterday when we were young,' he
sighs, casting his eyes down onto the grass, and we walk
on for a few seconds in silence.

'Do you still sketch?' he asks.

'No, I gave up years ago,' I say. I never picked up a
paintbrush or drawing pencil again after him.

'Oh, that's such a shame. God, you were so gifted, I
always wondered if I'd ever come across your work in
galleries.'

I feel sad that I didn't meet his expectations of me,
that the future he dreamed of for Rosie Draper wasn't
the path she took. I'd almost forgotten about my 'talent',
my ability to sketch and paint and how it singled me out
from all the other teenage girls I knew – and how my life
was going to be so different.

'No, I've been too busy bringing up kids and working

69

in the shop,' I say, braving it out, hoping he'll believe me even though I'm not sure I believe myself.

'That's such a shame, but understandable.'

'What about you? Do you still take photographs?' I ask, keen to move on from the subject of my talent; it reminds me of what I once had, what I'd hoped to become. It's painful all over again.

'Yeah, I'm a photographer, I do the odd show, a stint at various art colleges, teaching, lecturing. I could never imagine doing anything else really. I haven't done any shoots for a while, but my work's been in magazines, had a few exhibitions, I still make a living, you know . . .'

'That sounds exciting . . .'

'How are you? I mean . . . really? I'm so sorry, Rosie . . . for everything. I can still see you, that dress covered in forget-me-nots. You looked so pretty . . .'

We stop walking and he touches my arm. I keep my head down, my eyes away from his, and take off my sandals, feeling the grass warm under my bare feet. I slip the straps of my sandals through my fingers while I think of how to respond.

'You don't have to say anything, it was a long time ago.'

I straighten up, playing with the straps and avoiding his eyes. All the pain is flooding back and I wonder why I'm even talking to this man who came into my life and changed everything. In another life he swept by me, throwing up a fistful of dreams like gold dust, but before it even landed he was gone.

We both walk on a little further in silence, and I can't help but think how in tune with each other we still are. Our lives were entwined for one lovely summer and we have so much to say, yet neither of us seem to know where to begin.

We're different people now – perhaps the past should stay in the past?

He still has the energy, that infectious enthusiasm he always had, and the lovely voice, though now it has more timbre. He's looking at me with delight on his face, like he just found the most beautiful flower, but his eyes are tinged with something else. Sadness? Regret? I can feel myself burning up, the heat whooshing through my body. And I'm horrified to realise I still feel something for him.

'I never forgot you,' he sighs. 'I know it may seem like I'm just saying this now, but I thought about you every single day.'

'I thought about you too.' I don't add that sometimes those thoughts weren't love or fondness, quite the opposite.

'I made a mistake, Rosie . . . the biggest mistake of my life.'

'Peter, it's in the past, let's not rake over it all now.' I lift my head and try to brighten my voice. I don't need this heaviness, this awful reminder of a past I've tried to forget. 'You're at a wedding, I'm at work, we haven't seen each other for such a long time, let's just say hi, and talk about the good times. No need to go over everything, it's not like we need to . . . it's just good to see you, that's all,' I say, hardly believing it myself.

'I just feel like I need . . . to talk . . .'

'Why? What's the point in dragging everything up now? We were very young, we've both lived a lifetime since, we're different people now,' I say. We continue to walk in silence. We are both alone in our thoughts yet there's a pull, drawing us together from the past. Has it always been like this?

I am overwhelmed by a need to touch him, to reach out and remind him of how much I loved him. At the same time resentment is bubbling away under the surface and I want to push him away. I don't want to face the past, why should I?

'Let's sit down a moment, the wedding can wait a few minutes, even if my sister can't.' He smiles, settling down on the lawn, holding out his hand for me to join him, his eyes staring into mine. I haven't sat on grass since the grandchildren were small and as I try to sit down gracefully, it occurs to me I may not be able to get up again. But I join him, and throw back my head, feeling the sunshine on my face – I'm once again soothed by his presence. I always was. And despite all the conflicting thoughts, all I can think is, Peter's here, he came back.

'You haven't changed,' I say, making small talk. 'You look the same – and I guess you still don't follow the rules. I don't know many men of your age who'd sit on the grass in a wedding suit.'

'I try,' he laughs, 'but breaking rules isn't sexy in your sixties, it's just seen as eccentric or annoying, and it plays havoc with your back.' He rubs his lower back with his hand as if to demonstrate.

I laugh in recognition. I never imagined him old with aching joints – I still see the eighteen-year-old boy in his eyes and find it hard to reconcile this with the steely grey hair, the weathered skin.

'With you in your wedding finery and me with ferns and oasis sticking in my hair, we *both* look eccentric and annoying. If we're not careful our kids will put us into one of those twilight homes for the old and bewildered,' I laugh.

'You will never be old, Rosie – not to me.' He looks me up and down. 'Eccentric, a little crazy perhaps, but never old.' I laugh and nudge him in a mock reprimand. He always teased me, and it's amazing how quickly we're slipping back into our former roles. Despite everything

73

that happened, after all this time – we still fit. It strikes me that I still like this man sitting next to me on the grass in the sunshine. I would like him even if I'd never known him before. I am older now, I'm not that teenager in his thrall, I'm in control, yet … I know I'm vulnerable to his charm, his attention. He always made me feel like I was beautiful and interesting, it was so infectious I believed it myself.

'This is nice …' he says, and I'm not sure if he means the gardens or us, but it doesn't matter. His smile and easy laid-back way still have the power to seduce me, and my quick responses and confident façade aren't doing anything to smooth over my mashed-up thoughts, torn between wanting to kiss him or slap him hard across the face. I try to drive these feelings away, smiling up at the sunshine as we sit and stare out at the gardens together. I'm probably in shock, it's like the past just suddenly appeared and grabbed me by the throat saying, 'Hey, you … do you remember this?' And the crashing wave continues to overwhelm, enveloping me with the memories and the sheer thrill of it all – along with the fear of drowning.

I see some of the guests milling around the garden area near the bar. 'I think the wedding is about ready to start,' I say, not wanting him to miss anything.

'Meeting you is kind of bigger than a wedding.' He

looks at me. We make no move to go and I wonder what the people in the bar think when they see us here together, just another old couple, I suppose, nothing extraordinary. If only they knew – the strength of passion, the decades of longing and all that happened between us.

He turns toward me, hand on forehead shielding his beautiful eyes from the sun.

'It's not every day one meets the ... well someone who ...' He seems suddenly awkward.

'Yes,' I say quickly to cover his embarrassment.

'You're married, I take it?' he says, now staring out at the gardens again, not looking at me any more.

'Yes. I was, well, I still am in a way. Mike ... my husband ... he died, just over a year ago.'

'I'm so sorry.' We gaze ahead, watching two children chasing each other around the lake. They are dressed in wedding clothes and look like something from an Edwardian photograph in this setting. He's smiling – he always liked children and I wonder fleetingly if he has any of his own. It makes me think of what we might have had, what might have been – thoughts I've revisited countless times over the years.

'How old was your husband?' he suddenly says, breaking the thick silence.

'Only sixty-four. It seems funny saying "only". I

remember when I was younger I would think someone dying in their forties had had a good innings.'

'I know, crazy, yes? I always thought if I got to fifty I'd done well and could die happily of old age.' He shakes his head, smiling in disbelief. 'We hadn't a clue, had we?'

I shake my head in agreement.

'Then again, life seems to go on for so much longer these days.'

'For some of us . . .' I say.

'Oh, sorry, Rosie. I didn't mean . . .'

'No, it's fine. It's been a huge loss, to me and the girls, but we're starting to regroup and I'm beginning to feel more positive about life. Oh, it's a cliché, I know – but Mike's death has made me realise how short life is and how we make all these plans and . . .'

'Life happens while you're making them?'

'Yes . . . something like that. Didn't someone famous say that in the sixties?'

'It was probably me,' he laughs with a twinkle in his eye.

He's gently teasing and in spite of myself I can't help but tease him back . . . he's bringing out the teenager in me. I can feel her around me, the way I'm holding my head to one side, looking at him under my lashes, playing with my hair. I feel like the girl I used to be – she's putting her hands over my eyes, 'Guess who?' she says, and I'm happy to see her. I thought she was long gone.

'Was it a happy marriage?' he asks, and though I'm surprised at the question I'm not offended by it. Peter and I were once so close it feels natural to ask quite personal questions of each other even after all these years.

'Yes, it was. A very happy marriage. Mike was a wonderful husband and though we married young and had our ups and downs, it was good. He was always there for me . . . and now suddenly I'm lost.' I hear my voice break, and to my astonishment, my eyes fill with tears. 'I'm sorry, I don't know where this has all come from.' I wipe my eyes with the back of my hand. 'We haven't seen each other for all this time and I'm now blubbing everywhere. This is the first job I've been on in a year and the girls are worried sick I'm just going to collapse in a heap . . . and you turning up . . . it's just a bit of a shock.'

'No, it's me who should be apologising, I shouldn't have asked you about your husband, it was thoughtless.' He reaches into his pocket and hands me a beautifully ironed handkerchief. I take it gratefully and remember he has a wife who probably ironed it lovingly for him.

I wipe my eyes and I'm aware time is marching on but I don't want to move. I don't want to say goodbye to him again, I'm not ready to finally close the door on something I'm not finished with. I wonder if he feels the same.

'Did you ever get to Paris, Rosie?'

I shake my head. 'No, I suppose it was just a teenage fantasy, and once I was married with kids and a mortgage I found it harder and harder to imagine a real life spent sketching in a café on the Left Bank.' I wish he hadn't mentioned it, the thing that held us together. I remember a map of Paris he gave to me – I still have it, but opened it up so many times it's now held together with sticky tape. I still devour articles on Paris and I've bought a million guidebooks, always meaning to go, but in truth the thought of it was never quite the same after.

We sit in silence again. Every word has to be carefully chosen, I don't want to say something that might set us on the wrong course and ruin this one meeting with my vintage hurt. I want this to be my moment, the day he walks away from me knowing what he lost and regretting what happened, because that's how he made me feel. I want him to feel it too, to know the pain he put me through.

'I'll go, I'll go to Paris one day ... before I die,' I say.

'Shall we go now? Let's just run away to London and get on a train to Paris,' he says, and I see the excited boy under the steely grey hair. 'It may be a little different than we planned, we probably can't walk as far, for a start, and there's my back to consider,' he adds.

'Mmm, I'm not sure sleeping on the floor of an artist's garret would be good for my back these days either,' I laugh.

'What's the line from *Casablanca*? Bogart says to Bergman, "We'll always have Paris", and we will.'

I smile. 'I suppose so, no one can take away your dreams, can they?'

'It's somewhere I've dreamt about a lot over the years ... with you, Rosie, always with you.'

I smile at him indulgently, I can't help myself. I'm remembering again what a dreamer – and a charmer – he was and how impressionable I must have been to go along with it all.

'I think Paris is a state of mind,' I say. I won't be seduced by his twinkly smile and fond reminiscences.

'In Paris we're teenagers, the sun's shining and we're walking hand in hand through the streets. Let's be teenagers again, Rosie. After all, it was only the day before yesterday ...'

'You haven't changed.' I'm shaking my head and smiling at him. He's still full of life, but somehow he's softer, less arrogant than the eighteen-year-old I fell in love with.

'So let's book into a hotel and do it in style ... who cares how we do it, Paris is Paris.'

He's refusing to be put off his idea – he is joking, of course, but with a little encouragement I imagine he probably would run away to Paris now, a few minutes before the wedding. He always loved an adventure, something new to discover and sod the consequences, he'd deal with those later – or not. He never wanted to be in the same place for too long, and being Peter he never had to be – he was one of life's lucky ones and always managed to get his ticket out.

'As much as I'd love to join you on this impromptu Parisian odyssey, there's the small matter of a wedding.' I smile. 'And sadly I have the van keys so I can't run away to Paris today, the girls won't be able to get home. One of us has to be responsible. Let's leave running away until next week?'

'Okay, next week it is. I was about to grab your hand and make a run for it now over the rose garden.' He looks at me, his cheeky grin still firmly in place.

'How romantic,' I say, but what I really want to ask is, *What happened to us? Why did you never try to find me? How could you do that after all we'd been to each other?*

But in keeping with my sixty-something respectable businesswoman and widow persona, I keep it light and appropriate, if a little flirty: 'I don't think your wife would be too pleased at you abandoning her at a wedding to run off to Paris with an old girlfriend.'

'My wife? Oh … Camille, you mean? She'd be delighted, she's always trying to get me fixed up, I think she feels sorry for me.'

'Really?' I was horrified and intrigued. 'Do you have

one of those open marriages I read about in my daughters' magazines?'

'No. Oh God no,' he laughs. 'I'm sorry – I still refer to Camille as my wife, force of habit, I suppose. We were married for twenty years then estranged for ten, never bothering to get divorced. We both agree we should never have married, but finally got around to divorcing when she wanted to marry someone else.'

'Oh, was that difficult for you?'

'Yeah. Very. He's more handsome than me, and he has a lot more money. Can't think what she sees in him.'

He obviously doesn't want to go into his marital break-up and is trying to play it down with humour, so I don't pursue it. But I have to confess my spirit lifts to hear he's divorced. Okay, perhaps I'm understating my response slightly when I say my spirit lifts – I mean it soars and dances around the gardens shouting 'Yess!' I have this urge to run along the grass singing, 'Oh what a beautiful morning,' but my daughters will, no doubt, be watching through the window and at the sight of this would be also dialling for an ambulance.

So I abandon the song and dance, sit on my hands, lift my chin and try to look seventeen instead. I don't know why I'm so pleased at his single status, it's not like anything would happen between us now, we're both on the wrong side of sixty – it would be ludicrous.

81

'So, you're on your own now?' I say.

'Yes, I live in Oxford. Camille had the house in France ... and so she should, her father paid for most of it.'

'That sounds nice.' So he married one of his kind after all.

'Oh it is, the house in France was featured in a magazine recently; Camille insisted I do the photos, which was nice of her.' He smiles at the thought. 'She has a real eye for interior design, very French chic, I think you'd call it.' I wonder if he still has feelings for her. Did she break his heart like he broke mine? Was she his nemesis in the same way he was mine? 'I have some of the photos here.' He takes out his phone and opens up a world of huge, high-ceilinged rooms in eggshell blues and greys. Big sash windows framed by floating white curtains flood the rooms with light and tease glimpses of lavender in the gardens. He shows me a bedroom with an enormous bed, deep, fluffy pillows and beautiful ornate framed photos and paintings. And here I am, looking at pictures of the life he chose instead of being with me.

'It's stunning.'

'It was a wreck when we bought it but within a few months Camille had created this wonderful living space – she's very talented.'

He continues to scroll through the photos, our heads close together as I peek into his world.

'Is that your artwork on the walls?' I say, keen to move on from his 'amazing' ex-wife.

'Some of it, the photos mainly – the paintings are hers.'

'Oh, she's an artist?' I say, amazed at the vague feelings of envy that tingle through me. I could have been an artist. I could have lived with him in a house like this.

He puts away Camille and his phone and we sit in silence for a little. We've caught up on the immediate stuff of life, but underneath the smooth and smiley sur-face so much more is thrumming in my head: *Did you really think about me over the years? Have you any idea what happened to me afterwards? Did you even care?* But I've told him I don't want to talk about these things and he's respecting my wishes.

So I just keep things as smooth as his French pillows, and smile politely, continuing our story swap but unable to excavate the depths. 'Where ... when did you meet her?' I say, wondering how long after me she came into his life.

'I met her when I was at art college ... in London. Her parents were friends with mine, we'd known each other since we were kids.'

'Oh, so you went to London after all?' *Why didn't you*

tell me, why didn't you get in touch? Why didn't you write to me and share the experience I never got to have?

'Yes ... I worked for a few months at the vineyard in Italy that year, then I travelled for a while but my father wanted me to come home and start my "real life", as he called it.'

He looks at me and he's about to say something and so am I though I'm not sure what, when Pamela appears and calls out to him.

'Peter, I'm so sorry, darling, but the wedding's about to start.'

'I'm not going to lose you again ... not now I've found you,' he says quietly, waving a hand in acknowledgement at his sister. 'Can we meet up ... just lunch, a coffee?'

And I know I shouldn't, he's the last thing I need in my life right now, but I feel seventeen again, as we stand gazing at each other for a few seconds. I melt, my heart in a puddle on the ground until Pamela calls again, reality seeps into the rose garden and I remember the last time we said goodbye. Crowds of people, tears streaming down my face, the nauseating smell of burnt sugar heavy in the air and my chest tight with hurt and shock. Then the loneliness, the endless nights lying awake, imagining him far away, living his life – and missing him so much the pain was physical. And here he is now inviting me for lunch or coffee but I can see he wants more. I'm not being presumptuous, I still know him so well, he's here, asking me to love him a second time, but he's forty-seven years too late. I'm too old to love again.

'I don't know, Peter,' I sigh. 'Perhaps we should just say goodbye and walk away. I want to remember the good times we had.'

'Why goodbye when we've only just said hello again? And who's to say there aren't more good times to come? I thought we were running away to Paris next week?'

I laugh. 'I hope there are some good times to come for both of us, but perhaps not together. You and I already had our time. I have to be realistic, I'm not seventeen any more and neither are you. It would be foolish to go down the same road. I'm a grandmother of sixty-four and I should know better.' I really *should* know better, but even as I say this I feel like I'm on emotional sinking sand, rapidly slipping under.

'I understand. This has all come out of the blue, for both of us, but I'm not asking for anything more than friendship, a remembered past. As I've got older I've thought more about those teenage years, and I would love someone to share them with. Well ... you.'

I nod, reluctantly, shrugging and feeling myself being gently swept towards him into the vortex of our past.

'Look, Rosie, why don't we arrange to meet once, just once? We can laugh about how naive we were and share some lovely memories. Please say yes?'

After everything that happened I'm discomfited to hear him talk of us being 'naive' and sharing 'lovely memories'. My naivety was in loving him and our happy memories were burned in the wreckage – along with the future we'd planned. But he's looking at me now with that old smile and the past and the present are twisting together and I want to know his story.

'Okay,' I say, unable to resist the pull.

'Perhaps you could give me your phone number and I could call you sometime?' he says.

I suddenly feel hesitant. I waited a long time for that telephone to ring. Am I being stupid even contemplating waiting for another phone call just so we can meet up and open all the old wounds? But his eyes are still so blue, and he still has that 'something' he always had, and the seventeen-year-old girl who's now by my side begs me to say yes.

'So, your phone number?' he asks. He's taken out a small leather notebook and I wonder fleetingly if there are already other women's names and numbers in his little book.

But I give him my number, what harm can it do? I can always say no if he does ever call. Can't I?

We walk slowly back towards the hotel in the sunshine. I am with Peter and I'm fizzing with excitement but a cloud covers the sun and I can't help but feel a little shiver.

Chapter Six

After meeting him again I feel unsettled. I was beginning to contemplate a kind of life without Mike, but now the past and the present have crashed into each other and I'm thinking more and more about Peter. I know there are issues between us, things we need to say, but it's like someone has blown a dandelion clock into the air, and for now I just want to grasp at the wafting memories. My work is second nature to me, so it isn't affected by these distracting thoughts laced with tantalising and sometimes painful memories. But my head is full of him and the past and I'm talking to people on autopilot, nodding and saying 'lovely', or 'that's nice', when they might be telling me something horrific. I was talking to a customer only this morning telling her 'how excited' she must be as she booked flowers for her grandfather's funeral. I feel like I'm in limbo, living in the now, but taken over by the past.

Alone in the back of the shop I add white baby's breath to a bouquet, marvelling at the delicate, frothy flower heads while my mind is drawn back once more to Peter.

I remember him walking me to my bus stop, after college, when he suddenly said: 'Rosie, I'm going to paint you naked one day.' I was shocked at this and felt myself blush from my toes. At the same time I felt a flurry of something inside, a new and wonderful sensation, like a trapped bird in my tummy. I wasn't as outraged as I knew I should have been and felt a warm tingle go through me. I'd never had these feelings before and I wasn't sure I should be having them then either.

'Pierre Morton, you are very forward,' I said, with half a smile. We arrived at the bus stop and as I leaned against it he faced me, looking straight into my eyes.

'Yeah, I am. But you can call me Peter.'

'Do you always ask girls if you can paint them naked . . . Peter?'

'I didn't ask,' he said, a smile playing on his lips. 'I told you I would. And I will.' His confidence sometimes bordered on arrogance; unlike me he had no self-doubts and along with his laughing eyes I found this self-assurance so attractive.

'You're very sure of yourself, aren't you?' I said, afraid my legs would give way.

'No, just sure of my subject.' He was looking me up and down. 'Has anyone ever told you, you look a bit like Marianne Faithfull?'

'No ... not really.' I remembered my brother's friend Mike had once commented on the likeness, but I hadn't taken him seriously.

'You could go to London and be a model.'

'I don't want to. I want to go to Paris and be an artist,' I said, a teenager unable to accept a compliment. I was flattered but trying not to show it.

'Yeah, you could earn a living as an artist – you're good enough.'

I blushed again and felt a stab of disappointment as the bus arrived. But by now I knew we were more than just friends, a bud was growing between us, and as we said goodbye I waltzed onto that bus like I was Marianne Faithfull.

I smile to myself now, thinking about that girl. She was young and beautiful and talented and for the first time she had a slight inkling what it might feel like to be in love.

And sitting on the bus she allowed herself to imagine

Peter kissing her, his tongue probing her mouth, his hands moving all over her. But it was the sixties and she was torn between feeling terribly wonderful and terribly guilty. And despite it being a cold, dark December afternoon in the north of England, she was so hot she had to take off her cardigan.

The Monday after the wedding I'm working at the shop when the phone rings, and I have a sixth sense and just know it's Peter.

'Hello, Rosie?' And I remember again how I always loved the way he said my name, gentle and soft.

'Ah, so you called?' I smile. Anna looks up from a pile of carnations with a questioning expression, assuming she must know who I'm talking to. After all, my life is hers — and hers is her own.

'I know it's so soon after we met, but I was scared we might lose touch again. I wanted so much to meet I couldn't wait and didn't want to leave it any longer.'

'Well, it's been forty-seven years, I don't think a few more days would make any difference,' I say, feeling a little put out. He calls me now when nothing is at stake, when nothing's expected of him, yet he never called me when I needed him, when he said he would.

'Rosie, just tell me to go away if you'd rather not. I

just thought we should talk and I really want to see you again . . .'

This older Peter seems hesitant, slightly unsure of himself and I find it endearing. I want to talk too and hear myself say, 'Yes, that sounds good.'

Peter is a big part of my story and I will regret it if I never see him again, even if it is only once, just to find out the rest of *his* story.

'Okay. As it happens I'm up near you later this week.'

'Oh, I'm not sure about meeting here,' I say quietly, aware Anna has stopped what she's doing and is now looking at me. She mouths 'Who is it?' and I wave my hand at her as if to say 'It's nothing,' and take the phone into the back of the shop. 'What about somewhere further – halfway, perhaps?' I say, preferring not to meet him here in the town where we used to be us. I'd rather see him somewhere we've never been together, I don't want the past to crowd in on the present.

We agree on Friday at New Street station in Birmingham, halfway between Manchester and Oxford. Despite my older self telling me not to get carried away, I feel a frisson of fear and excitement as I put down the phone.

I compose myself, and wander back into the shop where Anna is now dealing with a customer. As soon as the customer is gone, she whizzes round.

'Who was that on the phone?'

'Oh . . . just then, you mean? It was an old friend . . .'

'You mean that Peter, the guy you met at the Parker wedding?'

'Yes.' I can feel my colour rising, so silly at my age, but I feel like a kid again. I really want to see him, I hope I'm not being stupid.

'I thought he lived in Oxford?'

'He does. So we're meeting up on Friday . . . in Birmingham. Will you be okay with me having my usual Friday off?'

'Yes, I suppose so, we're quite busy though – but Izzy will be here and Mrs Jackson is doing a few hours on buttonholes, God help us. I'm hoping there isn't too much damage she can do.'

I slip back into Peter reverie and Anna continues with what she's doing, but I know her and she's dying to know more. Sure enough, a few seconds later she's thought of a way of hacking back in.

'Birmingham, that'll be nice, there are lots of new shops and nice restaurants there now.'

'Yeah? We're just doing lunch. It was such an amazing coincidence to meet up again, we had such a good time at college and I think we both want to relive it a little, just as friends, you know? Pure nostalgia really.'

The door clangs as another customer comes in and

Anna goes to greet them. I put the kettle on, hoping the steam might conceal the mottling that is sure to be covering my chest.

'I can drop you off at Piccadilly for your train on Friday, Mum,' she says later, when the customer has left.

'That would be great, thank you. It's just a lunch,' I add unnecessarily, wondering who I'm trying to convince. I don't want to discuss my conflicting feelings yet with Anna ... well, with anyone. I have a good relationship with my girls but they have their own lives, separate from mine, and it will be good for all of us if I now try and do things independently from them. After Mike died they formed a wall around me to protect my feelings, but I feel ready to start taking down the bricks. My life is an open book that my children assume begins and ends with their births, which is partially true, but I had a life before them, and in meeting Peter I'm going back there and it's something I must do alone. I've been thinking about the next stage of my life a lot recently. I can't rely on my kids too much, it isn't fair on them and it isn't good for me. The girls are both settled and happy now and don't need me like they may have done in the past, so where does that leave me? Even the grandchildren don't need me any more except for the odd lift to dance class or to join them for an evening when Anna

94

goes out. So what am I left with? Work and walking the dog? I'm beginning to think there must be more than that.

I keep thinking about Friday when I'm seeing him again and I go from being deliriously excited to being petrified and doubting my sanity. Last night I woke about four a.m. and seriously considered calling him first thing and saying 'I can't make it, and I never will,' and just putting down the phone. Today I'm like a teenager again, deciding what to wear, how to have my hair, and holding conversations with Peter in my head. I can't read a book, settle down to watch TV or even talk to customers without my mind drifting towards the rose gardens and his beautiful smile.

I keep asking myself why him, why now? Is it fate? Are we the same people we were? And can I bear to excavate the past, delve into my own bottled-up feelings?

The train ride is pleasant, I buy a magazine and a black coffee and leaf through the glossy pictures as the world goes by through the window. I can't possibly read or think because if I do I might just call him and cancel. I'm having a wobble, wishing Mike was here and everything was as it used to be. If he were still alive I wouldn't even contemplate this meeting, but he isn't, so why am

I feeling guilty? It's not a date, it's lunch with someone I used to know well. That's what I keep telling myself as I get off the train and walk to John Lewis, the landmark where we'd arranged to meet.

I scan the area quickly and my heart jumps a little – there he is, waiting. I see him first, which gives me the chance to observe him unaware as I approach. He is still quite delicious in jeans and a white linen shirt, looking at least ten years younger than he actually is. Standing in the doorway of the store, he's looking at something in the window and I am able to observe him unaware. He's tall and still very slim with a full head of thick, dark grey hair – and I see he still has that something as a passing woman gives him a second glance. A familiar wave of mild jealousy washes over me. No wonder I was sometimes insecure with a man like Peter; I can see it now through older eyes, my teenage love, stinging jealousy enhanced by hormones. I am safe now, on the shores of sixty-something, and I can only pity the poor, helpless girl I once was – jelly in his hands. I'm close to him now and as he looks away from the window he suddenly sees me and his face lights up like it used to. We walk quickly towards each other, our arms open, and when we come together we embrace warmly for a long time. And I shouldn't feel like this, but I don't ever want to extricate myself from him.

Eventually we pull apart and do that thing people do when they are at a loss: we talk about lunch, where to go, what to eat. I can't imagine either of us is hungry, but it's the accepted thing to do and gives us a purpose, a structure. So we drift aimlessly towards the restaurant area, making meaningless comments: 'I can't believe it,' and 'after all this time,' and 'is it really you?' Eventually we wander into an Italian chain restaurant which I'm sure he wouldn't usually be seen dead in.

We sit down, gaze briefly at the menu and both choose a pasta dish. He orders a bottle of red and when it arrives the waitress pours it into huge round glasses and we sip it slowly, gratefully.

'Thank you for meeting up today,' he says, putting down his glass, meeting my eyes.

'Thank you for inviting me.'

'Well I did wonder if you'd say yes, I had to take a deep breath. Even at my age rejection isn't easy.' He smiles that lazy smile that begins in his eyes and works its way to his mouth.

'I wasn't sure whether to meet you, but then I just heard myself say yes.' I smile. 'I don't know if I would have suggested it though.'

'I suppose I'm old-fashioned – I believe the man should make the first call.'

'My granddaughter would be furious to hear you say

that,' I sigh, 'and me too – I'm not that seventeen-year-old any more, who swoons if you open a door for me.'

'No, I can see you're a woman now. You've lived a life and you look good on it.'

I blush like a young girl. 'I didn't want you to feel obligated to call me to meet up.'

'Why on earth would I feel obligated? I've been looking for you . . . for ever.'

I look at him and the tenderness in his eyes, the sincerity in his voice softens me.

'We had such great times, Rosie. All those hopes and dreams, all the plans we had.'

I nod. I want to remind him that he was the one who crushed those plans, who wrecked those dreams, but I just take a large drink of wine and smile.

'I wanted to see you, because – well, I wanted to see you. But apart from that I just feel like I need to face what happened, the way I behaved towards you . . .'

'You were young and you wanted so much more . . . but then so did I.'

'I was young, yes, and I was stupid and selfish and cruel.'

'I suppose that comes with the territory when you're eighteen,' I sigh, trying to be grown up about it. 'I really thought you'd save me . . . I needed you.' I blurt this out, accusingly, it wasn't my intention, I couldn't help it.

Instead of forgiving and letting the past stay where it was, the feelings have all bubbled up when I wasn't looking and I can feel my eyes stinging.

'Oh God, Rosie – I'm sorry . . .'

'No, no, I'm sorry. I didn't want this meeting to be about apologies and regret . . . there's really no point.' I take a tissue from my bag and pretend I have dust in my eye. After all we had I don't want it to end up as some confrontation in a pseudo-Italian chain restaurant in the middle of Birmingham. I have no intention of being the scorned woman who's held onto bitterness and resentment all her life, because that's not who I am. 'I agreed to meet because I'd like to talk, I want to know where you've been, what you've done, what happened after me. But for the sake of what we had I don't want us to be unkind to each other. If this is the one time we meet again, let's make it a happy one, or it will all have been for nothing. We've both had happy lives, of course there have been the "what ifs?" But doesn't everyone have those?'

He nods, raises his hand to my cheek and strokes my lips with his thumb.

I am stunned by the intimacy of this and shocked at how it makes me feel. He seems to realise my surprise and immediately removes his hand. I take a large glug of wine and we both smile awkwardly.

'I've thought of those lips for over forty years,' he says, staring into my eyes.

I never expected this, I already feel completely out of control.

'So as this is a first and last lunch,' I say, trying to wipe away the intimacy and keep things on a friendship level, 'let's just be happy and remember only good things. To no regrets.' I raise my glass.

He raises his. 'No regrets.' He takes a sip. 'I take it that means Paris is out of the question?'

I laugh and shake my head. 'You were always such a dreamer, Peter ... or should I say Pierre?'

'I'm horrified even now to think I called myself Pierre.'

'I know, and you smoked French cigarettes.'

'I'm going red. I was so gauche, why did nobody tell me? Why didn't you tell me?'

'I was too busy wearing black polo neck jumpers and pretending I was an existentialist who lived on the Left Bank. You weren't the only gauche kid in town.'

'God, we were so young, weren't we?'

'Yes, and while you were being Pierre I was doing everything I could to shock Margaret – I thought I was a wild-child rebel.' I laugh as I remember my mother.

As a strident almost-seventeen-year-old determined to make her mark, I couldn't see the vulnerability behind my mother's folded arms and disapproving face. I would have no truck with what I wrongly perceived to be Margaret's sheer meanness. 'You're just jealous,' was my clarion cry as I stormed upstairs and slammed my bedroom door following yet another row about the length of my skirt/lashes/hair.

I can see now that she was perhaps frightened of the unknown. She hated the idea of me going to 'that college' and longed for me to settle down and marry a local lad, someone who would keep me in the same town I'd been born in. This, she believed, would also bring me to my senses and stop my 'silly dreaming'. But the times they were a-changing and the more Margaret expressed her concern at losing her only daughter to the debauched student life she'd read about in the Sunday papers, the more that daughter dreamed.

We both take another sip and look at each other.

'I don't suppose Margaret's still around?' he says.

'No, she died a few years back, not long after Dad died. My eldest brother David died too, thankfully after Mum and Dad.'

'You had another brother . . . was he called Mark?'

'Yes,' I nod. 'Mark's only a couple of years older than me – he and his family moved to Australia. We send Christmas cards, but we were never that close. I don't miss my brothers, but I miss Margaret. Funny, I never thought I'd say that.'

'She was a tour de force, I'm not surprised you miss her – I imagine she left quite a void. I lost both my parents too . . . Sad, but part of life, I suppose.'

'Mmm, I remember your mother,' I say, trying to hide the dislike in my voice.

'Enough about everyone else. How are *you*, Rosie?' he says, probably keen to move off the subject of his mother. He is leaning forward, taking it all up a notch and looking earnestly into my face.

'I'm doing okay. I'm just getting used to being alone again . . . though I have a little dog, Lily, she keeps me company.'

'I always wanted a dog, my mum would never let me, said they were dirty and would ruin the furniture. Mind you, I think she felt the same about her children,' he laughs.

'And her son's girlfriend,' I say as the waitress puts down matching plates of pasta. Peter smiles to acknowledge my comment and after we've both been sprinkled with parmesan we pick up our forks to eat. The food is rather bland and tasteless, but what did we expect?

'Not quite Napoli?' he says, lifting a forkful of orange gloop.

'I know, it's a shame, no little Italian restaurants off the beaten track with candles in dusty bottles and tomato sauce made with tomatoes. Everything's so homogenised now, isn't it?' I agree.

'Yes ... I don't think anyone's fooled by the faux Italian surroundings or the Tuscan crockery,' he says, looking around him. 'That's what was so special about our time in the sixties ... it was all so diverse, new energy, established ideas being challenged – it was a time of great change, but we didn't realise it then.'

We talk some more about old music and our days wandering through Manchester with his camera and reminisce about some of the people from college.

And then at some point in the conversation we abandon the flabby pasta in glutinous sauce and just sip wine. Peter orders another bottle and I'm vaguely aware I'm being irresponsible if I drink any more. 'I have to get a train back to Manchester at six p.m.,' I say.

He looks disappointed. 'Really? Why?'

'Well, my daughter's picking me up at the station and I have to work tomorrow.'

'But you own the business ...'

I look up from my wine glass. 'Yes, but I still have responsibilities.'

'Oh.'

We sit in silence, my comment hanging heavily over the table.

'I'm sorry. No regrets, remember?' I raise my glass again and he looks wistful.

'How can we not have any regrets? We should have

lived in that garret overlooking the Parisian rooftops. We should have drunk coffee on French pavements ... When I let you go I said goodbye to all that.'

'So did I,' I say wistfully. I take a large mouthful of wine and swallow down the tears, the regret, the years of not knowing.

He is shaking his head slowly, tears in his eyes. 'But now, I just feel like it's kismet – what are the chances? We are being handed another opportunity to be together. Don't tell me it isn't meant to be, Rosie ...'

'Whoa. I agreed to meet up to have lunch, I don't see this going anywhere, Peter, how could it?'

He looks at me and sighs, his eyes beseeching me.

'Peter, you can't just waltz back into my life talking about "kismet" and second chances. You had your first chance and you blew it, and I'm now happily widowed and I'm not looking for love again, ever.'

'I understand.' He's running his fingers through his hair, something he always did when he was put on the spot and didn't know how to respond in a difficult situation.

'Can you ever forgive me?'

'It's not really about forgiveness. Yes, I'm still hurt, but I've been happy. I loved you, but I was lucky enough to love someone else too – it took a while, but Mike was the right one for me to marry.'

'I'm glad, I'm glad you had a happy marriage. I'm so relieved I didn't ruin your life with my stupidity.'

'We both were stupid, we were young and in love ... at least, I was.'

'I was too. I know it might not have seemed like it at the time ... but I still cared about you and I miss you, I've always missed you.'

He casts his eyes down and we sit in silence.

'It's my biggest regret, but then it's easy to look back and say why did I do that? At the time it seemed like the right thing to do – I had so many plans ... art college in London ... and travelling the world. In those days I just thought of myself.'

'And all I thought of was you. Even after everything, when my whole life stopped on that day at the fair, I still loved you and if you'd come back to me I'd have welcomed you with open arms ... then.'

'Oh, Rosie ...'

'No. I was the idiot, Peter, not you. And when I finally managed to pull myself up I went on to live a different life as a different person ... It was a wonderful life with Mike and we were so happy.'

Mike's joy at just being with me was an antidote to Peter's cruelty.

'I just sometimes wonder if I'd been in a different environment with a different person what it would have been like, what would I have been like? I wonder if I'd have made it as an artist?' I muse.

'Yes, what might have happened to the girl who planned to exhibit in Paris, haul her canvases to San Francisco and sell them on the bay, live and paint like a Native American in the desert?'

I'd forgotten about San Francisco and the desert, I'd forgotten my own girlish dreams, yet he'd remembered them for me, kept them safe all these years. I'm touched by this but do I really want to be reminded of all the things I didn't do?

'I chose a different path,' I say. 'Yes, I still clung on to the remnants of what I'd hoped for, but what happened changed me and showed me what I needed and not what I wanted. I think I learned over the years that the two things are quite different.'

I sip my drink and feel a lump in my throat thinking of the early days with Mike, when I still belonged to Peter, but Mike had enough love to wait for me to catch up. Sometimes the past would come crashing in and he'd hold me in the night as I cried myself to sleep. He was always there, always loving me. And I will always miss him.

'Yes, I spent much of my life chasing what I wanted, never what I needed. I didn't know the difference then,' he sighs. I wonder if he knows the difference even now.

'You were always chasing the light.' I say. 'Like a kitten dashing after a butterfly, and I always worried you'd get bored, so I had to keep moving and be glittery for you. I wondered later if that's all Paris and I were, a sparkly idea, a moving concept that kept your interest for a little while.'

'Rosie, our plans were real to me, and I wanted to do all the things we'd talked about, but suddenly that day there you were, telling me it wasn't possible, that we couldn't do it.'

'It's funny how we see things differently. I felt it was you telling me I couldn't have what I wanted, what I needed, and I had to run away. It was hard at first to adjust, but I have never regretted the choices I made.'

He doesn't speak, just puts his head down again, and I am surprised to see years of heartache etched in his brow.

'Margaret always said you'd leave me and she was right. Your talk about living abroad always excited me but it scared me too. I only wanted to do that with you. It was *our* dream, you and me and no one else's, and I didn't want to do it alone. What happened to you ... after the fair?' I ask.

'I spent the summer at the vineyard in Italy,' he sighs. 'After the first few days there I realised what a terrible mistake I'd made but my father refused to pay my fare home. You know what he was like, he wanted me to "be a man".' He says this in a gruff voice and I'm reminded of the awful blustery pomposity of his father, who seemed disappointed in his artist son.

'You didn't go back to college after the summer, did you?'

'No, I did a year travelling and working and my father insisted I get back to Britain and do a course or start a job ... What he wanted, not what I needed,' he laughs, echoing our earlier conversation. 'So I went to art school in London, then I lived in Europe, spent the next forty years travelling the world. I have spent my life running away; I've always been looking for something.'

'We are different, so different. I'm beginning to understand why it would never have worked, you and me,' I say, thinking about the way he just packed a bag and walked away, from me, his family, his life. And now he hops on planes and trains, still searching for something else, a more sparkly existence. 'I hope you found what you were looking for,' I add, and I mean it; time has made it bearable for me to hope he's been happy.

'I've been happy enough, but I've spent a long time looking for something that was once right under my nose. You went on to have a good marriage, a family ... I have nothing. I spent the rest of my life looking for another you. And now I know, there isn't another you ... just you. It's only ever been you. Do you want to talk about what happened ... ?'

'I have talked about it. With Mike,' I snap, suddenly overwhelmed by the memories of the past.

'Of course, he was your husband, of course you'd talk to him,' he says, but I can see that hurts him and I'm angry because he wasn't there and Mike was, he has no right to be hurt.

'I just want to make it all up to you ... that's why I was so desperate to meet you again. People often get second chances in life, and here we are being handed this wonderful opportunity to wipe the slate clean, start again. I was young and stupid and I thought I was invincible, that we were invincible. I assumed whatever happened you'd always be there ... that I'd fly off to Italy and you'd be waiting on my return. I didn't show you enough how much you meant; I didn't realise it myself until we were apart. I want to make up for that, I want to love you again, Rosie.'

Chapter Seven

On the train home after meeting Peter I drifted off, thinking about the first time we'd gone out together. I'd been standing at the bus stop and he'd happened to be walking past. He'd smiled at me and I'd pulled my coat around me to cover the red blooming up from my chest to my neck. I was trying so hard to be cool around this fabulous human being, but I was awkward, unable to pull off the sophisticated-woman-of-the-world act. I couldn't play games, there was no point in hiding this blossoming inside me.

'Cigarette?' he said, wandering into the bus shelter like he had no particular place to be and offering me the packet. I nodded, despite an earlier attempt making me cough. I wanted him to have an excuse to cup his hands around mine. I wanted the flame reflected in his eyes as he looked into mine and in that moment, as the soft, relentless rain came down, I knew I'd do anything for this boy.

I took the cigarette from the proffered pack and when he'd lit it, our eyes meeting over the naked flame, I sucked gently, tasting the acrid smoke. It was still unpleasant, but it was also illicit, seductive, and just when I thought it couldn't get any better, he turned to me, his breath smoky, and said, 'The bus isn't coming. Why don't we get out of this rain and go for a coffee?'

I nodded, helpless to resist as he hailed a taxi, which was exotic in itself, I'd only ever seen people do that in films. He asked the taxi driver to take us to the Kardomah, a coffee bar in Albert Square, and we sped along the rainy streets to the city. Once in the café, he pulled out a chair at a table, and I sat down feeling like Audrey Hepburn.

I'd never been in the Kardomah, but I knew it was a special place. Known then as 'the artists' quarter of Manchester', it was cool, exotic, and totally the place to be. Thinking back now I realise how important he was, not just to my emotional growth but my cultural awareness. I remember he explained the Venetian Gothic architecture of the Kardomah's exterior, pointing out the table where L.S. Lowry always sat when he went there for coffee. The waitress came to our table and Peter ordered two black coffees, the sophisticate's drink of choice. When they arrived I breathed in the rich, nutty aroma thinking I had landed in heaven, sipping elegantly whilst trying not to let the bitter taste show on my face. I have only ever drunk black coffee since that day – another small but significant beginning of my metamorphosis brought about by Peter Moreton.

'I like it here, but it's nothing like the coffee bars in Paris where artists paint and draw and novelists talk about their work,' he said, stubbing out his cigarette in the ash-tray. Long, beautiful artist's fingers twisting the stub into the base until every spark was gone.

'Gosh, Paris – that sounds wonderful,' I gushed. I'd dreamed of living in Paris, in a studio in Montmartre, overlooking the city. I longed to place my easel in a Paris street and draw the intricate Gothic buildings, the inter-twining lace structure of the Eiffel Tower.

But I didn't say any of these things. Instead, what I said was, 'I've never been to France, but my uncle went to the Channel Islands once.'

'Oh,' he said, sipping his coffee, while I prayed he didn't ask me any searching questions about the place. I hadn't a clue about my uncle's trip or where the hell the Channel Islands were, I'd just wanted to sound worldly.

Despite my nervousness I found him calming, and was thawing in the warmth of his eyes, the strangeness of his beautiful vowels. All the same I was keen to move away from the subject so I launched into a complaint about my mother, hoping it might explain some of my rather artless behaviour. 'Most of our family comes from round here and as Margaret won't let me do anything or go anywhere I doubt I'll ever visit anywhere outside Manchester,' I said. 'She's convinced a Woodbine and a French kiss will be a passport to eternal spinsterhood or damnation – or both.'

He laughed loudly. 'I presume you're referring to your mother? Why do you call her Margaret?'

'Because it annoys her ... and I can pretend she's not my mother,' I said, enjoying his attention, basking in his laughter. Who knew that my irritating mother could be the icebreaker in a conversation with a man?

'And who would you like to be your mother, if not Margaret?'

'Oh, someone I could talk to about art and the world ... Simone de Beauvoir or Sylvia Plath – or even one of those women who are striking down at the Ford Dagenham plant.'

'I like you, Rosie Draper, you're ... different.' He said this like I was interviewing for a job and he'd decided to give me the post. 'You don't put on any airs and graces, you're not bragging about "Daddy's new car", or where you went to school ...'

113

'I could hardly brag about my school,' I laugh. 'It wasn't Eton.'

'Exactly, you aren't a snob. But you're really talented, your drawings are really good, you should be thinking about becoming an artist when you leave – don't end up wasted in a typing pool somewhere.'

I was delighted, I knew I had a talent, but no one had ever really commented on it except Mike, who always seemed to be at our house just lately.

'Yes, you're a brilliant artist, Rosie, but you're so modest – I like that, but I think you should push yourself more.'

'Push myself? I'm not sure what you mean.'

'And that's exactly why you're special.' He smiled, reaching out his hand across the table, the tips of his fingers brushing mine – it was like touching a firework.

I see now that I was as different to him as he was to me – and he was enchanted by my gaucheness and perhaps what my granddaughters would describe as 'an inability to filter'.

A couple of hours flew by, basking in his appreciation. We talked and talked and it was after six p.m. when I left to catch the bus home. I took my seat and I couldn't stop smiling, then just as the bus was about to pull away he jumped on, leaping into the seat beside me. I giggled and he put his arm around the back of the seat, causing the

114

hairs on the back of my neck to stand up. The journey home that evening was glittery with stardust and beating hearts and when he drew a heart on the window with his finger I thought I might just die. And I still can't believe he's back in my life after all this time.

Anna is interested but wary about my lunch with Peter and after asking where we'd eaten and what we'd eaten she doesn't mention it again. Isobel, on the other hand, likes to talk about emotions and feelings. She's quite perceptive and when she accompanies Lily and me on one of our walks she is gently inquisitive.

'What's it like seeing someone after such a long time, did you feel anything, Mum?' she asks as we walk through the park together.

'Scared stiff!' I laugh. 'And yes, I still feel a fondness for him, we were together for less than a year, but it was a significant time in my life and he made a huge impact on me. We often dismiss young love as puppy love, telling kids they aren't old enough to feel anything real, but at that age feelings shape who you are, what you become. And Peter was such a huge part of me back then I think I've always carried a little bit of him around with me.'

I can see that now, even as I say it; I hadn't even realised it myself, but he's been with me even after we parted. I remember wondering what he would think of punk art in the seventies, I've asked myself if he'd like the colour I painted the walls in 1983, the new roast of coffee beans I started drinking in the nineties. It's all been subconscious, but still so much a part of me. People you love leave bits of them behind, in the same way Margaret and Mike have stayed with me even though they aren't here any more. We carry on through the people we love though I sometimes wonder what my mother would think about certain things if she were here.

'It must be weird. I can't imagine seeing a boy I went out with at that age now.'

'It's like meeting a ghost,' I agree. 'Someone you've remembered for so long has just materialised before you. He looks different, but the same. I couldn't quite believe it was him at first.'

'Wow. And what on earth did you talk about after all that time?'

'It's funny really, we talked about what we do and where we are in our lives, families and things like that. The last time we met we had a terrible argument and it all ended very badly, but the years have softened things, and I'm not so crazy in love with him now so I can see clearly. It was good to catch up.'

'Yes ... I bet you had a lot to talk about. Would you like to see him again?'

'Perhaps, for lunch or a coffee if he's in the area, but that's all. I'm not sure I'm ready for another man, not sure I ever will be ... I want to be just me for a while.'

She laughs. 'I know what you mean. I love Richard but sometimes I long for a rest, just some time alone to think – away from his latest "project".'

I feel for Isobel – she suffered several miscarriages in her late thirties and now at nearly forty says she's accepted that children won't figure in their life. Richard said recently that they are both happy and fulfilled and don't need a child to mess everything up, but I know he's just saying this to make Isobel feel better. I understand how Isobel feels, and sometimes I watch her looking at Katie and Emma and I worry if she leaves it much longer the small window for treatment or adoption will have closed. It's not easy being a mum, you absorb all their hurts and worries like a sponge until you can't take any more ... then that one more thing comes along, and you're amazed at your own capacity to absorb. I feel like I've spent my life kissing grazed knees and broken hearts better – and I wouldn't have had it any other way. I adore my girls, and as much as I've looked after them all their lives they look after me, particularly now they're older. The three of us have always been close, and when he was sick, knowing he wouldn't be with us much longer, Mike said he knew we'd be okay. 'The Carter girls look after each other,' he'd said. I wonder who will look after Isobel when she's my age?

'So you haven't made arrangements to see him again?' she asks, throwing a distressed old tennis ball for a very excited Lily.

'I gave him my numbers, but I'm not sure it's wise to try and go back,' I say, still lying to myself as Lily drops the ball at my feet. Since we met some old wounds have reopened. I still feel little nubs of sharp resentment and I'm torn between wanting to be with him and wanting to stay away, to preserve the past – and perhaps myself? A part of me would like to re-establish – as friends – the happy Rosie and Peter who talked about Paris and art, but that would lead to deeper discussions and I'm not sure I'm ready to hurl myself into all the emotional turmoil that would involve. The sensible, grown-up Rosie doesn't know if she should even consider another encounter, or if it would be wiser to leave him behind, the way he did me.

'We always talked of living in Paris, Peter and I . . . silly really,' I sigh, throwing the ball back across the grass.

'It's not silly, who knows, you might still go one day. Not with Peter, perhaps, but you and Corrine could do a weekend?'

'Yes,' I say vaguely.

But it's not about the place, it's about the person, and

the one I wanted to be with in Paris was always Peter. I realise now that's why I've never been – I could never go there without him.

I remember one night when we were lying in a field, gazing up at the stars, we'd only been together a few weeks and he asked me to run away to Paris and get married. My mind had soared up into the sky, it was all I'd ever wanted since our eyes first met.

'Yes, of course, yes,' I sighed and kissed him. The air was thick with lust and silence as he kissed me gently, his hand sliding up under my top as I lay back on the cool, dark grass.

'Don't. We can't go any further,' I whispered, against my own desire.

'I know but . . .'

'We can wait, Peter. Let's wait until we're married.'

And so we stayed under the stars, imagining our wedding in a little church in Montmartre and all the children we'd have.

'You can sketch and I'll take photos and sell our art so we can go to little bistros on the Champs-Élysées. We'll spend all our money on champagne and frogs' legs and snails . . .'

'And the patisseries . . . we'll buy up all the croissants, let's live on croissants . . .' I'd never even seen a croissant, let alone eaten one, but I'd read about them in books and imagined the flaky, buttery deliciousness on my tongue.

Over the years, this memory has stayed with me and sometimes I take it out when I'm alone and wrap it around me like a warm blanket. Thoughts of Paris have always kept me warm.

In spite of my long-held dream to visit, I never suggested that Mike and I go there. If I had he would have made it happen, because that's the kind of wonderful husband he was, and he'd have done it all for me. But even after everything that had happened with Peter, I didn't want Paris with anyone else.

I pick up the ball once again at my feet, Lily panting deliriously at the mere prospect of another throw. It's wet and disgusting and I pull a face at Isobel before throwing it gently across the grass. Lily's enthusiasm overcomes her arthritic joints as she staggers after it, breathless but happy.

'Lily runs just like me,' I say, pointing at her, and Isobel laughs.

'You love that dog, don't you?' she says.

'Yes I do. I didn't realise just how much I appreciated someone waiting for me at the end of the day. She's always so pleased to see me, I love her stratospheric levels of excitement at the smallest thing.' I smile, giving her a stroke. 'Unconditional love – there's nothing quite like it.'

'Is that how it feels to have a child?' she asks, and my heart twists.

'In a way, but a child is everything, there's nothing quite like having a child,' I say, looking at her as she gazes ahead into the distance.

How I wish my younger daughter had known the joy of holding her baby close, and the contentment of motherhood that runs so deep. It's so hard to describe the love you have for your children, but there's also the love you have for the children you lose and I understand Isobel's pain. Each time she miscarried she lost a longed-for child, and the memory of those children will never leave her. She'll wonder what kind of people they might have turned out to be: kind, funny, good at sports, talented . . . the next prime minister? But she'll never know because their lives ended before they'd begun and I hurt for her and for what might have been.

Chapter Eight

I'm driving into town to meet my friend Corrine for dinner when my mobile rings so I pull over to the side of the road. I put on my glasses and see 'Pierre' flashing on the screen, which makes me smile.

'I know it was, at times, a little difficult, but it was good to see you last week,' he says.

'Yes, you're still good company.' I smile.

'Rosie ... we talked about it being a one-off, a lunch where we just said hello again, but I was wondering if you'd like to meet ... again?'

'Oh, Peter, that's lovely, but I don't know ...'

'I just feel we have a lot more to talk about ... things we haven't said.'

'Yes, but if we met every day for the next hundred

years I think there would still be things we wouldn't say.'

'I know, and I'm probably being selfish, looking for answers, trying to understand myself, and okay, even redemption maybe? But ...'

'Peter, please don't be offended, but I don't want to spend my future going over my past. It was all too painful and I just don't need—'

'I'm sorry, I shouldn't have even suggested—'

'No, it's fine. I'm only just processing the loss of my husband. I've been through a lot, and now meeting up with you has brought back some memories I'd like to forget.'

'Of course, of course, and if you'd rather not talk then that's fair enough, but I just thought if we talked things through it might help. I don't want your memories of me to be dark – we had some happy times, didn't we?'

We did, we had wonderful times together, being part of a couple with Peter Moreton was good for my soul and also my confidence. With him I wasn't invisible any more – I dyed my hair blonder, wore strawberry-red lipstick, talked about art and pretended to understand politics. He made me stronger, more confident, I began to believe in myself and I was so much happier than I'd ever been. In spite of everything, Peter had been good for me – but now? I'm not so sure.

'Yes, we had good times and I went on to have a lot of

happiness in my life, and now I have my priorities. I've got my family's future to think of.'

'But that has to include *your* future too, Rosie. What about your artwork? You don't sketch any more.'

'No I don't, that's all in the past, I have a business and other, more important things to do now,' I say. And I can hear Margaret's voice, she never understood how I could sit and sketch for hours, and saw it as rather pointless: 'You don't want to be wasting your time with pencils, there's housework to be done.'

'You had such a talent. It might be the past, but it doesn't mean you can't go back there, it's never too late, Rosie. I often wondered what had happened to you and I always imagined you painting the pyramids, drawing the Taj Mahal, showing your work in big white galleries in NYC. Okay, so life got in the way then ... perhaps it wasn't your time, but I don't care how old you are, at our age it's even more important to do what *you* want to because there may not be that much time left.'

'You're right, and I've thought about sketching, travelling, doing stuff I want to do ...'

'Then you must.'

'Oh, Peter, the world doesn't work like that. You've never had to worry about anyone but yourself, so it's easy for you to hand me a list of clichés and tell me life's short so why don't I get on a plane, or spend my time sketching instead of earning a living. I have a family, and responsibilities, something you don't have and so can't possibly understand how it is, how it can pull you apart sometimes.' As I say this I know it sounds unkind, critical of his advice and of his lifestyle, but I can't help how I feel.

'No. I probably don't understand. Who am I to try and tell you how to live your life? I haven't exactly made a success of my own, I've always felt like an observer and that's what I am. I take pictures of other people living their lives and I don't really have one of my own, except for when you and I were together. I took pictures of you then, you were part of my life – and you'll always be my flower in the rubble,' he says. 'And, if we don't meet again, promise me you'll never lose sight of that girl with the crooked smile, the long blonde hair, and the big dreams, because I never will.'

The phone clicks and he's gone and I feel terrible. I miss that Rosie too, and I didn't mean to upset him, I just wanted him to realise that I'm not the teenager in thrall to him as I once was. I wanted him to know that he can't just click his fingers, say a few magical words and I'm off on his magic carpet again.

I wipe away the tears and start the car engine, my thoughts flipping constantly. I probably overreacted, he was only trying to inspire me, make me see things positively – he was always so good at that. I wonder if I should call him back but decide it may not be wise, he probably resents me for pointing out that he has no family and doesn't understand what it means to be responsible for others. He talked of possibilities and futures and how I once had all these plans, but that was Rosie then, it isn't Rosie now, and it strikes me that I'm not really sure who Rosie is any more.

I thought being in love with him at seventeen was complicated, but meeting him now is bringing back all the conflict in my head. I don't need this, I think, and I pull out onto the road as my mind trips back to two young people wandering through dirty streets, exploring the ghosts of buildings that were once homes, now just rubble on the ground. Me in my best powder-blue dress thinking I had all the answers and the world at my feet.

'I want to see you standing against that wall,' he'd said, making square shapes with his fingers, scrutinising with his eyes while taking out his camera.

'You don't want a picture of me against a grey wall – I'm no model,' I laughed.

'You're *my* model. Come on, baby, imagine I'm David Bailey, do your model poses,' he said in a funny cockney voice.

He snapped away, shouting 'Yes, yes' as I pulled funny faces, throwing my arms above my head, flattening my palms against the wall and pouting over my shoulder into the camera. I couldn't do anything for laughing but he just kept shooting.

The streets were empty, the slum clearances had left the area bleak and grey and as dusk began to fall we'd headed back home. Tripping over the grey rubble I spotted a wild flower, a tiny daisy in the dust, pushing through the broken bricks. Despite all the destruction around us here was a new life, fighting against the odds. I bent down to get a closer look while Peter continued to photograph me.

'I can't believe it . . . a flower, in all this,' I said, opening my arms up to the bleak landscape.

'A flower in the rubble . . . just like you. It's a reminder that life just has a way of working stuff out, babe,' he said, putting down the camera and smiling at me.

At the thought of the flower I return to our phone call, touched that he'd remembered that day too. I wish now I'd been more gracious on the phone instead of being mean and bitchy, but that's how I felt when he started telling me how to live my life. How dare he? I've lived a life and it's been full and happy. This Rosie runs a florist, she picks grandchildren up from dancing class and picks daughters up when life knocks them down. This Rosie is trying to make a new life from the ruins of her old one and it isn't helpful of Peter to turn up in the middle of it all with his crazy talk, opening up old wounds and awakening old fantasies – making long-forgotten dreams feel like reality again.

'You said what?' Corrine is open-mouthed. I've arrived at the wine bar in a bit of a state and she is, as always, ready for a drama.

'Look, he has my number, if he wants to he'll call.'

'So, let me get this right, you just told a gorgeous, single guy that he has no life and should get out of yours? And now you think there's a chance he might call you? Good luck with that.'

When she puts it like that my heart sinks and for the first time since we met again I face the possibility that we really have said our final goodbye. And it hurts.

'No ... I don't suppose he will call me after I said that.'

'And doesn't that bother you? I mean there's every chance he's on the phone now to some woman who isn't rude or unpleasant. She hasn't told him he's nothing and he's inviting her to dinner, or New York for the weekend.'

'Paris ...'

'Paris who?'

'That's where he wants to take me.'

'Oh, I'm sorry, why didn't you say? Horrid old Paris?

128

Ooh, he starts off with nasty old clichés about how you're still young enough to live your life then he tries to force you into going to Paris? The bastard!'

'Stop, Corrine.' I'm laughing. 'It's not as simple as it seems.'

'Nothing ever is. Give me his number, I'll go to Paris with him – don't say I don't do you any favours,' she says, taking a glug of her raspberry martini.

Corrine is one of my oldest friends, and unfortunately for me she always tells it like it is. For example, a month after Mike's death when I opened the door to her in pyjamas mid-afternoon her opening gambit was, 'Hello? Rosie, wake up, smell the coffee and stop pretending it's you in that graveyard.'

And that was the gentlest remark she made, so if there's one thing I can count on with Corrine, it's honesty.

'Give me your phone, and tell him you didn't mean it,' she's saying, making a beckoning gesture across the table. She's had one too many raspberry martinis and while I'm the designated driver tonight there's no way she's getting my phone.

'But I did mean it, I'm not a kid and he's not my hero any more.'

'If you don't call him and arrange another date, I will.'

'It wasn't a date ...'

'Of course it was. Stop kidding yourself, Rosie, your

face lights up when you talk about him. You've spent the last forty years worrying about everyone else in your life and what's going to happen if – and now it's time to have some fun.'

'But it won't be fun, we had a terrible break-up and I don't want to go there again.'

'Okay, so he broke your heart when you were twelve . . . '

'I was seventeen . . . ' She never listens.

'Twelve, seventeen, who cares, it was a hundred years ago. Look, just see how it goes after a few drinks. Be nice, forget what happened then and see what's happening *now* . . . the clue is "now", Rosie. Stop living in the past and just call him.'

'If I do I might regret it.'

'And if you don't you might regret it.'

She is tipsy and funny and very Corrine and I laugh along.

'And anyway, don't take this the wrong way but there isn't a queue forming to go with you on a date. What have you got to lose?'

I can't answer this.

'At our age, Rosie, our tomorrows are fewer than our yesterdays.'

This hits me right between the eyes and after a few minutes she's convinced me to call him. I am completely

130

sober and can't believe I'm doing this, especially with a heckling Corrine egging me on in the background.

And when he answers and I tell him I would like to meet him again, he seems so delighted my heart melts.

'Peter, I know you're right – I need to look to the future. I like that you feel comfortable enough to advise me but you can't just tell me how to live my life. And if I'm honest it stung a bit when you said you'd imagined me doing all these wonderful things in galleries in New York, when the truth is I've been here – and I've never picked up a pencil since we parted.'

'I just wanted you to remember who you were and who you could be again. I really didn't mean it as a criticism of you or your life.'

'No, and I didn't of yours either – we both went down different paths and sometimes the grass may look greener, but I wouldn't swap my husband or my girls for a lifetime of galleries and travel.'

'No, trust me, you wouldn't. It's a lonely old road,' he sighs and I wonder at the reality of his glamorous life. After seeing the photos of his home and learning about his travels I imagined a happy and fulfilled life – but his comment has made me wonder just how happy he really is.

Chapter Nine

The next day at work Anna is worried about being a mum – and I worry Isobel's worried about not being a mum. Consequently, as their mum I'm now worried about both of them. Being a mother is not just about me, it's about balance and sacrifice, and Corrine's rousing speech about me looking after me and chasing those tomorrows fades slightly along with Peter's 'inspirational' speech about my dreams of showing in galleries in NYC. It all sounds very lovely but I'm not sure when I'd have had the time, with nappies to change, hearts to mend and children to love and care for. I have to smile. And to think I believed it had been me who was the naive one who knew nothing about the world.

'I can't talk to Emma,' Anna's saying. 'She told me to get out of her grill the other day.' She shrugs.

'What's a grill?'

'I presume it's some teen-speak for "get out of my face", who knows?'

I smile. Emma and Katie's dialogue is often peppered with words no one over twenty-five seems to understand.

'I can only imagine what my mother would have said if I'd suggested she "get out of my grill",' I laugh.

'Good old Margaret,' Anna sighs.

'Oh, talking of Margaret, I'm meeting the boy she didn't approve of ... I'm going to see Peter again,' I segue nicely. I don't want to make a big thing about Peter because we're just old friends, but at the same time I feel I should let the girls know I'm seeing him again.

'Oh ... good. Don't get too carried away,' Anna warns, in my mother's voice.

'I won't, Margaret, and thank you for your advice, but I'm old enough to look after myself.'

'You say that but you haven't "seen" anyone since before you married Dad. I worry it's too much too soon.'

'Anna, it's lunch with an old friend. I won't be leaping into bed with him or running off to Vegas for a quickie wedding.'

'I hadn't even thought of that,' she laughs, but I know she's worried I'm going to get myself into some kind of emotional turmoil. Perhaps she's right, but I'm beginning to realise that to really live your life you have to some-times step out of your comfort zone.

'I wish I was your age and could float off for nice lunches,' she sighs. 'But when I'm not a taxi service for kids, I spend my days working, shopping, cooking, clean-ing and arranging orthodontist appointments.'

'Yes, being old has its upside. I thought I'd never get used to living without you girls but there are bonuses to having grown-up kids who've flown the nest. I can stay home and do just as I please, or go out and not worry about picking anyone up or getting back to cook chil-dren's teas. I've seen the timetable on your fridge, and it's a bloody matrix,' I laugh. 'But as much as I like my freedom, you know I'm here when you need me to taxi, cook, take to orthodontists . . . whatever.'

'Thanks, Mum, but no need for both of us to live like taxi-driving hermits,' she sighs. 'You get out there and enjoy yourself . . . but just be careful.'

Later, Isobel calls me. 'Anna says you're going out again. Have a lovely time, but if you need a lift back or anything just call me.'

'Thank you but I think I will be fine.' I say this kindly but wish they'd stop mollycoddling me.

'And don't get into any compromising situations.'

'As I told your sister, we are merely going for lunch, I'm not going to leap on him, I'm not a panther.'

'I think you mean cougar, Mum.'

'I'm not one of those either.'

'I should hope not!' she laughs before putting down the phone. I wish everyone would stop telling me what not to do. Peter, Corrine, the girls – has anybody bothered to notice that I have got to the age of sixty-four, which indicates that I am capable of looking after myself? And as for Isobel's instructions re the compromising positions, I don't think either of our backs could take it.

Today I'm working on a huge birthday bouquet in pale pinks and blues and find myself staring at a cluster of blue hydrangeas and remembering a date I once had with Peter. We met at the cinema, he was waiting on the steps clutching a spray of them and I thought I might die from sheer joy at the sight.

I held the pretty blue flowers to my chest with one hand, as he offered me his elbow to link my other arm through. I felt like a queen with Peter by my side – that's how he made me feel, that with him I could be anything, anyone.

It was so cramped in the cinema our shoulders were touching, and I was overcome by the intoxicating after-shave warmth emanating from him. I'd never been this close to a real man before – my brothers and Dad didn't count – this was something quite different which came with new sensations. Still holding the hydrangeas I gripped the stems as his arm snaked around my shoulders during the film. It stayed there for ages and I desperately hoped this was a prelude to a kiss. My dress was sleeveless and as his hand moved down to my arm and rested on my bare skin I had to catch my breath. After a little while he slowly, gently, began to caress my arm, running his fingers up and down my skin, causing my stomach to flip and my flesh to prickle with delight. Then just when I thought I couldn't take any more he leaned into me, his breath hot on my neck. My chest went into spasm as the dampness of his lips brushed against my collarbone and I was overwhelmed, wanting to scream with pleasure at this strange and wonderful magic. I ached for him to kiss me and turned my head towards his, our lips almost touching, when the man next to me stood up and asked if he could get past. Peter pulled his arm away as the man climbed over us, almost knocking over what was left of our popcorn and ruining a beautiful moment. After that, Peter took out a cigarette and left my shoulder naked and unloved and I was so frustrated, just longing for him to touch me again.

But, too soon, the lights went up and I dreaded having to move apart and end any chance of being kissed by him that night and I think he felt the same. Everyone was moving around us but it seemed like we were the only

136

two people there, groggy from the warmth and the dark and a mutual, unquenched desire. I couldn't tell you what the film *Oliver!* was actually about, I'd thought only of Peter's hand on my arm. I have never been able to watch that film without recalling the erotic intensity yet simple innocence of that moment between us.

Today, Peter and I meet in Albert Square. It's his idea to go to where the Kardomah Coffee House once stood. The name is still on the side of the doorway and we touch it and remember the way we were and I appreciate the romance of it all. He hands me a large head of blue hydrangeas, as he did all those years ago, and I'm moved – he remembers the little things. For a while we are lost in time, standing in the middle of Albert Square, the centre of our swirling past and our gentle present. Our then, and our now.

'I used to tell Margaret I was knitting with Anita when really I was meeting you,' I laugh later at lunch as we stay on safe ground talking about the happy times. 'I got away with it too – though she did scrutinise me on the intricacies of the purl stitch when I left the house in my new dress.'

'You were quite a rebel,' he says.

I think of the constant tussle between Margaret and me

during that time, and what used to make me mad with frustration now makes me smile. 'That's a bit short to go knitting in . . .' was her opening remark as I'd tried to leave the house without an inquisition.

I was always so uptight and excited about meeting Peter I just wanted to escape. I wished I could have told my mother I was going out with a boy — after all, I was seventeen. Some girls could share things like that with their parents, but Margaret wasn't one of those mums who smoked or danced to music on transistor radios in the kitchen. No, Margaret was a God-fearing 1930s matriarch brought up on bread and dripping and no sex until you're married — and probably never again after you'd conceived. I knew if I told her about Peter, she'd want to control the relationship in some way, she couldn't leave anything alone.

'Do you think she knew you were lying to her?' Peter says, opening the lunch menu.

'Oh God, I hope not. I feel bad now just thinking of the awful way I spoke to her — she couldn't do or say anything right as far as I was concerned. I still feel guilty about that even now.'

'Stop blaming yourself. Your mother wasn't easy. You gave her a hard time, but she did you too. She never let you out of her sight and everything you did was met with suspicion. No wonder you lied to her.' He makes me feel better about myself, my behaviour back then; he is gently erasing the guilt I've lived with.

It's nice being with someone who's known you for a long time, before life changed you. I miss the shared history I had with Mike and take comfort in Peter's easy references to Margaret and the girl I used to be. I don't have to explain anything to him, and I love that he knows my story and the people from my first few chapters. He knew me then and knows me still.

'But as a mother now I can see Margaret's side of things. She was just trying to protect me,' I explain when the waiter brings the wine. We both choose the same meal, a roast vegetable wrap with guacamole and sweet potato chips on the side.

He's now looking at me. 'She did everything out of love, in the same way my parents did, but sometimes it was hard to swallow. I came to your house a few months after, you know. Your mother told me you didn't want to see me again.'

I am shocked at this revelation. 'Really? I had no idea ... I often wondered if you'd write ...'

'I did,' he says.

'I never saw any letters,' I sigh, feeling tears spring to my eyes. He wordlessly hands me a napkin and I discreetly wipe them away. I am upset that Mum would do that, knowing how much I'd loved him. I thought he'd

139

just given up on me, that everything we'd had together had meant nothing. To hear that this was not the case upsets me now after all those years of hurting.

'If you'd seen them, would you have written back? Called me? I included my contact numbers.'

'I honestly don't know what I would have done. I wish I'd known because I would have thought better of you over the years, realised that I meant something to you, but in other ways it could have been disastrous. I was a mess for a while ... and then I met Mike. I think if I'd seen a letter when I was first married, it would have been terrible for me and him. It would have been unsettling at best – and who knows, I was so mixed up I may even have tried to find you and where would that have left me?'

'Perhaps with me? Together again ... a happy ending?'

'I had my happy ending, eventually with Mike. After you I needed someone I could rely on and who I knew wasn't going to run out on me at the first sign of a problem.'

'You must have hated me.'

'I did – but I loved you too.'

Margaret was so supportive of my relationship with Mike, she didn't want Peter coming back and causing me pain. She knew I'd be torn and if I was married and pregnant when he wrote, it would have been so distressing for me to read the letters, to see him. In a funny way she knew me better than I knew myself. She kept me safe from Peter and instinctively knew that Mike was right for me at the time.

'You thought that I'd simply forgotten you?'

'I did for a while,' I say, 'but my new life was happy and that wiped away much of the hurt and resentment.'

'Yes, but you may have chosen a different life if you'd known I still loved you.'

'Perhaps – but I've no regrets. We get what we deserve in this life and our fate was sealed that day, when I told you . . .' I can't finish the sentence, can't bear to hear myself say it. He seems to understand.

'I thought you hated me, resented me.'

'I did, for a while . . . quite a while,' I say.

I see the regret in his eyes. I know now he's suffered as much as I have – but perhaps it's been worse for him because he was the one who caused the break-up. It's probably the wine but I can't help it, I reach out and touch his hand.

'Don't do that,' he says.

I flinch and pull my hand away.

'Oh, I didn't mean . . . it just brings back memories and makes me want what I can't have, what I threw away.'

'Now it's my turn to give you advice – let's just enjoy the now. I think you and I are about good times – the minute there's a problem you panic and leave.'

'Do I?'

'Yes, you always have, but that's okay because this is just a friendship, no strings, no blame.'

He looks at me and nods slowly. I need to lighten the mood, there's no point having lunch with an old lover if we're just going to bicker and make each other feel bad.

'Hey,' I say, resting my head on my hand, 'remember our first kiss at the bus stop?'

He smiles and we wander back together, to a bus stop years ago in the soft, relentless Manchester rain.

About two months into our friendship he walked me to the bus stop, put both arms around my waist and gazed into my eyes. 'I can't wait until tomorrow, it's at least ten hours before I'll see you again,' he'd said, his breath on my face, his cheek touching mine. I swear anyone passing must have heard the pounding of my heart as he leaned in and kissed me with those soft, warm, smoky lips. Suddenly there was no rain, no dirty pavements, no graffiti-decorated bus stop. I was on a beach, the waves lapping around me as his mouth gently opened mine. My legs almost gave way, and I wanted to sink into that imaginary sand with him. My heart was stuffed with candy floss and I glittered with love and lust and happiness – and standing at that bus stop in the rain, I knew this was what I'd been waiting for all my life.

'You were my first kiss,' I say now as we order coffee.

'I remember it so well,' he sighs. 'Your hair was damp and your eyelashes had raindrops on them.'

'Looking back it was all so intense: you were too handsome, too clever and far too much for my young and fragile heart,' I say with a giggle. 'I was all over the place.'

'Ah, but we were teenagers and that's how love is when you're young – it's a vivid swirling of emotions you can't harness. I felt it too, I was just better at covering it up – I swaggered around a lot in those days.'

We drink our coffee and I think of that kiss and I swear I hear the rain on the plastic roof of the bus stop and feel his lips on mine all over again. The years have faded the memories, like sunlight on silk, and I can't always remember what I was wearing or what was said, but the strength of those feelings will always be imprinted on my heart. I've come to imagine that time in pale watercolours on thick, white paper. Soft, gentle strokes of the past, muted pastel shades of the blossoming of spring, first love, now faded and patchy in parts, but the picture is still there.

By the time we've drunk our coffee the mood has lightened, and I'm starting to enjoy reliving the lovely moments we shared. If I don't there's no point in doing this, no point in us meeting up and being miserable.

'Shall we have another glass of something?' he says,

a sign he wants to make our lunch last longer – and I'm glad, because I'm having a good time. We're only having a drink, just two old friends, it's nothing.

'I hope you're not trying to get me drunk, Peter Moreton.'

'I can't believe you'd think that of me, Rosie Draper.'

'Carter . . . my married name is Carter. And I have no intention of climbing into the back of your Morris Minor like I used to, so don't get any ideas.'

'Damn, and it's parked outside, waiting for the moment. Okay, Mrs Carter – I shall keep myself to myself as your mother would wish.'

He orders us some drinks and I scold myself. Why would I even say that . . . about climbing into the back of his car? I'm the one saying 'just friends'. The alcohol is talking; I must stop now.

'Talking of Margaret, I think you said your dad died – did she ever remarry?' he asks.

'Oh no. There was only ever my dad for Margaret.'

'Oh that's sad, did she pine for him?'

'Pine? Margaret? No, I meant there was only my dad who'd put up with her. Margaret never pined for anyone.'

He laughs.

'Except Princess Diana. She never quite came to terms with "Poor Diana's death" . . . you'd think she was related to her. First there was that tell-all book with the "wicked" revelations,' I say in mock horror. 'Then the candid TV interviews, the "Squidgy" tapes, the tragic death, followed by all the conspiracy theories. Margaret never got over it.'

He laughs, his eyes dancing, enjoying my silly story. My family have heard all my silly stories and it's nice to have a new audience.

I feel my eyes prick with tears as I think of Margaret now. She was so loyal, always a staunch supporter of those she loved, she was there when you needed her and there when you didn't. And it never fails to take my breath away at how much I miss her.

'I always say to the girls, thank God your nan never lived to see Prince Charles marry "that woman".' I say this mimicking Margaret's 'outraged' voice and he laughs loudly. I like that I can still make him laugh.

'One can only imagine the hand-wringing scenes,' he joins in, adding in mock seriousness, 'Makes one think God may have a plan after all.'

'Don't you dare talk about God in a wine bar,' I say in Margaret's voice and we smile at each other. He gets me, he always has.

I don't know what will happen next, I don't even know if it will involve Peter, but meeting him again has reminded me I had a life before. I had a 'me' once …

and despite my greying hair and sagging flesh I'm not so different to the girl he once loved. Here with him I feel like we're slowly morphing into the people we were. Or perhaps we never really changed.

'So what are your plans?' he suddenly asks.

'You mean tonight?'

'No,' he laughs. 'I mean for the rest of your life.'

I blush. I keep saying 'no strings' and 'just friends', and then I go and say something that could be misconstrued as slightly suggestive.

'I have some thoughts about where I'd like my life to go, they aren't fully formed yet, but I'm thinking I'd like to travel. For once I have this crazy idea about following my heart instead of doing what I *should* do.'

'And what do you feel you *should* do?'

'I *should* stick around for my family; even if I went away on a holiday without them I would be missed, and I'd miss them too. I'd like to retire, hand the shop to the girls, but I *should* stay and work, because . . .'

'Why? Can't they manage without you?'

'Yes, but they need me around.'

'Yes, of course, but what do *you* need?'

'I don't know . . . I honestly don't know.' And I realise that I'm not going into work for the girls, I'm going for me. 'Perhaps I *need* to stay at work because I'm scared of leaving,' I say, surprised at my own revelation.

'So you'll carry on working? Indefinitely ... because you're too scared to stop?'

'No. I know what I *need* to do is shake it all up – but I'm just saying I'm cautious about doing that just yet. Everything has changed so much recently I'm not sure I want to throw it up in the air and try to catch it. I might drop it.'

'And you might not. You might catch it, you might just do something completely different and it could all work out for you.'

'It's a lovely thought, if a petrifying one, but I've lived a very ordinary life, Peter. Worked six, sometimes seven days a week, a fortnight's holiday booked the same time each year. If you looked at my wall calendar from 1980 and one from 2000 they would be marked with exactly the same things on the same day. That's how it was and how I wanted my life to be – as a wife, a mum, a grandmother, I needed to know what was happening every day. But now I must confess a part of me would like to see how it feels when anything could happen.'

'That's more like it, the girl I used to know. You sound like me – or like I used to sound. I never wanted routine, always the adventure, but rather ironically I think I might be ready for a bit more security in my old age.'

'I can't imagine you ever giving up the chance to

chase something glittery, however old you are,' I say. 'My daughters want me to grow old gracefully. They couldn't handle me having a late-life crisis, running around the world, online dating . . . joining a girl band.'

'Sounds like fun to me.'

'Yes, well, those are things you've done – apart from the girl-band bit . . . '

'Actually, there was one time in Russia in the late eighties . . . ' he jokes.

I smile too. 'Well, what I'm saying is you're used to jumping on planes and trains at a moment's notice, you can just fly away whenever the need takes you, but I can't. And as much as I'd love to do something new and exciting, for me that would also be new and scary. Do you know I've never been on a plane on my own?'

'Really?'

'Yes – why would I? I've always been with the family – I've never really done anything on my own. This past year is the first time I've ever even lived on my own.'

'Rosie, you've got a lot of catching up to do,' he sighs, with a smile.

As our wine is now finished, and it's early evening, he suggests we perhaps find a bar and have another drink. A few months ago the idea of having no one to get back for would have upset me, but no one's waiting for me and I think good. So why not make the evening last?

'We've never got drunk together before,' I say as we sip from our second bottle in a trendy wine bar full of bright young things.

'I remember once sharing a couple of bottles of beer. We thought we were wild.'

'That *was* wild in those days,' I laugh.

'There's still a lot we haven't done together.'

'I'm sure there is,' I say, feeling slightly tipsy.

'So you agree there are lots of reasons for us to have another date?'

My heart lifts. I'm enjoying this, and I'd love to see him again, but am I being foolish? I *should* say 'Let's leave things as they are – there's too much rubble to sort through and I'm not sure I'd survive,' but I just smile. I can't help but smile when he's around.

'I know we did lots of things together when we were younger,' he continues, 'but this is now, this is Rosie and Peter in the present day, and we should celebrate that. We are now getting drunk together for the first time, and there are other things we can do for the first time that we couldn't when we were kids. We could cook together, read together, learn a language ... paint?'

'We used to draw and paint together a lot,' I offer.

'Yes, but we never finished a picture, it often ended with you taking my shirt off.'

'You took your own shirt off as I recall ... and mine,' I laugh.

'Oh yes, I'd forgotten about that.'

'I hadn't.' I bite my bottom lip like a naughty child and he reaches for my cheek, taking me in like I'm a work of art. It's good to feel appreciated again.

'You haven't changed. Not one little bit.'

'Neither have you,' I say, unable to take my eyes from his. It's amazing how quickly we've slipped back into the connection we shared a lifetime ago.

Chapter Ten

'So, reasons for another date,' he continues. 'There's also the fact that I never got to draw you naked . . .'

'Mr Moreton, I do feel that may be a little forward for a second date.'

'Oh dear, I worry I may have offended you, Mrs Carter, perhaps the naked drawing will have to wait.'

'Sadly, it's too late for me to model naked,' I sigh.

'It's never too late. To model naked or dance in the rain . . . or run away together to Paris?'

We both giggle conspiratorially. 'Ah, Paris,' I smile. 'I've often thought of the two of us in Paris, a summer evening dining under the stars on a café terrace . . .'

'The sunset over the Seine . . . sharing candlelight and a bottle of Alsace Pinot Blanc tasting of honeyed pears.'

'Even the reliving of our teenage dreams has become more mature. Fancy wines, expensive cafés ... back then we'd have been happy sitting on a wall with a couple of baguettes.'

I think back to those early dreams we had of Paris. We used to talk all the time about the kind of life we'd live together, the children we'd have, the pictures I'd paint. 'Tell me about Paris,' I used to say.

'Our studio will have easels and a darkroom for my photos,' he'd start. 'At first we may even have to sleep in there – we'll be poor, struggling artists but I'll bring you freshly baked croissants and hot coffee in a huge cup every morning.'

He'd tell me all about the gardens and the galleries and the little cafés that spilled out onto the pavements and the patisserie shops, their windows stacked with exquisite cakes and pastel macarons, which later became my favourite confection. Peter had been to Paris and he knew the French words for things – and I was so impressed.

I look at him now in his white linen shirt, steely grey hair and those laughing eyes that have seen the world and taken its photo, and I'm impressed all over again.

He reaches his arm around my shoulder and his face is close to mine as he whispers into my ear, 'Have you any idea how much I've missed you?'

I turn and look at him and we are silent for a long time, until one of us breaks the mood.

'I'm not surprised we're here, together,' he says. 'It never occurred to me that we wouldn't meet again, that I wouldn't know how things turned out for you. Our lives are entwined, aren't they? Do you feel it too?'

I nod, telling myself I should stop drinking wine, it makes me talk too much and I feel disloyal to Mike even thinking this . . . but the thought of Peter and me in Paris has got me through some tough times. Even in the happiest marriage you wake up some mornings and think, 'Is this it?'

We are sitting close together, his arm still around me, and I know if I look up at him he will kiss me. So I mustn't, because it's getting late, I'm tipsy in a wine bar in the city with a man I once loved, who broke my heart into a million pieces. I eventually look up at him but I pick up my drink so as not to give any sign that I will be receptive if he tries to kiss me. Suddenly he takes his arm from around my shoulder and he's holding both his hands in the air, making a square with both forefingers and thumbs.

'What are you doing?' I say.

'Sorry, force of habit – it comes with the job. I'm just framing that bar over there. I like the way the glass bottles are lit from behind and the way it looks so glitzy and pretty – but look at the girl.'

I glance over to the spectacular bar made from coloured glass enhanced by the lighting and the bottles and beautiful old-fashioned champagne saucers stacked high. Just beside it is a beautiful young girl, with long dark hair, her head resting on her hands, she looks incredibly sad.

'What do you see?' I say.

'The flower in the rubble ... like you.'

'I haven't seen her for a long time,' I say, my heart jumping.

'I'm looking at her now.'

'You always saw something in me that no one else ever did,' I say.

'No, the only person who didn't see it was you.'

He is looking at me like he used to, and I'm seventeen years old with long blonde hair and everything to live for.

'I still have the photographs I took of you, laughing, skipping through the rain, posing like a model,' he laughs.

'I remember those photos ... we took one together, sitting on your Morris Minor,' I laugh back and we both return to a Saturday afternoon, me on the bonnet of his car, my best powder-blue cardigan over my shoulders.

'Two of my favourite things,' he'd said, 'Rosie and Morris.' He took ages to set up his tripod with his new-fangled timer and with only seconds to go surprised me by throwing himself onto the bonnet of the car. I had to hold on to him so we both wouldn't fall off and as the light bulb flashed we were holding on for dear life and laughing. We laughed such a lot back then.

Peter could see beauty in everything and even as the clouds began to swell until they burst, he stood with his hands out, just feeling the rain.

'Come on, Peter, let's go back to the car, we'll catch our death,' I called from under my thin cardigan – a makeshift umbrella. A storm was coming and I was terrified of storms. But Peter just laughed. 'It's only a summer storm, you can't catch a cold from getting wet, just feel the rain on your face.'

I was sheltering against a house, which seemed to amuse him as he grabbed my hand and pulled me towards him.

He held me close and began to kiss me, our faces becoming wetter and wetter as the rain continued to beat down, puddles forming around us. Then I caught a glimpse of lightning and cringed.

'You're scared of everything,' he laughed, taking my hand again and pulling me down the road. We ran along the pavements lining the terraces, dodging the puddles, me screaming loudly – but not in fear now, it was pure joy as we splashed along the roads banging into each other and laughing as we did. Eventually he led me to a gaggle of houses half torn down, vague shapes of what they once were. We slowed as we approached to look through the mists of the storm.

'They're like ghosts.' I shuddered, gazing at the broken shapes, eerie against the deep, gunmetal clouds.

Peter put his arm around me. 'Hard to imagine this wasteland was once a community,' he said. 'Families lived here, babies born in the bedrooms, people had sex and fought and loved and died here . . . such history. I wonder if it's retained any of those lives within the walls . . . their souls trapped in the brickwork?'

I looked at him, he was so poetic. 'You have a really beautiful mind. You say things I don't even think.' I leaned my head on his chest and smiled.

He kissed the top of my head. 'Come on, let's try and capture some of this rain and light . . . make some history of our own.' He took out his camera and we walked towards the spectre in the storm. And I watched him thinking, There goes Peter, always chasing the light. He put his hand in the small of my back to guide me across the rockier terrain and as we walked into the emptiness we found the shapes of rooms.

'The rain's stopped,' I said, holding out both hands without feeling pricks of water.

'No, it's a ceiling,' he said, pointing upwards to half

a ceiling with a broken light fitting still dangling. We stood for a while looking up.

'Someone must have bought that light fitting,' I said.

'Yes, the wife loved it but the husband hated it and they rowed over it. Sometimes he hated it so much he couldn't speak to her.'

'Yes, but at night they'd get into bed together, just up there ... ' I said, pointing. 'And they'd snuggle up together with a cup of cocoa and a hot water bottle and he'd forget the awful light fitting downstairs because he loved her so much.'

'I'd forgive you the light fitting,' he said, kissing my neck. 'I bet they had an amazing love life in that bedroom up there.'

He pulled me towards him and, sheltered under the broken ceiling, we kissed, our kisses becoming more passionate, his hands moving all over me and I knew this was crazy but I couldn't stop myself.

'No ... we mustn't ... we have to wait,' I gasped.

'We can't wait, go on, Rosie, please, it'll be okay, I promise.' He gently pushed me against the damp bricks, kissing me softly, tenderly, and I was his.

He lifted me up, and I wrapped my legs around him, desperate to take him as his hips pushed against me, holding me up against the wall with his body, neither of us able to stop. How wonderful it was to be in this secret place alone together, his breath on mine, cool, damp bricks on my naked back, the joy of his kisses, his body with mine together as one.

'I love you, Rosie,' I heard him say as the storm gathered itself and a fiery wind rushed through the gaping broken arches as the rain lashed down. I lost myself in this wild and wonderful place, of rolling thunder, and flashes of lightning that lit up the whole world.

And as the storm eventually subsided, a long trickle of rain escaped from a crevice above, dripping on my head, running onto my face. I opened my mouth and let the water in and the storm slowly moved on.

'I've never been scared of thunder since ... that day,' I say, looking at Peter.

'That was a fierce and beautiful storm,' he sighs. 'I've photographed electrical storms all over the world since then – just spectacular, the way they light up the sky is surreal – but none of them as beautiful as that moment ... the flash, the sheer exhilaration.'

I feel a tingle go through me at the memory of the first time. I'm touched that after all he's seen and all he's done this still runs deep for him too. I can't help it; I squeeze his arm and look into his eyes.

'I remember it so clearly,' I say, and he nods, never taking his eyes from mine. 'You've seen so much,' I say, bringing us both back into the present. If we stay in the past any longer we may do something we'll regret. 'I can't imagine the things you've seen, the places you've been to.'

'I've got some storm shots here.' His eyes are on fire as he turns on his phone and talks me through some of the photos. 'I used a slow shutter speed to capture these,' he says, scrolling through the Congo, South America, Australia, zigzags of lightning stretching across navy blue and purple skies. They are stunning: the composition, the way he's captured the spark of lightning, harnessed nature in one millisecond of a shot. He's so talented, and I can feel his enthusiasm, his sheer passion for what he does. I haven't drawn or painted for years but I remember a time when I felt like this about art – I wanted to build a future on my talent and nothing else mattered. Back then I couldn't imagine a life where I didn't paint or draw, a life in which I never appreciated a photograph, a piece of art, and seeing how his whole life is caught up in this makes me realise how much I've missed it. I've been thirsty for this for a long time.

'And, Rosie,' he says, putting his phone back in his pocket, 'don't believe anyone when they tell you that lightning doesn't strike twice – because I know it does.'

Chapter Eleven

'I'm staying in a hotel,' he says one evening after dinner. For the past few weeks we've been meeting regularly for lunch in the city centre, once or twice a week, but tonight we're having dinner for the first time and it feels more serious. I think I'm developing feelings for Peter. I don't know if it's love, perhaps I'm just reliving my youth and being thrilled all over again to dip my toes in the past. Either way, I'm beginning to think that if we ever wanted to take this further, we should address the elephant in the room and talk about what happened after the fair.

'It's lovely,' he's saying. 'It's a Malmaison – we could go back there after dinner for a drink in the bar?'

This is unexpected; I don't quite know how to take his

suggestion. Does he mean just a drink or does he want more? And what do I want?

'You don't have to rush back, do you?' he says.

And it hits me again, after a lifetime of rushing I don't have anywhere to rush to. No one's waiting for me, no one needs me, everyone's safely ensconced in their homes, in their lives, even Lily is with Anna and the girls, so what harm would it do to have a last drink with an old friend?

He's standing up and looking at me, waiting for an answer. 'Come back to my hotel, we'll have a drink, and I'll ask hotel reception to call you a taxi. I'd feel happier doing that rather than dumping you in the first black cab that comes along – you can never be too sure these days,' he says.

'Okay, yes, that would be nice,' I say, telling myself it's the perfect end to a perfect evening, but already the other side of my mind is jumping ahead, wondering if I might be tempted to stay.

We leave the wine bar and meander through Albert Square, past the Royal Exchange Theatre, a lunar pod encapsulated in the old Edwardian Cotton exchange. We stand and stare at this for ages. 'I remember the exchange closing in 1968.' He turns to look at me. 'It was a year that changed everything.' He grabs my hand and I melt at the warmth, the feel of his flesh on mine.

I am both comforted and saddened by his remark. I know the impact he had on my life, he was the one that changed everything for me. And though he says things changed I can't see where I impacted on his life at all. After me he just continued on his rather self-indulgent path of travel with a career paid for by Mummy and Daddy. When I think about this it makes me think of all the years Mike and I toiled together to make a life, and my love and respect for my husband bulldozes the re-emerging feelings I have for Peter. Then I remind myself that Peter was young and his abandonment wasn't as total as I'd believed over the years. I'm trying to pretend this is all about friendship, but in spite of everything and after all these years, I think I still love him . . . I think I always have. And I'm as mixed up as a teenager.

It's like fate sent him here to spend another summer with me just when I needed him. It's a hot, breathless summer just like our first – a time of real freedom – when all I had to worry about was what lipstick to wear and whether to let him kiss me. And as the sun melts over the city tonight I look at him and realise this might just be my time to enjoy the lipstick, the kisses and the freedom, all over again.

'I still love this city,' he says as we head over to his hotel, just off Piccadilly, which gives us the chance to walk down Market Street hand in hand as we used to. 'It's like literally walking through the past for me.' Having left Manchester the same year we parted, he's lived his life elsewhere for a long time, whereas I stayed here in the same life. I've been steeped in the memories, unable to forget.

'It's family that's kept me here – once you have children your world shrinks – in a good way.' I smile. 'Schools and friends and of course Mike's work and then the shop, we had no choice but to settle here, it never occurred to us to go anywhere else. I've often wondered what it would be like to live in another city, another country . . . I wonder how different my life might have turned out.'

'I often wonder how different my life might have been if I'd had children,' he sighs.

'Are you really saying this to me?' I ask. I feel a frisson of anger ribbon through me. He had his chance – I'd have married him and had ten children if he'd asked me.

'I'm sorry, that was insensitive . . . but I've spent much of my life kicking myself and wishing things had been different.'

He smiles wistfully and I wonder if his wife begged him for children and if he said the same things to her that he'd once said to me.

'You sound like you feel you missed out, but you had a career, a lovely life and the money and opportunities to see the world. Would you ever have been ready to be a parent?' I ask, echoing his own words from the past. Maybe it was Camille who rejected the idea of children. Perhaps it was her wish to put her career before family. From what he says she certainly seems ambitious and I really can't imagine her changing a nappy or wiping baby vomit from designer clothes. And having glimpsed her immaculate home, medication would be required at the very thought of a sticky-fingered child near those chiffon-grey walls. She really does seem to have lived a charmed life, moving seamlessly from the wonderful Peter to a newer, richer beau in her later years. While the rest of us are worrying about our pensions, winding down work and hoping we have enough money to leave the kids, she's painting walls and canvases, creating beautiful living spaces – a stage on which to set her perfect life. Women like Camille make me feel rather inept and not for the first time I wonder what someone like Peter ever saw in someone like me.

We arrive at the Malmaison and I feel immediately comfortable. The entrance is dark and sultry with plush velvet sofas and dimmed mood lighting, a perfect setting for seduction.

Peter orders us both a brandy and I go to the Ladies to reapply make-up, where I come down to earth with a bump. Seeing the wrinkles in these brighter bathroom lights is a stark reminder of what I am – a grandmother who should know better. Because I'm with my old lover I feel more relaxed, familiar, but at the same time I'm still vulnerable. We've been seeing each other for a while now but I won't just hand over my heart to him again. Mind you, at my age I'm more likely to regret saying no than saying yes – to pretty much anything.

I think about my mother and wonder what she'd think of me in a fancy hotel with Peter almost fifty years on. I know her advice would be to run home, lock all the doors and never see him again, and along with Margaret's voice come the old self-doubts. Am I enough for someone like Peter? I'm not well travelled, I haven't had adventures, I'm not sophisticated like Camille. Hell, I hadn't even lived alone until Mike died. And if an idyllic life on dove-grey linen sofas in the French countryside, with an intelligent, glamorous wife, wasn't enough for Peter – then how could I ever be?

'Oh, shut up, Margaret,' I say under my breath.

I couldn't wait to get away from her comments and her nagging. I remember sitting in the passenger seat of Peter's car gazing up my street, covered in cherry blossom. The spring sunshine peeping through Persil-white clouds in a tight blue sky, the car smelling deliciously of leather, stale smoke and aftershave. Peter climbed into the driver's seat and started the engine and I felt a rush, a breeze through my bones as we pulled away, leaving

Nightingale Road behind. I was shaking off my mother's judging and fretting and fussing and my father's grunting and the 'me' I didn't want to be who lived in that little terraced house with the net curtains and the matching plumped cushions.

And Margaret knew how I felt, she knew I didn't want to stay around here, that I wanted a bigger life. But she was scared for me and scared of losing me, so she fought me over everything.

'I don't want to lose you, Rosie,' she'd once said in a rare moment of weakness after a huge row. She'd stopped scrubbing and was looking at me, a trickle of sweat moving slowly down from her forehead, and in that moment I felt an unexpected pang of love for Margaret. She worked so bloody hard with so little thanks, not even an acknowledgement from my father, all she had to look forward to was the bingo, and a bit of gossip. This wasn't a life I wanted, I couldn't live like this knowing I'd never see the world beyond my back yard, never feel a foreign sun on my face. She'd never known the passion of art, the way it filled you up and gave you something to live for when there was nothing but dirty streets and grey skies.

Margaret's vulnerability that day crystallised our relationship and I saw what was happening: she was fighting to keep me and I was fighting to leave.

As a mother I can see it's probably the main reason

mothers and teenagers fight – we want our children to stride out into that big wide world, do all the things we never had the courage or opportunity to do. But our instinct is to hold them close, keep them safe – and never let them go. I think perhaps it's time for me to finally let go.

167

Chapter Twelve

I flick my hair, spritz some perfume, leave the ladies'
toilets and walk back into the bar where Peter is waiting.
I sit down, melting into the soft, red-velvet sofa. The
brandy is warming and intoxicating – and so is he.

'Tell me about Mike,' he says. I'm surprised at this, but
I suppose it's natural he would be interested.

'Mike was kind, and he loved me. He was a good dad
and he lived a decent life – he wasn't rich or famous or
special, but he was special to me.'

'And you were special to him, I'm sure. You gave him
his family.'

'Well, Mike wanted children from the outset. His
own father died when he was only young and he just
wanted to make a family and so did I. Once we were

married the girls came along in the first few years.'

'Are the girls coping . . . having lost their father?'

'Yes, but they were so close, it's not been easy.'

'Are they okay about you seeing an old boyfriend?'

'They have some reservations. They don't want me getting hurt, I suppose. My eldest, Anna, is like my mother and has been a mother hen since Mike died. Isobel's a little more laid-back but prone to influence from her big sis, but all they want to do is protect me. They both know you broke my heart.'

'Oh God, do they? Do they know what happened?'

I shake my head. 'No, but they would both be horrified if they thought I was now in a hotel bar with a man old enough to be my lover.'

He laughs. 'Rosie. You spent your youth worrying about what your mother would say. Don't spend time now worrying about your daughters . . . it's your life, no one else's.'

'It's easy for you to say. I swear the minute I turned sixty they started to see me differently. Mind you, doesn't everyone? People want to define you, put you in a box and label you "old" like you have no right to have fun any more. As far as my girls are concerned I'm too old to take risks, make mistakes – but isn't that how we learn . . . from our mistakes?'

I think about what happened with Peter all those years

ago and realise it was the biggest lesson I ever learned and it taught me a lot about myself.

'We're never too old to learn on this journey, and along the way we discover ourselves – some of us may take the road less travelled, which in its own way is a sign we understand who we are and what we need.'

'You took that road, but I've lived with other people ... travelled with other people,' I say, acknowledging his metaphor. 'So I've never really had the chance to know me, what do I feel? What do I want? And I don't just mean the big things – I buy mint choc chip ice cream because it was the girls' favourite, and I eat it too. But I don't really like it. So what's my favourite flavour? I don't really know because I've never stopped to think about it. I've been too busy stuffing the freezer with bloody mint choc chip.'

He laughs again. 'Perhaps that's the first thing on your list – find out what your favourite ice cream is?'

'I suppose. It's just that having a family is wonderful, but it's also compromise: you're involved with a group of people who all want something and as a parent, a wife, you want them all to get what they want and you don't think about yourself. I still don't know what I really want.'

He settles into the sofa. 'So apart from ice cream perhaps you need to try on a few things for size. Look around and decide what happens next for Rosie?' I appreciate this, and I'm reminded again of his thoughtfulness – he's always interested in what I think, he cares how I feel.

Mike and I didn't always have the time and space for discussions like this and perhaps it would have been a little too esoteric for us to talk about life in this way. When you spend your time together discussing mortgage payments, car insurance and what to have for supper, those 'us' moments in a relationship become fewer as the years go on. Consequently, my relationship with Mike was reality-based, it didn't involve hopes and dreams and what ifs. Our life involved getting things done, the important stuff like looking after the kids, buying a house, building a business, creating a good life for ourselves.

'I still don't know what I really want,' I sigh. 'I know I don't want to waste a minute of what I have left, and I still want fun. I want to open up the box of things I used to dream of doing and look through them. I may not be able to do everything, I may not be able to do anything, but I want to feel like I made a good fist of it, you know?'

I look at him and he's smiling, nodding, he understands me, we don't need to explain.

'It's hard to define a future for people like us, it comes

with the sixty-something territory,' he says. 'We're too old for sports cars and too young for stairlifts.'

'Speak for yourself, I'm not too old for a sports car,' I say, and I suddenly see myself driving down country lanes in a red MG, sunglasses on, the wind in my hair.

'Ah, The Ballad of Lucy Jordan,' Peter sighs, referring to a song Marianne Faithfull sang sometime in the seventies. It was about a woman who had once dreamed of driving through Paris in a sports car and how marriage and kids had ended her dream. It's a song that's always made me feel incredibly sad, but now the image fills my mind and makes me feel euphoric. Peter's right, it's never too late and unlike Lucy Jordan, this wife and mother may one day live her dream of Paris after all.

'I think the real tragedy is that I'm wiser, stronger and probably a damn sight more interesting than I was at seventeen – I just don't look it to the outside world,' I say wistfully.

'You'll always be seventeen to me; a stronger, wiser girl, but still beautiful.'

Being with this man who sees my seventeen-year-old self makes me want to be her again. I don't want the lack of confidence and the vulnerability that came with youth – but I would like to taste some of that freedom, a flake of happiness without responsibility, without consequences.

I smile, thinking of what Anna and Isobel would say to this. Like most kids they only see the wife, the mother, the grandmother. And until recently, so did I.

'I adore the girls and when I think about what my future holds, they are a huge part of it. But if I want to change and make a life for myself, whatever it may be, I will have to make it clear to the girls that I have to be allowed to make some mistakes.'

'I suppose you'll just have to alter their perception of you. I'm sure they'll understand.'

'Yes, first I need to convince them that I'm capable of leaving the house without a police escort. Like now, they would much rather I was tucked up safely in bed than drinking brandy in a hotel with an old boyfriend.' I say this as though I have lots of old boyfriends, when in reality he is the only one. 'If one of them calls me in the morning and I don't answer there's hell to pay – our Anna called the police recently and I'd only gone to Sainsbury's.'

'A wild, supermarket adventure, eh? You rebel,' he laughs.

'You may laugh, but it's such a role reversal. I've spent most of my life protecting them and guiding them through life's ups and downs, but now they do the same for me. Don't they realise I've been there and done that and I know best?' I'm joking but sometimes it's how I feel.

'Ah yes, that scientific fact: Mum always knows best,' he jokes.

I think about my own mother and how she warned me against falling for him, but I thought I knew better.

'Having children makes you think about your own parents,' I say. 'Margaret said you'd never marry me because you came from a different world. I told her that's why I wanted to be with you – because you were different.'

'And that's why I love him,' I'd screamed in her face. 'Because he's different ... and I'm different.' I told her I wasn't going to live her life, slaving away in the kitchen waiting for a man to come home from the factory every night, never going anywhere, never doing anything except bloody bingo every Friday and polishing the front room on a Wednesday ...

He shakes his head. 'It was quite tough for you, wasn't it?'

'It was tougher for Margaret. I try not to think of all the cruel insults I hurled at her, I just remember the pain in her eyes and it hurts even now over forty years later. She was protecting me and I hated her for it. I just hope after everything that she knew I loved her and in the end I know she was right.'

'I'm sure she did. I suppose having your own children helps you work through the relationships you had with your parents?'

'Yes, in a way it's a kind of therapy, but we never learn. We all think we'll be perfect parents but we bring our own flaws to the party.'

'And now, with your girls ... what would you do differently?'

'That's a tough one. It's hard to identify let alone reveal what you didn't get right. I think if anything I've been too involved in their lives. Margaret wanted to be involved in mine, but she did it through control; she thought if I stopped seeing you I would stay in her orbit for ever, marry a local boy and she could keep me close.'

'And you did.'

'Yes, and it worked, because in the end she knew best.'

I may have *wanted* someone like Peter, but she knew I *needed* someone like Mike. I get a tight knot in my stomach just thinking about him. Without him I still feel like I'm in the middle of the ocean and there's no one to rescue me. Perhaps I need to rescue myself?

'I know the girls are grown up, but I still sometimes feel like a single parent without Mike at my side. Take Isobel, she's had problems having children and she sometimes talks about it, and I know she's hurting, but she doesn't feel she can share her pain with me because she doesn't want to upset me. Likewise, I don't want to tell her I'm worried about her because I don't want her to feel like she can't tell me if she needs to – it's a complete conundrum. But if Mike were here I could talk it through with him.'

'It must be difficult to lose that kind of relationship, that trust and sharing . . . but if you need to you can talk to me, Rosie. If you're worried about your family I will listen and—'

'Thanks, Peter, but although they are a huge part of my life my time with you should be about us, not everyone else.'

'Yes, but being in a relationship is about sharing your problems. When we were younger you told me about your mother and I listened . . . it's the same thing.'

'I suppose you're right, I just feel a bit territorial about my girls – especially where Mike's concerned . . . and what you said just then about a relationship?'

'Yes.'

'Are we . . . having a relationship?'

'I don't know. I'd like that but I don't know how you feel . . . I know I couldn't bear another goodbye.'

And in the middle of this lovely moment, surrounded by velvet sofas and candlelight, a frisson of irritation shimmers through me.

'You're the one who said goodbye the first time,' I snap. And I realise that however wonderful this new relationship is on the surface, we need to excavate the past in order to build new foundations. We are both on a different footing now and I feel so much more in control the second time around. If we are beginning a new relationship then we need to deal with the detritus of the old one first. If we don't talk about what happened I will always feel a twist of pain, a vague stab of resentment at his abandonment, which sometimes feels like yesterday.

I can remember it all so clearly. The day we broke up from college we ran out into the sunshine, the summer stretching out before us, a long, glistening sea of time together – until he dropped the bombshell.

'Rosie,' he said, 'I'm really sorry, but I have to go away with my family – we're going to our house in Italy.'

I was devastated and it didn't make it any easier to hear that he'd be gone for three weeks.

'Stay here – you're eighteen, they can't make you,' I said, panic-stricken at the prospect of being without him.

'I have to, it would break Mum's heart if I didn't go,' he sighed.

My own heart was now in shattered pieces on the ground. This was the first time real life had encroached into our perfect bubble and I realised later that this was our first test – a summer with me or a holiday in Italy – and he chose the holiday.

I hated everything in that moment, except him, which

shows how in love I was. I never saw his flaws back then. I was more angry with Peter's parents for taking him thousands of miles away from me.

'Italy?' my mother said when I told her. She said this like he was going to the moon.

'Yes.'

'Three weeks?'

'Yes.'

'Who goes to Italy?'

'Peter does. His family have a house there.'

'Oooh, very nice. It's all right for some,' she'd said, picking up her cloth and continuing a very vigorous polish of the front-room window. 'And I expect you're going to wait for him?'

I was angry that she even needed to ask the question. 'No, I'm going to run off with the first boy I see the minute his plane leaves the ground,' I hissed as fresh anger swept through me.

'I'm saying nothing,' she said, which usually meant the opposite and I could feel a tsunami of 'counselling' coming my way from 'Margaret Draper, Advice Columnist'. 'All I'm saying is, once he gets in that heat, with loose young foreign women throwing themselves at him ...' She left it hanging, digging straight into my basic teenage fear. I wanted my mum to reassure me that my boyfriend would be faithful and soothe my fears, not

178

rip me open and leave my insides to bleed all over the front-room carpet.

I've been reassuring my own girls ever since to make up for the sometimes brutal way Margaret blurted out exactly what she was thinking or predicting.

Over the next few days she worked herself up into a frenzy, conjuring up images of dark-skinned señoritas with wild eyes and dancing hips. And thanks to her, so did I.

'He's only going on a family holiday. He'll play cricket on the beach with his brother and swim in the pool. Then they'll have dinner and drink Chianti under the moonlight.' I smiled to myself at his description. It sounded idyllic.

'Mmmm, wine, eh? Very fancy.' This was followed by a murmured, 'Not for the likes of us.'

'Actually, Mum, it *could* be for the likes of us. There's no reason why we can't drink wine and have holidays abroad.'

'Oh yes, lady, there is. Money, for a start – it doesn't grow on trees, you know. We're not rich like the la-di-da Moretons,' she'd sniffed.

Looking back, she was right: whatever the politicians were telling us about class mobility I couldn't really see the Draper family drinking Chianti under any moonlight. I understood only too well what she was saying, I felt it too, that chasm between Peter's life and mine. I'd tried to close it and at the same time distance myself from Margaret and Nightingale Road, but I was as entrenched in that life as she was. I know now Margaret and I were more alike than I ever would have believed, we wanted the same things – the safety and security of marriage, and a family.

Mike was later to provide this for me and the girls, and during Peter's holiday in Italy Mike had already begun to feel like a support. He was someone to lean on when I was missing Peter. I'd play cards with him and my brothers, we'd watch TV and we laughed a lot that summer. Looking back I can see now that I was myself with Mike, I didn't pretend to be 'an art student', I was just Rosie Draper. I remember one evening I was hanging over the kitchen sink washing blonde dye from my hair and asked him to help me rinse it all off. He did so happily and it turned into a water fight with me screaming the place down and for a little while I was able to forget about Peter. Later I sat with a towel around my head and I never gave it a second thought because I just felt so comfortable with Mike around, like I'd known him all my life.

So while Peter lay on a sunlounger under an Italian sun, my days consisted of lying on my bed daydreaming, playing cards with Mike and just waiting, waiting for Peter's return. Apart from a postcard in which he talked about pasta, there was nothing, and by the third week my heart was droopy. I was tired and emotional and when I looked at the calendar I realised, to my horror, that my period was very, very late.

Chapter Thirteen

'I missed you so much when you were on holiday in Italy that summer,' I say now to Peter.

'I missed you too . . .' He starts to say something else but my mobile rings, and before I can find it in my bag and put my glasses on to see the ridiculously small buttons to answer it the damn thing stops ringing.

'Where were we?' I say, abandoning the phone and sinking back into the sofa and his arms, at which point the bloody thing starts beeping, which makes me jump.

'Oh God, what now?' I sigh, putting my glasses back on and checking the voice message.

'Mum, it's me, Anna. I've called you at home and I'm now calling you on your mobile . . . I suppose that's obvious, well, not necessarily because you don't have a clue what's going on with your phone. Where are you? I thought you were only going out with Peter today … surely you should be home by now? Call me when you get this – I'm beginning to worry.'

'I'll just give her a quick call, put her mind at rest,' I say, feeling very guilty that I've put her through such worry. I want to text to avoid any confrontation in front of Peter, but in this light I could end up texting anyone and at least if I speak to her I'll know she's got the message. I dial the number and explain to Peter, who probably thinks I'm mad checking in with my daughter at my age, 'As I told you, if I don't call her she'll panic and call the emergency services again.'

'Good grief, you could arrive home later to a house full of police and firemen.'

'A girl can dream,' I say, as Anna picks up. 'Hello, darling.' I'm smiling down the phone at her. I love my girls.

'Mum? Thank God for that – I've been worried sick.'

'Oh, Anna, I'm fine, I'm sorry to worry you, I should have called but we were chatting and time ran away. I'm still out with Peter.'

'Out? Where?'

'In Manchester. We're just having a last drink, in the Malmaison. Peter's staying here. You'd love it, Anna, the interior is just lovely, it's all in shades of red and—'

183

'Mum, I thought you were only going out for dinner . . . I've been frantic. I hope you're not being silly.'

I bristle slightly at this but try not to react. 'No, I'm not being silly. I'm having a lovely time,' I say calmly, without smiling.

'Good, don't go doing anything—'

'Anna, I don't think we need to have this conversation. I'm fine and I'm safe, thanks for being concerned.'

'Well, now I know you've not been sex-trafficked, I wanted to know if you can pick up Emma and drop her off at work in the morning at her Saturday job. I've got to take Katie to her dad's.'

'Yes, of course.'

'Don't be late back, you'll have to be up at eight to get Emma to work by nine.'

'Oh, I've never had to do anything like that in my life before so thanks for the advice.' I say this good-naturedly but I'm feeling slightly angry at her attitude.

'I can't believe you're still out in Manchester on a Friday night,' she's saying, ignoring my sarcasm. My kids are fed up with my sarcasm; they've had it since birth and they aren't amused by it, but Peter's smiling at the side of me, and I think how nice it is to have a 'new' old friend who finds me amusing.

'I know, Anna, I know. I shouldn't be out late at night, I should be in my stairlift whizzing up and down the stairs in my own home. But that's next Friday evening's entertainment.'

'Very funny. Seriously though, Mum, I hope you're not planning on driving if you've had a drink. Are you getting a taxi back home tonight?'

'Who says I'm going home tonight?'

'What? What do you mean . . . ?'

'Oh, you're breaking up. Look – I have to go. I'll pick Emma up in the morning, but I'm turning my phone off now so please don't call me again.'

'You're not in his room, are you, Mum?'

'Not yet, darling.'

'Not yet?'

'We're going up to his room now to have mad passionate sex. If I'm a little late in the morning explain in detail to Emma, won't you?'

Peter almost chokes on his drink.

'Mmm, you are hilarious, Mother,' she says in an irritated voice. She always calls me 'mother' when she disapproves.

I put the phone away and take a large sip of my drink. Anna doesn't think for one minute I might spend the night here in this lovely hotel with this handsome man. After all, I'm sixty-four and at my age I couldn't possibly do something like that. Could I?

'Did you mean that . . . about going up to my hotel

185

room?' Peter says as I put the phone back in my handbag.

'No, of course not.'

'Oh, how disappointing.'

'Well, I hadn't planned to, but who knows? The night is yet young and life has been quite surprising recently.'

His eyes light up and his lovely, sexy smile takes over as he leans towards me.

'Hang on a minute, Peter Moreton,' I say, my hand on his knee in a temporary holding motion. 'I can't help but feel this has all been planned.' I hold my hands up at the beautiful surroundings. 'It's not the obvious place for a man to stay on his own – were you assuming I'd sleep with you tonight?'

He becomes slightly bashful, not something I'm used to seeing in Peter.

'No, not at all. I wouldn't be so presumptuous. I like nice hotels, I like nice things and I refuse to stay in those awful one-roomed cells that sit along the motorway edge. I confess that it crossed my mind that if things were going well, a decent hotel to have a last drink might be a good idea but only so you could call a taxi from here.'

'Okay, I believe you.'

'Anyway, if you're not prepared to run away to Paris with me you're hardly likely to stay in a hotel in Manchester – let's face it, they don't compare.'

'What's the line? We'll always have Paris, Peter,' I laugh.

The awkward, besotted teen is dissolving, as is the woman who held onto hurt for over forty years. I can blame the wine and the candlelight, but I think it has more to do with a rediscovered desire to cast caution to the wind. I've had a lifetime of playing it safe, and tonight I feel outrageous. The call from Anna telling me I was too old to be out after dark brought out the rebel in me the same way Margaret's comments did about me being too young to do anything. Tonight, I have an uncontrollable urge to tell them all where to go, and just go with the flow.

Peter leans in and kisses me full on the lips and I'm taken aback and complete mush in his arms.

'I don't want you to think this is all about my evil plans to get you into bed,' he says, emerging from our kiss.

'At my age I'm extremely flattered by the idea of some-one – well, anyone – having evil plans to get me into bed.' I smile. 'As I said, it's been a while.'

'Can you blame me for booking a double room and imagining your scent on high quality cotton sheets, your blonde hair spread on the pillows like a golden cloud?'

'You are and always were the most outrageous flat-terer,' I laugh. 'It's a good job I'm older and wiser and not taken in by your poetry as I once was.'

'Damn,' he says wryly. 'And there's also the slight problem of my back.' We both laugh heartily at this, recognising the difference between us then and us now. Little has changed, yet so much has changed.

'Well, I do have a few conditions. I need another brandy for courage, the lights have to be off . . . and I need an alarm call at dawn so I can take my grand-daughter to her Saturday job.'

'The glamour of it all.'

'Yes . . . welcome to my world, Mr International Photographer.'

'Okay, but do you have to leave me at dawn?'

'Yes – it's called being a grandparent . . . it starts when you're a parent and you realise the world doesn't revolve around you – it revolves around your children . . . and now their children.' I realise how full my life is and it's mostly picking up after others, but they are my others and I don't mind.

'She could get a taxi perhaps?' he says. 'I could arrange one from here.'

'No, you couldn't. Peter, she's a sixteen-year-old girl going to a job in a burger joint that pays minimum wage. Turning up in a taxi would be ludicrous.'

'No more ludicrous than you leaving here at dawn to drive back and . . .'

'Peter, you don't get it, do you? I *want* to take my

granddaughter to work. The kids are my world and they grow up too soon. My time being a grandparent is precious.'

'Of course, it's all a bit new to me, this grandchild thing.'

The prospect of being responsible for anyone but himself is still new to him, I think, marvelling once more at how he's lived a life of such freedom.

He calls a waitress and orders another two large brandies. I'm still slightly irritated that he wanted to try and organise a taxi for Emma; she's my granddaughter and my family will come first whatever happens between Peter and me. That's the way I am and if he wants to pursue this relationship that's going to be the deal.

'We can take these brandies upstairs. I'll show you the room and you can decide if you want to stay,' he's saying. 'I just think it would be good to talk. We only ever meet in restaurants and bars and we need some privacy. I feel there's still so much unsaid.'

I soften at this. He's been feeling the need to talk too and I'm relieved we're still in tune on most things as we always were. He seems nervous so I make light of things.

'If I decide to stay,' I raise my eyebrows, 'I need you to know that I expect sex to be athletic and last all night.'

'So, you're as flexible as you always were?'

'I do Pilates . . . I do okay.' I wink.

Chapter Fourteen

Once in the bedroom it seems my confidence was fleeting. I stand in the middle of the room looking at the beautifully made but imposing bed.

'I haven't ever ... Mike was the only one, apart from you,' I say.

He walks towards me and takes me in his arms. 'There's no pressure. You don't have to stay and if you do we can just lie together, we don't have to do anything. It's time to let go a little, Rosie ... there are no rules.'

We take our brandies and lie down together on the bed hand in hand.

'You're smiling,' he says, turning to me.

'I'm almost happy.'

'Almost?'

I nod. 'You said earlier that perhaps it's good to share and work through stuff in a relationship and if we're going to try again I really think we need to clear the debris of the past. Can we turn out the lights and just talk?'

He reaches for the lamp, plunging us into semi darkness. I can just about make out the shape of his face next to mine.

'After forty-seven years, it's good to hold you,' he says tenderly.

'This is nice, but weird because you're not Mike – stupid, isn't it?' I say, suddenly wondering what I'm doing here lying on a bed with someone that isn't my husband.

'No, it isn't. It's perfectly understandable. You were with the same man for over forty years, it's bound to feel a little strange.'

'I never imagined this happening again ... me and you,' I say into the darkness.

'I feel like I've been given a second chance to make it right with you, Rosie, and I won't mess it up.'

'It took me a long time to get over you the first time,' I say. 'For years I went over and over that day in my mind and for a while it was the end of everything.'

'You have to talk to me about it. I wasn't there for you then but perhaps I can be now.'

I'm still not ready to talk about this, but then I don't

191

know if I'll ever be ready. It's haunted me for a long time and no matter how hard it is to dig up all these feelings again I know I must. I have to share the past with Peter and clear up the mess before I begin to think about a future, with or without him. So I take a breath, steel myself and return to that long, hot summer of 1968.

'When I found out I was pregnant I was terrified. Back then it was the worst thing that could happen, especially to a working class girl like me. Not to mention the shame I brought on Margaret! But the more I thought about the baby – our baby – the more real it became and I started to believe it might be a wonderful solution to everything. You and I could get married, I'd be able to leave my mother's control and we could start our lives a bit sooner than we'd planned.'

I talk through the parts he doesn't know and some of the parts he does and take him back to the day the course of my life was altered for ever.

I was too scared to tell Margaret my period was late. I wanted to wait until Peter was back from Italy so he could be with me when we told her. We'd hold hands and stand before her, defiant in our love, nothing and no one coming between us and our baby. She'd complain that she'd never be able to hold her head up on Nightingale Road ever again, but Peter and I would move away and get married before the baby was born. We were going to live abroad anyway, so she didn't have to worry about her precious neighbours.

Peter's parents would have to accept me because I was carrying their grandchild and Peter and I could be married as soon as he got back from Italy. I wouldn't give up my art, I wouldn't need to – we'd just carry on with our lives, we'd be a family, something I now realised I'd always wanted for us. Even more than Paris.

I'd think about his face when I told him our news and those days would be soft, pastel pink, edged in lace. But other days I'd worry that his parents might try to keep us apart, and mine would be so racked with shame they'd throw me out. And the more I thought about this little seed growing inside me the more attached I became. I'd disappear upstairs in secret to look at myself sideways in the full-length mirror in Mum and Dad's room. I was sure I could see a slight bump, and my tummy felt hard as I caressed the new life inside me. I couldn't wait to share it with him.

The day after Peter was due back was the local carnival, a big event in the Salford calendar and Peter had suggested we meet at the fair. I was excited and nervous and I couldn't sleep the night before, knowing he must be back in the country, just a few miles down the road. I lay awake for hours in my little single bed, imagining our reunion, desperate to see him and tell him my news.

I didn't feel well the following morning when I dragged myself out of bed, and after my bath I had to sit down on the bathroom floor. I was so excited about seeing him I felt dizzy and a fleeting twinge in my stomach told me his child felt the same way. 'Yes, you're excited to see Daddy, aren't you?' I whispered. I wore my new dress that day, I'd saved it specially for him. It was sprigged with tiny forget-me-nots, a little tight around the waist and bust, but I hoped my new curvier figure would please him. I finally felt grown up, a mother-to-be, my secret still safe under the forget-me-nots. For the first time in my life I belonged, I had a defined place in the world. There was a name for me – mother. I didn't think too much about the fact I wasn't married, I just thought about the loveliness of it all – well you do at seventeen, don't you? And wandering to the fair to meet him I felt as beautiful and blooming as the blowsy pink roses in gardens along the way. I couldn't help smiling openly at passers-by, longing to announce to complete strangers that 'my boyfriend's home and we're having a baby'.

Arriving at the funfair, my heart danced on ahead of me, my eyes darting everywhere looking for his dark, curly hair, those piercing, twinkly blue eyes. I knew if I looked long enough he would appear above the heads of the clowns and the kids and the trombone players. As I waited I suddenly had a dark feeling, one of those passing clouds, an inexplicable sensation that sweeps through, like a ghost. It was then I began to worry he was late, or wouldn't turn up and that he might not be as pleased as I was about the baby. I suddenly felt very alone in the swirling crowds, clowns dancing by me and children with balloons running past, screaming. I discreetly put my hand to my belly to protect her as a brass band appeared, moving loudly in my direction, hurting my head with its noise. I was standing in its path as the cacophony grew louder, like thunder as the players enveloped me. And I stood there in my lovely new dress, in the middle of the carnival madness, holding a sudden despair in the pit of my stomach.

Then I saw him and the clouds parted, the sun came streaming through and I ran, my arms open, throwing him my heart to catch. I pushed my face into his neck, wanting to breathe him in. He smelt deliciously summery: salty sea air, sunshine and sandalwood.

'I love you,' I whispered in his ear as he held me tight. I pulled away to look into his face, I'd forgotten how beautiful he was, and his Italian tan made his eyes seem bluer, his teeth whiter. His forearms looked golden, strong and weather-beaten and I just drank him in, unable to take my eyes from him, or the smile off my face.

The air was still thick with crazy. Music was playing,

kids screaming, people laughing as clowns with huge feet slapped by, but for me there was only us and eternity, the rest of the world dissolved like candy floss on my tongue.

'I missed you so much,' I said, touching the plaited leather bracelets he was wearing on his wrists. I ran my fingers around them, suddenly feeling a little shy. 'You look like a hippie artist who just left the beach,' I laughed.

'That's how I feel.' He smiled. 'Like a hippie! Being in a different country changes your whole perspective. I was so much more creative, took a million photographs.'

'I can't wait to see them ... I've been drawing too ...'

'I just feel so free, like anything's possible, you know?'

I nodded vigorously, vaguely disappointed that he hadn't asked me about my drawings. Mike said they were the best I'd ever done, but Peter was the only one who could validate my talent back then.

I took his hand and we wandered towards the big field surrounding the site. It was so busy with shouting children, dogs without leads rampaging over picnic rugs as mothers handed round sandwiches to their kids. That'll be us soon, I thought, watching a young mum holding her baby close to her chest, rocking and smiling amid the madness, her husband's arm around her, the picture of contentment.

We sat down on the grass and I spread the skirt of my dress out so he could see it. I was waiting for him to say how pretty it was, he always complimented me on what I was wearing, but he was too busy laughing at a fluffy little dog that was running around in circles. I couldn't help but notice he seemed closed off, and I wondered fleetingly, instinctively, if something had changed for him.

He took out a cigarette and lit it, blowing the smoke high.

'It sounds like you all had a great time in Italy.'

'Amazing . . . just amazing, an incredible experience,' and it occurred to me that he might not be talking about just the weather or the pasta.

'I mean, it's our house, I've been there before and everything, but I never really appreciated it when I was younger. It was different this time, and now it feels strange to be back here. You get used to swimming every day and being in the sun. I'm not used to grey old Salford.'

I smiled. He'd soon cheer up when I told him our news; he'd leap up and kiss me and twirl me round and we'd talk about where we'd live. If he wanted to leave grey old Salford, that was fine by me.

'Peter, I've got wonderful news,' I said. And before he could ask or I could tease him I heard myself blurting it out, too excited to wait. 'We're going to have a baby.'

He turned to look at me, and I waited for the penny to

drop, the lazy smile to go from his eyes to his lips and the million kisses to follow. But I couldn't see any twinkle, just the blood draining from his face as he held his cigarette mid-air before putting it to his mouth.

His face darkened. 'Is this a joke?' he said, stubbing out the half-smoked cigarette.

I was still smiling inanely, waiting for the joy. But he was looking at me with such intensity, such horror, I began to realise he wasn't sharing my happiness.

'I think I'm about two months, maybe more. Look,' I said, gesturing to my abdomen. Surely when he saw my tummy, touched it with his lovely gentle hands, he'd feel it too? But he didn't move, just looked down at my stomach with no expression on his face.

'Just feel,' I said quietly. 'Peter, our baby's in there.' I took his hand and gently guided it to my stomach, but before it reached me he pulled his hand away.

'Don't. This isn't real. We can't . . .'

'But you said we were getting married anyway and it didn't matter if I got pregnant. It's why we didn't wait.' I couldn't believe his reaction, I'd worried he might be surprised, it wasn't like we planned it. But this? I never expected this, not from Peter, not from this wonderful artistic boy who was loving and gentle and had asked me to marry him. This was going to be our beginning, the start of our life together, I thought we'd be wrapped around each other by now, making plans for the future. Not this ...

'Rosie – I'm not ready to be a dad ...'

I started to cry. Did he not love me after all? Had I been stupid believing in him? This wasn't the boy I loved, the one I'd have given everything up for – this was a stranger.

'Oh, Rosie, don't do this. You know it's the last thing we need.'

I was still in shock. 'But we're going to live in Paris. We can still do all the things we talked about, we'll just have our baby with us,' I said, blindly hoping that if I kept reminding him of what we'd said he would see this the way I did – as a blessing. 'Peter, this doesn't change anything.'

'Rosie, it changes *everything*.' He said this slowly, clearly, as though he was explaining maths to an impatient child. 'I don't have any money, we've nowhere to live and I'm not staying round here ...'

Tears were streaming down my face by now and I'd never felt more alone in my life. How had I got this so wrong?

'I know we're not staying around here, but ...'

'I mean I'm leaving Salford ... I'm going back to Italy. I'm sorry, I can't take you with me.'

I felt the ground move under me, I saw children

laughing, dogs barking, but I couldn't hear them, just sensed vague movement around me.

'I made some friends on holiday, and they just travel around Europe and they're working in a vineyard in Italy. It's a wonderful place, with a beautiful lake, surrounded by mountains, I stayed a few nights there ...'

I sat, open-mouthed listening to this. While I'd been home crying myself to sleep each night he was out with new friends having fun.

'But you can't ...' was all I could say. And I thought of my mother's warning about 'loose foreign women' and 'dark-skinned señoritas' and I just knew.

'Is it a girl?'

'Oh, don't be jealous, it's not like you. They are friends and yes, a couple of them are girls, but they're just friends.'

I didn't believe him, I just knew when he was lying.

'Rosie, I've got my plane ticket back there next week. I thought you'd understand.'

'Understand? You thought I'd understand that after promising marriage and a life together you go away for three weeks and everything's changed? What is there to understand about that?'

I had just spent the longest three weeks of my life waiting for him. I was carrying his child, I'd kept our secret safe, nurtured it, protected it, and now he was abandoning me and our unborn child ro run away to Italy?

'It's only for a few months. I'll be in touch when I get back.'

'In touch?! But you can't leave me now ... not now.'

I'd stupidly hoped if I talked to him long enough he'd come back to me, but looking at his eyes, he was already gone.

'My dad's paid my air fare, thinks it'll be good for me, you know, "You have to stand on your own two feet, my boy" and all that ...'

Even then, in the thick mist of confusion and disillusion, it didn't escape me that he'd found enough money for his air fare. He never had to try too hard at anything.

'We could go together ...' I was now desperate. In a few seconds I'd contemplated the awfulness of life without him, and the bleakness filled me up like dirty water in a glass. I couldn't bear the prospect of the physical pain of being apart.

'Rosie, I only have one ticket and your parents wouldn't let you go to Italy anyway. Imagine your mother's face.'

Thinking about this comment now angers me – how dare he blame my mother for me not being on that plane to Italy with him – but back then I was just so fraught I couldn't think straight. I just kept hoping that any

201

second now he'd change his mind, that it wasn't too late.

'I don't care. She can't stop me, I'm seventeen now, I can do what I like. I can come with you to Italy and you can pick grapes and I can sell my drawings, I'll meet your friends. I don't mind if some of them are girls. We can move to Paris once the baby's born.' Even as I said it I knew it was a fading dream, but I was so desperate to keep him I was in denial of what was happening, refusing to take on what he was saying to me. I would have done anything, gone anywhere, and even though I knew he had someone else I was so sure of our love I thought it would burn out any other feelings he might think he had for someone else. 'This is our chance, Peter, we can run away.'

'No, you can't go anywhere at the moment. But we'll still see each other when I'm home. When you've sorted things out.'

'Sorted things out?'

'Yes. You have to get rid of it, Rosie.'

Now I felt like I was in a boxing ring, being punched to the floor, staggering back up and being punched again. An abortion? I couldn't even say the word out loud. In all my daydreams and even in my worst fears I'd never contemplated this. It had never occurred to me that he would suggest something so cruel, and in that moment, when I realised he wanted to destroy our baby, a little light went out in my heart.

'It's for the best, I won't be here and if we're not together it would be foolish to try and bring up a baby on your own.'

'On my own? You're breaking up with me.'

My shock and hurt was slowly being overcome by a wave of anger. I was horrified to think that I'd spent the best part of a year listening to this boy, giving everything only for him to sweep me away like dust under the carpet.

'You can't, you can't do this … it's your baby, Peter. You can't just walk away.'

'I'll help you, I'll pay for it … It's not you, Rosie – we've had a great time, but I need to go and do things with my life … on my own. I can't be a husband to you. And I can't be a dad.'

I was rocking and crying and holding my stomach and Peter was now cautiously putting his arm round me, not knowing how to deal with this. Gone was the lazy, easy physical contact we'd enjoyed before. He was now polite, already distancing himself from me and the 'problem'.

'Let's just get this sorted and we can both get on with our lives, eh?' He was touching me under the chin like I was a fond sister and I wanted to smack his face, shake him and scream that he'd let me down. I was distraught, not just because of his reaction to what had happened, but because he wasn't who I thought he was. It made me question myself and every moment of our relationship and wonder if he'd ever loved me. I'd loved him, but perhaps I'd just loved who I thought he was.

I looked into his eyes, still waiting for a flicker of the boy I hoped was there, but nothing. He looked through me, which was the most painful thing of all. And I was reminded of something his father had said a few months before. *Our Peter's like a bloody magpie, sees something glitter and he's off chasing it.*

'So that's it then,' he said, brushing dry bits of grass off his jeans, keen to seal the deal and fly away to his better, brighter glittery life.

I just nodded. What more was there to say?

'I'll "sort it",' I said through my tears and grabbing my handbag I stood up and marched through the grass. I heard him call my name and I began to run, tearing through the carnival crowds. Better to never see him again than have our next 'date' at an abortion clinic with him handing over money and telling me it was for the best so he could walk away from the mess he'd made.

I fought my way back through the laughing kids, the candy floss, and round the carousel. The smell of burnt sugar and hot dogs permeated the air and I felt sick, staggering like a drunk, blinded by the pain and the tears.

All I could think was 'I will never get over this' – and I realise that a small part of me never has.

Lying here together now, so many years later, I'm still struggling with the past, but I'm beginning to feel strangely lighter.

'My heart breaks just hearing you talk about that day,' he says. 'I don't recognise that boy and I would give my life to turn back the clock and change everything.'

'I wouldn't,' I say. 'Yes, it was devastating, it broke me and it took me such a long time to move on from losing you. But the baby ... it's not something you can ever move on from, you hold them in your heart.'

He puts his hand on my stomach and I feel the years rush through me.

'I got to Italy and realised I'd made a huge mistake. I could only think of you. I kept imagining the clinic, the surgery, the awful operation ... and you alone and scared, then I thought of the baby and it suddenly all meant so much.'

'I didn't have the abortion,' I say. 'I'm afraid fate took care of that for us.'

Chapter Fifteen

The night of the fair the blood came. I lay in bed in agony, knowing what was happening, feeling the loss as the little life ebbed away and left my body. I cried for my mum and she came running. Her baby was losing her own baby and I could see she was hurting almost as much as me. She held me through the night, mopping my brow, telling me not to cry as she wept with me. 'It's okay, love, everything's going to be all right, Mum's here.' Sometimes I can still hear her saying the words softly in the night.

After the miscarriage I lost myself for a while. I could think of nothing but the baby and Peter – grieving for him, our child and our future. And for a while I felt I had nothing.

I'd switch from being heartbroken to furious, imagining Peter living his life, still fulfilling those amazing dreams without me while I was left with the dust. And I'd lie on my bed imagining him in a vineyard, a beautiful waterfront, gazing at the mountains with someone else. And the more I conjured up these images to torture myself, the more angry I became until all I could see when I thought of him was a burning rage. It was this, along with Mike, that ultimately made me stronger.

No one knew about the pregnancy except Margaret, who amazed me with her motherliness and love and during this time we grew closer. I learned to respect her, and appreciate her wisdom which in turn softened her towards me.

I knew now that her meddling and controlling wasn't about hurting me or spoiling my life – quite the opposite: she'd known more about life and people and could see what was coming. Whereas I, in my youth and naivety, couldn't.

I was now dealing with the fallout, the terrible loss of my baby and wondering if I'd ever come to terms with that. How do you say goodbye to someone you've never even said hello to?

Peter is holding me now as I tell him about that night. He's lying next to me, tears streaming down his face, and I finally feel released; in acknowledging the grief, he's acknowledging the existence of his child. But sharing the loss with Peter after all this time brings a fresh splash of grief. I realise I have never fully come to terms with what happened because I needed him to know too. I needed him to feel this loss as keenly as I have, as I still do because there's no headstone, no little blanket, no life to celebrate. And I cry along with him for our baby, who never knew what it was to feel sunshine on her face.

Later, we talk about the baby that might have been and Peter asks if I think it was a boy or a girl.

'A girl,' I say. I've always thought of the baby as a girl. 'And her name would have been Daisy.' I smile.

'Our own little flower in the rubble,' he says.

'Daisy gave me so much,' I say. 'She showed me how it felt to be a mum, and made me realise that's what I wanted – a family and children. All my teenage talk about painting pyramids and running around the world showing my pictures was real at the time, but it wouldn't have been right for me back then. Becoming pregnant made me realise that all this was meant to be, I had found my role at last, and this was what I needed *and* wanted. I just hadn't realised until Daisy came along and showed me the right path to take.'

I think about Mike and how he also taught me that it was okay to love again and I know he was my fate and helped me move on.

'The day I married Camille all I could think about was you,' says Peter.

We are both silent. Cars pass outside, a police siren screams in the distance; I'm not used to the sounds of the city. I see a chink of light through the curtains – it must be almost morning, we must have been talking for hours.

'Why did you think of me on your wedding day?' I say, remembering how I had spilt mascara tears on my cream suit just wishing it was Peter waiting for me at the registry office.

'I wished I was marrying you. I hadn't seen you for more than ten years, but I imagined you in a white veil and when I lifted the veil to kiss Camille I was filled with an overwhelming sadness ... and it was my own stupid fault.'

'It wasn't meant to be, Peter, we were both with the people we needed then.'

He sits up slightly, on one elbow, resting his head on his hand. Even in the darkness I'm aware he is running his fingers through his hair. I know him so well, this stranger.

'You chose your path, Peter.'

'I'm not making excuses, but I feel like I'm apologising on behalf of someone else. I hear you now and I agree, and I hate that stupid, arrogant boy who wanted it all. But believe me when I say I'm different now.'

'Do people really change?' I ask, probably sounding cynical but it's a genuine question. After all that happened can I ever trust him enough to really love him again?

'I probably had to live a little before I became me,' he says. 'I never had to try too hard for anything and when the sea got a little rough I let you go, I wanted to ride my own waves. I made the biggest mistake of my life – but that was the beginning of me growing up and it changed me. I had houses, cars, a beautiful wife and a great career – and every day I would wake up and my heart would sink a little, because all I ever wanted was you.'

Oh, how I wished he'd said that forty-odd years ago. And why do I suddenly feel so guilty for feeling that? I loved Mike and always will.

'Are we really meant to be together now, or is it the great tragedy that we were meant for each other once, but missed our way? Is it too late for us, Peter?'

'No, it isn't. As I'm beginning to know you again I feel like I'm coming back to life. My feelings for you are as strong as they ever were.' He turns his head to look at me.

'I didn't expect to ever feel like this again ... not at my age,' I say.

We lie in silence for a while, both thinking; apart, yet together. Then, eventually he pushes on through the silence.

'Thank you for telling me, Rosie, I needed to know what happened.'

'And I needed you to know,' I say, feeling like a huge weight has been lifted, glad I've finally been able to share this with him.

'What about you? How do you feel?' he suddenly asks in the darkness.

'I feel better. I feel like everything happened for a reason and though things don't always make sense to us at the time, we sometimes realise that they were meant to be.'

'Life has a way of working out,' he says.

'Yes, you often said that, and you are right.'

'So, let's talk about tomorrow and the day after that and the day after that,' he says. 'If you could have anything happen, what would it be? What's your greatest wish?'

'I wouldn't want to change the past, but I do wish you'd known me at twenty-five, I wish you'd waited long enough to love me in my thirties and forties. I wish you'd seen how good I still looked then and how my breasts stayed pert and my waist stayed trim. I wish you'd held my hand and those of our children when my skin was fresh and I was young and vital with energy and still had so much life to live. But that's just fantasy and it wouldn't have worked, and it's better that you waited until now to come back.'

'I think we're both ready for this. I was never a great believer in fate, but what were the chances that Pamela would choose your florist and we'd meet that day at my niece's wedding?'

'I know, I've been wondering recently if Mike set us up. I think he'd want me to be happy again and he'd want me to have a man in my life, if only to take me out for lunch and treat me well, make me happy – and you do.'

'I've never been happier. I feel like I've been looking for something all my life and I've finally found it and at the ripe old age of sixty-five I'm in love again with my first love, for a second time,' he says.

My heart softens when I hear this. I'm not ready yet to say I love him, but in a teenage way I'm delighted he said it first.

'This is different from the first time though,' he says. 'The only way I can describe it is that it feels like home.'

'That's so lovely, I know what you mean. It's calmer,

we're both older, more accepting. But I do wonder what my kids would say about me lying in a hotel room with you – "At your age, Mum?" I can hear them now. I should be babysitting grandchildren and sucking on boiled sweets with a copy of *The People's Friend*.' We both laugh and I think how lucky I am that he's come along and saved me at a time in my life when I needed something else, someone just for me.

'I think we should give ourselves another chance, let's take this a little further and see where it goes,' he says. 'Let's go to the cinema this weekend and if you want to come back to my hotel again . . . ?'

'Okay, that sounds good. But I have to warn you I'm too old to worry about racy underwear and ageing cellulite and as exciting as it may be, the thought of having sex with someone new frightens me to death.'

'That's okay, I don't care about racy cellulite or ageing underwear.' He smiles.

'Oh, I have those too.'

We laugh, like we always did. I have a feeling we have a lot more laughter to come.

Just a few hours later my mobile alarm wakes me and I'm amazed not to be in my own bed alone. I reach out and there he is, smiling. 'I always longed to watch you sleeping, but never had the chance until now,' he says, his hand on my cheek. I stir slightly and smile back, aware my mascara must be blurry and the rest of my beautifully applied make-up long gone. 'You okay?' he asks.

'Yes. I'm sorry, I have to get up. My granddaughter ...'

'So, the cinema?' he asks.

I nod.

'And we're going to start seeing each other? You want this?'

I feel happy, but a little shaky. I think about Mike and the girls and I wonder if I'm doing the right thing, but if I don't do this now I never will.

'Yes, I do – if you do?'

'Of course.'

I dress in the bathroom. I still want to keep a little bit of me to myself and I'm worried how my sixty-something body will look in the cold light of morning to my old lover's eyes. Last night was a watershed, we talked openly and honestly and shared something very deep. I finally feel like I'm coming out of the darkness of the past, of all the grief and loss, and moving forward. And now we've talked I feel ready to take things further with Peter and perhaps become something more than just old friends.

I catch myself in the mirror and smile at the woman looking back. She's not too bad for her age and on closer inspection, there's definitely a little more light in those eyes than yesterday. And as we leave the room we kiss in the doorway and my tummy is filled with apple blossom again.

Chapter Sixteen

It's hard to imagine being without Peter in my life now, but then I suppose he's always been around in some form. His return has reminded me of Rosie – not the mum, the grandmother, or the widow – just Rosie.

Customers in the shop have been remarking on how well I'm looking and Anna just asked me if I'm using a different moisturiser. I want to tell everyone why I'm looking and feeling younger, why I'm walking with a spring in my step and why I've joined the gym and had my hair highlighted. Corrine has been telling me for years I need to 'go blonder'. 'Blondes have more fun, love,' she said last week as she slapped on acres of nose-stinging bright blue bleach. I hope she's right. I don't say anything to anyone other than Corrine, but I know it's because of Peter, he's put the light back in my eyes, the colour back in my life and I'm beginning to believe in myself again. I'm excited by him like I used to be, and hearing him talk about the things he's done, the places he's been doesn't make me sad or envious, it makes me want to do it for myself. I've no regrets about the way my life's turned out, my family mean everything to me and I wouldn't change my time with them for the world, but I've never done anything my granddaughters would post on their Facebook pages or tweet about.

Recently I've been thinking perhaps now is the time to do these things. Since Peter has swept back into my life it feels like I am slowly opening up like a flower. I want to leap into oceans and ride waves, to climb on a clapped-out lorry and journey through India, trek the Himalayas. I want to see all the places I once dreamed of, but never arrived at.

I don't say too much to the girls about Peter, they know he's a friend and they make jokes about 'Mum's new man', but they don't for a minute think it's anything more than a rekindling of an old friendship. And that's all it was initially: a few lunches, some nice times talking about how the world once was. But now it's much more than friendship, we've shared the pain of the past and I feel we've come through it together. I am interested in the possibility of much more with Peter, but it's never going to be just about what I want. I have to see how things go before I start making announcements and calling him 'my partner'. I'm older and it's so different from before because whether I like it or not more people will be involved in this relationship. I now come with a whole heap of baggage! For the moment perhaps I'll keep Peter's involvement in my life vague. I'll tell them soon – when it feels right. I'll hold him close to my chest, like a bridesmaid with a fragrant posy – my delicious secret.

I'm not sure my girls are ready for me to have a 'boyfriend'. I'm not entirely sure I'm ready. I know they're grown-ups, but Mike was their dad and introducing Peter as something significant will be changing the dynamic of our family.

Initially it may only be a slight shift, but it will exist, and it will be impossible to go back from that point. I'm terrified they may feel he's taking the role of their dad, something Peter could never do. He and Mike are like passing ships ... Peter gave me the thrill, the passion, showed me a world I'd never seen before; he taught me so much about life and art and people – and he was the love of my life, always will be. But I came to love Mike as much, in a different way, he was the calm after the storm, and he stepped in and loved me selflessly. The girls both know Peter once broke my heart and who's to say he won't again? But this time I'm older and wiser and I can look after myself. This time around I'm going into this with my eyes wide open.

If I'm honest, the young Rosie that still lives somewhere inside me is a little scared of entering into this relationship. I suppose I'm also worried if I tell everyone then real life will intrude and the magic will end, like it did before, and I don't want that – I want to escape hand in hand with Peter into our past, and that summer when life was simple and my heart was intact.

I am always honest with the girls and tell them when I'm seeing Peter, but I usually invent a reason: 'He wants me to help him choose some plant bulbs for his garden,' or 'He's passing through Manchester and we're meeting for a quick coffee.' I don't tell them the reason he's in Manchester is because he wants to see me and kiss me with a passion that takes my breath away – and that garden bulbs are the last thing on either of our minds.

It doesn't occur to my daughters that I might be having more than just a coffee or a nice lunch with an old friend. And when I look into his eyes I know my thoughts are quite inappropriate for a lady of a certain age with two grandchildren.

'Have you tried the new wine bar on Deansgate?'

Isobel asks as we prepare flowers for a funeral. Anna's doing the big floral tribute and Isobel and I are making up the smaller ones.

'No, I hear it's really trendy though. Apparently the Man United players go there. I'd love to go, but I'd feel old up against all those WAGs in their miniskirts and hair extensions,' Anna remarks.

Neither of them ask me if I've been and both look at me open-mouthed when I say, 'It's not that bad, the tapas is lovely and the wine's not overpriced.'

'How do you know?' Anna asks, looking at Isobel.

'I was there on Friday night.'

'Who with?'

'Peter. I did say I was going out with him.'

'Yes, but I didn't realise you meant you were going out at night. That's the second time you've been out late with him.'

'Fourth actually ... or is it fifth? Terrible, isn't it? We should really be indoors after six p.m., but sometimes we meet up in our zimmer frames after dark for a Horlicks,' I joke.

Anna is looking at me. 'But you never said.'

'But you never asked.'

'Mum, you should tell us where and when you're going out – what if something happened?'

'Then Peter would be with me. Anyway, you two go

220

out and you don't always tell me where and when and who with.'

'That's different . . .'

'Not really, I worry about you as much as you worry about me. The only difference is I've been worrying about you two a lot longer.'

'Well from now on I want you to text me when you arrive somewhere.'

'No, I'm not texting you every time I go to the bloody toilet. You're not my mother and I'm not sixteen, Anna.'

'I'm not asking you to text me all the time . . . I'm just saying you should let us know your whereabouts.'

'Okay, I shall furnish you with a laminated wall chart covering my social activities for the next month,' I say.

'I bet it would fill a wall chart too. You're never home these days, unlike me. I wish I could have *one* night out. I'm fed up of ferrying kids to dancing classes and back, and now Emma wants to go to parties – and they always seem to be on *my* weekend,' Anna starts. 'I told her, no more parties, you've got exams and I'm not spending another Saturday night sober, so she's going over to her friend Chloe's to revise.'

'Oh, don't talk to me about Saturday nights,' Isobel says. 'All Richard wants to do is hammer nails in walls and sit gazing at his Screwfix catalogue. And when I say screw . . . I don't mean . . .'

'Well, it's all relative, looking at DIY screws probably *is* porn to Richard,' I say, feeling slightly outrageous.

'Mother!' Anna laughs and gives me a mock disapproving look. 'When did you get so raunchy?'

'Ah, you'd be surprised,' I say.

They both laugh and I count my blessings they assume that on the whole I'm living a chaste life of garden centres and light lunches with another OAP. I suppose that's how the rest of the world sees us two older people – but when we're together, it isn't like that. With him I feel young again with the world at my feet. If the girls only knew the adventures we have in our heads they would be amazed. We talk of travelling the world and of course of living in Paris and I'm beginning to think the dream isn't dead after all. One day perhaps ...

So while Anna's worrying about Emma and Isobel's complaining about Richard's latest screw obsession, my life is not on their radar. This is a huge relief as it means they don't ask too many searching questions about what I'm up to, and I can have fun without explaining myself to anyone – for the first time in my life.

Chapter Seventeen

Peter's invited me to his home in Oxford for the weekend. It's the first time I've been and I'm nervous. This feels like a watershed in our relationship and sitting on the train I think back to that other time, when I first saw the house he lived in, and realised how different we were.

I'd been going out with Peter for several months and hadn't been invited to his house or to meet his parents. He'd suffered an afternoon with my mother and a plate of stale Battenberg cake, so the least they could do was return the favour, but nothing. It bothered me, and it crossed my mind they didn't think I was good enough, but then one day fate stepped in when Peter's car broke down and his father had to come and tow us back to his house, which is where I met his mother.

Once we'd arrived at his home I was immediately struck by the difference to mine. The hallway was the size of our front room, high ceilings, huge, ornate mirror and flowers everywhere. I followed Mr Moreton down the hall, and as we passed a doorway I caught a glimpse of a little blonde girl playing the cello.

'That's enough now, Pamela, time for bed,' Mr Moreton called as he passed.

He led me into a back room, which he referred to as 'the sitting room', and I followed meekly behind, taking in the art-filled walls, overstuffed sofas and groaning bookcases filled with foreign novels. He told me to take a seat and I was perched on the edge of the sofa when an attractive, older red-haired woman appeared in the doorway.

'Oh ...' she said, and curled her lip when she saw me. I felt like a burglar. She was holding a magazine and looked like she was dressed to go out in a smart tailored dress, backcombed hair and deep coral nails that matched her lips – she oozed old-fashioned glamour.

'This is Peter's friend,' Mr Moreton said, nodding towards the sofa. 'Pretty little thing,' he muttered rather inappropriately, but at the time it seemed perfectly acceptable.

'Oh, a friend of Peter's, how charming.' She smiled, but only with her mouth.

'Stupid boy's gone to the garage to get petrol, he forgot

to put it in again,' Mr Moreton grumbled. 'He goes around in a daze, can't commit to anything for more than five minutes, like a bloody magpie, doesn't do real life – sees something glitter and he's off chasing it. National Service, that's what he needs.'

I had never really considered Peter as anything but a god. So he forgot to put petrol in the car, but he was charming, intelligent and funny and I rather resented his father's version of him.

'It's quite true, my son would forget his head if it wasn't screwed on … How do you know Peter, dear?' his mother asked, looking into my eyes and trying to establish the nature of our 'friendship'.

'College.' She clearly didn't know my name, so Peter obviously hadn't mentioned me to her. I smiled inanely, pulling at my short skirt, not something I would have worn if I'd known I was meeting the future in-laws.

She was now circling the couch, weighing up her prey as she lit a cigarette. She let the smoke out slowly through her nostrils, while flicking the ash in a chunky glass ashtray. 'Coffee, darling, make some coffee – use the pot, it's been on the stove for a little while, should be nice and strong.'

'Will do.' His voice was less grumpy with her, she was definitely in charge.

'So how long have you and Peter been … friends?' she

said, joining me on the sofa, tilting her head and taking another huge drag.

'I've ... we've known each other since we started at college, last September,' I said, nodding too eagerly like those dogs people used to put on the back ledge of their cars.

'Oh you're a *student*?' she said, like this was now making sense. What did she think I was? 'I'm sorry, are you ... erm, your name is?'

I told her.

'So, Rosie?' she said, crossing her legs, warming to her elegant cross-examination. 'Do your parents approve of your choice?'

'My choice ... you mean Peter?'

She looked surprised, shocked even. 'No. Art ... how do they feel about you reading art?'

Fortunately I didn't have to respond to this as Mr Moreton was walking into the sitting room with a tray and three cups of coffee, a milk jug on the side.

'I suppose you like it black, all the young people drink their coffee black now,' he said, placing the tray on the table. He could have put arsenic in it for all I cared, I didn't want their bloody coffee or her patronising talk. I wanted Peter to come back, rescue me and take me home. More pertinently, my skirt was riding up by the second on their leather couch and to reach for the cup was difficult enough without showing Peter's parents my upper thighs. Where the hell was Peter – how long did it take to put petrol in a car?

'Tony, bring in the biscotti, they're in the Lavazza tin, darling. Rosie looks like she could do with something sweet. You're very pale, aren't you, dear? Are you sure you're okay?'

'Yes … thank you, just a little tired.' I smiled, my lips tight shut waiting for whatever Tony was going to bring in for my consumption from the strange-sounding tin in the kitchen. 'We always bring biscotti back from Sardinia,' she said in an aside to me as he appeared next to me, proffering the tin like one of the Three Wise Men.

Lavazza, biscotti and Sardinia – three words I'd never heard in my life before – she may as well have been speaking another language. She opened the tin with manicured hands and I cautiously leaned in to see what was inside, relieved they were only biscuits. Custard creams they weren't, but I could see a biscuity resemblance and thanking her I took one from the tin.

As she prattled on about Sardinia and the scenery I continued to nod and smile, balance my cup and saucer on my knee, try and keep my skirt decent and bite into the biscuit. As my teeth went down onto what I expected to be crumbly I almost broke a tooth, or several! What on earth was this? It was extremely hard and impossible to eat so I just sat clutching it with one hand, hoping at some point to discard it between there and the car. By the time Peter eventually turned up my cup was wobbling in my saucer and the skirt had ridden up my legs. And there, in the art-filled, book-stuffed, middle-class home, I saw myself for the first time as they might see me and I was overwhelmed by the disparity in our worlds. I must have seemed so gauche to them with my short skirt, flat vowels and inane answers and when the three of them launched into a political debate I just gave up trying.

I see now how immature I was, lacking in confidence, unsure of myself and my feelings. I was both impressed and daunted by these people, who allowed me to glimpse another world of continental holidays and foreign novels. I could observe the differences in our worlds, and naively believed we'd overcome them, that one day I might even be part of this. His mother resented me because of where I was from, the way I spoke and the little working-class mouse I appeared to her to be. I wasn't like the daughters of her friends with their educated voices and academic ambitions, I was just an unremarkable girl with a talent for drawing and that would never be enough for her son. Eventually, Peter caught the panic in my eyes and suggested he take me home.

'I can't believe you left me in there,' I hissed as we walked through the hall. 'Your parents hadn't a clue who I was. Why have you never told them about me?'

'I wanted to keep you all to myself,' he said, plucking a blue hydrangea head from a jug in the doorway and offering it to me. I wafted him away, I wasn't going to be that easy to convince. I knew it was more likely they'd think I wasn't good enough for him, and he knew it. I didn't exist in his real life and I was hurt and angry with him. I suppose I should have seen the writing on the wall then, but love is blind.

I was never invited to Peter's house a second time, and I never saw his parents again.

And now, as we pull up outside his Oxfordshire home, I'm reminded all over again of the different worlds we inhabit. His home is just lovely, as I'd imagined, a big old Edwardian place that he reckons he 'compromised' over after his divorce. Looking at it I can only imagine how gorgeous his house with Camille must have been if this is a compromise. The living room is large and airy with big comfy sofas, shelves lined with books and framed photographs covering the walls. The entrails of his camera stuff lie on the coffee table along with sketches, and charcoal and pencils litter every surface. It's untidy but cosy and I immediately feel at home, remembering the beautiful detritus of art that used to lie around my own bedroom when I was young. Pencils, paper, half-drawn pictures, watercolours, all waiting to be finished or mounted; I threw them away after we parted. I feel sad now that this didn't figure in my life after all.

'You really should be drawing again,' Peter says as I hold a piece of charcoal between my thumb and forefinger, remembering its silkiness in my fingers and the skill I once had.

'I think I will ... soon,' I say, picking up a camera and looking through the lens. I feel him at the side of me, he's suddenly a little on edge. 'Are you okay?' I ask, taking the camera from my eyes.

'Yes ... but it's a very expensive camera, it's special.' He smiles apologetically.

I put it back on the table; I'm not embarrassed, more amused. 'I suppose that's one of the joys of living alone without family popping in and rifling through everything. You're lucky to be able to leave such treasures around and not expect them to be picked up and played with ... until I arrive, that is.'

He laughs. 'Yes, I'm sorry. I'm not sure it's a good thing having the luxury of solitude – one can become a bit too precious when you're alone a lot of the time. I make my coffee a certain way, I like to sit in the same chair by the kitchen window to read my newspaper and I eat the same breakfast of muesli every day.'

'That's hardly a problem,' I laugh. 'I think that's pretty normal.'

'But not for me. So sometimes I shake it up and go wild: I read my newspaper in the sitting room and cast caution to the wind and have toast for breakfast.'

'You crazy bastard,' I say. 'What happened to the guy who ran away to Italy and woke up in France?'

'I woke up alone one day, and realised that running away isn't the answer. But a good breakfast is,' he laughs.

I can see he's changed from that reckless, selfish young man he was, but I wonder if Peter's life of independence, even selfishness, could ever be shared with another person. I glance at the camera now back in its place and wonder if he's destined to wake up alone.

'This is my most recent work,' he's saying as he shows me drawings and photographs that cover the walls, modern, structural photos juxtaposed with photos of old Salford slums.

'I remember you taking that one,' I say, looking closely at a black and white photo of kids playing cricket on Nightingale Road one hot August afternoon.

'That was the day we photographed the slum clearances.'

'Yes, not the obvious place for a romantic date – but don't tell my granddaughter. She'd say, "Nan, you are just so weird." She's always saying that,' I laugh.

I imagine what Emma would think about us wandering through bleak wastelands of graffiti and rubble, past red-bricked terraces turned black with soot. I realise now we were witnessing the post-war, post-industrial slump of empty warehouses, slum clearances, poverty and broken lives. But Peter had shown me something more than this – he'd revealed the stories in the graffiti, the kids with angel faces in the rubble, the pure, wind-blown beauty of clean washing dancing over cobbles in the sun. Then, as now, he taught me so much and changed my perspective on life.

'It must be fun to have grandchildren around – I always think you never really get old with kids in your life,' he says.

'Yes, it is. I adore them and when Mike died they missed him, but Katie, the younger one, didn't quite get that I was upset. About two days after Mike died she called round and said, "It's a shame, isn't it, but you're okay, aren't you, Nan?" I said yes and she said, "Oh good, are you better enough to make me pancakes then?"' Mike would have laughed with me about that, but Peter just smiles, like he's not sure how to react. I don't suppose he gets the funny little nuances of children.

'I'm sure your grandkids get you back on your feet,' he says. 'They aren't influenced yet by how society thinks we should behave.'

'They are my life, but it's bittersweet. In the past year we've had more birthdays, another Christmas, Emma has a boyfriend – all things that Mike won't ever see.'

'That must be difficult, but it sounds like you and Mike had a good relationship and he died knowing you were all okay. The girls are grown up and they're living their own lives now and—'

'Yes, that's true, but it doesn't really work like that. A forty-year-old is still your child, still your baby, and the older they are the more problems they have. For example, when Mike died Anna had just split with her husband. She was devastated, and it upsets me to think he never knew that she was okay in the end. But of course it isn't the end, there will be other problems, other stuff. And other wonderful things too,' I add before he thinks I'm a complete pessimist. 'We have graduations and weddings and lots of birthdays to look forward to; we love a party – any excuse to celebrate.' I smile.

'He went too soon. Ironic really, he's got a whole family who still need him, he had so much more to give, yet he has to be the one who goes. Here's me with no one depending on me or needing me and I'm still here – what's that about?'

'Oh don't say that, Peter. Besides, I've given up trying to work out the why-mes and the what-ifs,' I say. 'I just cling desperately to your philosophy that life has a way of working things out . . . it's very . . . Buddhist?'

'Very Peter,' he laughs. 'I learned a lot about Eastern philosophy and religion over the years, through my travels. I suppose I have a Buddhist approach to certain things, but as you know, I don't adhere to one ideology – I just make it up as I go along, like I do with life.'

'Yes, so I've gathered. You never even bothered to get divorced until you needed to.'

'No, that's true. I didn't get married until I wanted to either. I suppose I just go with the flow. I can't complain, I've had some great times and as you say, we shouldn't have regrets.'

It makes me smile now when I think about how he's grown into himself, he's fitted his life around him rather than the other way round, which I think most of us do.

'You are the complete opposite of Mike,' I say. 'He was organised, always meticulous, and while I was rushing around worrying and being a drama queen he'd deal with the problem in a practical way. I was in tears when Anna called me to say she was leaving her husband, but before I'd put the phone down Mike was in the car to bring them all home to us.'

'I can't imagine how I'd ever deal with something like that. I wouldn't have a clue,' he says, genuinely impressed. 'I suppose we look at others who have different lives than we do and admire them for their knowledge, their courage, their wisdom?'

'Yes, but you're just as knowledgeable and wise and courageous – you just show it in different ways,' I say.

'Ah but a family . . . a child? That's a mystery to me, and if I'm honest I find that aspect of life a little scary. I'd rather climb a mountain and photograph vast panoramas than change a baby's nappy.'

'Yes, because you've never done it. Trust me, it's easy – not always pleasant, but easier than that mountain.'

'Well, I never met Mike, but he was obviously a good father and he did know about nappies and children. I feel like I know him. I think I would have liked him. We probably had a lot in common – after all, we've both loved the same woman.'

I hadn't really thought about it this way, but both these men know things about me no one else does. And though they will never meet, through me they are inexorably linked. I think Mike would have liked Peter too, he would have been fascinated by his travels, his photography, and I'm sure they'd have shared an interest in nature and the stars. 'Let me continue to show you round the stately pile.' He laughs, but where I come from it might well be a stately pile, it's huge and beauti- fully decorated. I wonder if Camille has been here with her magic paintbrush, dusting the walls with Borrowed Light and Elephants' Breath. I have to smile at my own immaturity and admit I'm still slightly jealous of his ex, even though she's married to someone else. Damn that woman and her brilliant sense of colour and style!

He takes my hand and guides me upstairs into a bed-room where the wall is covered in prints from all over the world.

'Wow, you've been everywhere – and photographed it,' I say.

I'm gazing at sunsets spilling into endless oceans, huge white Italian churches, Gothic German architecture and shanty towns in South Africa . . . so many images of places I could only imagine.

'I wish I'd been there, seen those sights.' I feel wistful.

'You can. There's no reason why you can't get on a plane and go wherever you like.'

I look at him and smile. 'Oh, Peter, you're such a dreamer.'

'You were a dreamer too once, Rosie. Don't close the book on your life yet – you have to grasp it – be you and do what you want to do. Like she did . . .' He passes me a photo of us then, two beautiful young people sitting on the front bonnet of his Morris Minor, a powder-blue cardigan around my shoulders. We are laughing – I can't remember why. I don't think we needed a reason to laugh in those days.

'God, we were young, so young – and we both had such big dreams, didn't we?' I sigh.

'My mother always called me "Peter the pleasure-seeker", and I was. Still am, really.'

236

'Your mother knew you well. There goes Peter, always chasing the light,' I murmur, almost to myself.

I have my overnight bag with me. It's in the hall masquerading as a large handbag. It was Corrine's idea; as she said, 'If things don't work out you don't look too keen and can leave with your dignity intact.'

He makes dinner, a simple but delicious salad, followed by French macarons.

'These are my favourite, how did you know?' I said, biting into a pale pink disc filled with tart raspberry cream.

'I didn't know, but we used to talk about French patisserie, so I imagined you'd like them and it might remind you of Paris.'

'I don't need a reminder of Paris,' I say, taking a second macaron and offering him a bite. He takes it and in this sharing, this closeness, I feel the shock of intimacy, and realise how much I've missed moments like this.

'I won't have another glass,' I say as he is about to pour more red.

'Oh, why? Would you have preferred the Pinot?'

I smile. 'No, it's just that I may drive home . . .'

'Ah, but it's quite a drive, and I've made up the spare room just in case.'

I was glad to have the option, it felt less pressurised. 'In that case I'd love another.' I sit back and look at him in his own natural habitat. I still love looking at him, he still sets me on fire as I watch him through the soft candlelight. The easy smile, the way he gently teases me.

I know that he's travelled, seen some amazing sights, but I wonder if he has been truly happy. Has life been good to him, or has he lived with a sense of loss, of vague disappointment overshadowing everything wonderful?

When the dinner is finished and the coffees and brandies have been drunk, he asks again if I would like to stay the night.

'Don't feel you have to,' he says.

I take a deep breath and jump off the cliff. 'Yes, I'd like to spend the night ... with you,' I say. I'm nervous and as much as I want to there's a little pull inside asking me if I'm sure I want this. Am I risking being hurt all over again? Yes I am, of course I am, but I'm beginning to realise that anything worth doing has an element of risk, and I finally feel ready to take this one. And this time I'm old enough to deal with the fallout, I have my eyes open and I know where I'm going with this. It's about me and Peter and now, not years ago and not next week, it's about what I want, now.

He takes my hand and we slowly wander upstairs to his bedroom where I ask him to turn out the lights. We kiss and I'm back in the swirling summer storm. I never imagined I'd ever sleep with another man after Mike, but here I am, back where it all began with my first love. It's another summer, another place, but we're the same people, just older, wiser and as unsure, nervous and excited as we were the first time.

Now, in my older body, I have other concerns too. I'm worried about how different I must be from the girl he remembers. I climb into the bed complaining of being cold, but really I want to cover up, I feel exposed and it's not just my flesh, my heart feels like it's opened up too. Old, forgotten feelings and sensations come flooding back into me. I welcome them, but I'm also scared of what this means. I'm as vulnerable as I was then as I lie back and he kisses me all over, gently pulling away the covers and telling me I'm just as beautiful as I was.

'More, even more beautiful,' he says. 'I've missed you, Rosie.'

To sleep with Peter again is wonderful, thrilling, it's as though we're reaching into the past to grab hold of what future is left for us. And this isn't a friendship, or even a fling for me any more – this is another step towards healing the past and getting back my life.

Despite the fact that we're both older and wiser than the first time, it's a warm, feckless summer just like our first and I am falling again, like the teenager I once was.

Chapter Eighteen

The morning after our first proper night together I feel elated, and at the same time a little sad, like I've lost something. I suppose in some ways sleeping with Peter is like coming full circle for me – he was my first, and I can't help but wonder if he will be my last. At the same time I feel like this has been a step further away from Mike, another door closed on my marriage, but I am positive and this other door has opened and the light has come streaming through.

We sit in his kitchen and drink black coffee from huge blue pottery cups as croissants warm in the oven and Albert, Peter's old tabby cat, twists in and out of our legs. The sun comes down in an arc through the window and we are bathed in a pool of light, both thinking, not talking. Peter has always been a thinker. He likes to contemplate – he used to sit looking through the car window, imagining a photo, composing it in his mind. I'll admit I sometimes used to find it frustrating, I was impatient to get to where we were going, or just frustrated because I wanted his attention. Now I'm older I appreciate the thinking space we have together, neither of us feels the need to speak, we just enjoy being.

'You probably don't realise this,' I say into the thick, morning silence, 'but you've taught me how to let go, relax. I love the silence, I've come to realise how important it is.' I've always revelled in the noisy chaos of busy family life, I would miss the coming and going, the dramas, the falling out and the making up. And knowing I will welcome that cacophony again soon, I'm just enjoying the peace and quiet here with him.

'Yes, it's like oxygen. The world's so damn fast these days with computers and phones and people shouting over each other to be heard through some medium or other. I suppose that's why I'm a photographer, and I can live with silence: the only sound I need is the click of the shutter.'

'It's funny, because when I'm at home on my own I often feel the need to put the radio on, or I talk to Lily or telephone someone. But with you I don't feel that need, I just love this, now, me and you and silence.'

As if on cue Albert gives a little miaow and Peter gathers him up in his arms and talks to the little cat like he is his child. As I watch him gently stroking and cajoling, offering him various tempting feline titbits, it occurs to me that Peter really should have been someone's dad and the person he hurt the most, that day at the fair, was himself.

Later, we stroll into Oxford, wander through the University Parks in the sunshine, ending up by the river, where the late afternoon sunshine spills on the water and punters move their boats lazily by.

'Ice cream?' Peter asks, spotting a small hut selling refreshments.

'Lovely.'

'What flavour would you like?' he asks, as we walk towards the hut.

'Oh, any ... I don't mind.'

'Yes, you do. You hate mint choc chip and you need to discover your own flavour. Until we go to Italy and you can taste a million gelatos you'll have to make do with the basic flavours here, I'm afraid.'

'Okay, vanilla,' I say, laughing.

He lifts his hands in the air in a despairing gesture. 'There are at least twenty flavours on the list, from Brazilian Coffee to Black Raspberry. You can't have vanilla ...'

He starts laughing and I join in. 'I know I'm laughing, but I am honestly so overwhelmed by the flavour choice I have to play it safe.'

'Rosie, recently you told me that you liked the idea of seeing yourself in a red open-top MG wearing sunglasses, your hair flowing in the breeze.'

'Yes, but what's that got to do with ice cream?' I'm smiling, loving his attention and the sunshine, enjoying the warmth on my face as I look up at him.

'It's got *everything* to do with ice cream. What would that red, open-top MG-driving woman choose? It wouldn't be vanilla ... would it?'

'No, you're right, she'll have a scoop of the mojito and one of the Jamoca fudge almond, please,' I say, loving the way he constantly questions me, and pushes me out of my comfort zone. This isn't just about ice cream, this is the magic of Peter and the unsafe, recklessness of him compared to Mike, who chose the mint choc chip or the vanilla along with me. Peter hands me a cone and I taste the sharp limey zing of mojito and the rich jaw-aching chocolate of Jamoca and I long to try them all, to go back and taste every flavour that little hut has to offer. I look at Peter walking next to me, licking his own exotic ice cream concoction, and I wonder what else he could teach me. How much more of life can he open out to me, and lay before me – he is exciting and dangerous and always has been. Today it's mojito ice cream, once it was sex in a storm, who knows what's next? I feel a shudder of excitement go through me, and it isn't the chill of the ice cream. Still eating, we walk across the little bridge over the river and lean over when we're halfway across and watch the boats go by.

'I love being here,' I say.

'Me too.' He takes my hand. 'Could you ever see yourself living here?'

'It's somewhere I'd love to live, but it's not where my family are and that's where I have to be. It's not a rule, it's just me. But Oxford's just so beautiful, the architecture, the culture, the dreaming spires – you're so lucky to live here,' I say wistfully.

'It's the nearest I've ever felt to home,' he says. 'I just feel at peace here. You were saying this morning that I am comfortable with silence and that's what I've grown to love here – the quiet. The university students keep it fresh and vibrant, so it's never stale, but on a summer evening at home the only thing you can hear is a bird sing, and that's all I need now. I don't want to lead the fast-paced life I used to revel in any more. I like to dip into it every now and then, flex my photography muscle in another country, a big noisy city, and it's still fun – but I always long to come back here. I've been all over the world but here just feels like home.'

We both continue to watch the world in silence, safe in the knowledge the other one is there, but neither of us needing to speak or touch. And I envy him the freedom he's had to search and find his place in the world. Most of us have to compromise; if things had been different I doubt I'd have stayed in Salford. Mike and I talked for a while about moving to the seaside like people do, but we both knew it wasn't about what *we* wanted. There were our parents and our kids to consider, and we were rooted like trees to those terraced houses on old northern streets. I still am, and as long as the girls are there I will have to stay. But now, I wonder. Everyone has their own lives, no one's depending on me – could I dare to think about drifting away now, just for me, just for a little while?

Later we walk back to his house and sit again in his lovely kitchen eating pasta in his home-made sauce of tomato and ripped basil leaves and I feel like I'm in Italy. He tells me about his time spent living on the Amalfi coast working in a restaurant, lying under a hot sun in a rocky cove by day, serving tables and flirting with Italian women by night. His stories always make me want to visit the places he's been to. I want to taste the fresh shellfish straight from the sea, drink crisp white wine under that hot sun and walk hand in hand with him along a sunset beach.

I will miss him, after this weekend – our time together

here at his home has changed us, propelled us forward into a deeper understanding. And being in his home has given me a taste of his life. I'm getting to know this older Peter so much more. He isn't dashing around, he isn't arrogant – and dare I say, he may just have had his fill of chasing butterflies and glitter.

'Stay another night, there's no need for you to go back,' he's saying as we drink a last cup of coffee. I have that Sunday night feeling, as the carefree weekend edges back into real life, and it makes my heart dip a little to see my overnight bag packed in the hall, a reminder that this isn't my home.

I've just had the best twenty-four hours. He has been great company, the sun has shone, the food he made was delicious, and for the first time in a long time I've felt so relaxed. I have only had to think about me while here with him. Peter indulges me, he listens, he gives me his full attention and here there's time to sit and think and walk and talk and all the time in the world to choose ice cream.

'Oh, Peter, thank you, and you know I'd love to stay longer. Being here with you this weekend I've just felt . . . I don't know, free. You've looked after me so well and you have such a lovely home, you've no idea how much I'd like to open another bottle of red and sit on your lawn watching the sun go down.'

'Then let's do it.'

I laugh. 'I can't, Peter. I must go home. Anna has to go to the solicitor's first thing about her divorce and Isobel's in the shop, so I want to take the girls to school.'

'Oh, that's a shame, not that you're taking the girls to school ... I mean that you can't stay. Having grand-children seems as bad as having children.'

'Or as good,' I say, sending a gentle warning shot. I have already made it clear I *want* to do this, no one is forcing me to do anything, it's my pleasure. 'We want them to know that Mum and Dad are divorcing but everything's still okay. I think Katie the youngest has been affected most.'

'Oh dear.' He doesn't quite know what to say, he's not used to dealing with the fallout from divorce – all he and Camille had to worry about was their joint custody of the artworks. I know that sounds mean, and the reason I'm back with him is the way he embraces freedom and doesn't have any baggage. But unfortunately I do and he doesn't seem to be able to get his head round this.

'Well, if I can't convince you to stay I'd better give you your surprise now,' he says. 'Close your eyes, I'll be back in a minute.'

He goes out of the room and returns almost immedi-ately with a large, flat box wrapped with a large blue ribbon.

247

'You opened your eyes,' he says in mock chastisement.

'I hate surprises. Well, I love them, I just can't bear not to know what it is,' I say, unfurling the thick, silk ribbon and opening the box. Inside is some paper, a brochure with some pictures printed off the internet, and when I put my glasses on and read what it says I see he's made a booking for a two-night stay at a luxury French hotel just outside Oxford. I look up at him, a smile about to break on my face. 'This is somewhere I have always wanted to go,' I say. 'I've looked at it so many times on the internet, drooling over the amazing food. Oh and look, the bedrooms are just pure luxury . . . Peter, a weekend here must cost a fortune.'

'I just wanted us to do something special. I racked my brains wondering what we could do and then I remembered you'd mentioned the gardens there. And I thought where better to take a florist than a hotel with special gardens.'

'Oh, but it's so much more, there's a herb garden . . . and a Japanese garden with a bridge,' I say, clapping my hands together like a little girl. I am so excited. 'What a lovely surprise.' I am delighted. I've never been anywhere like this before and it will be a once in a lifetime experience – I can't wait.

'We can wander through the gardens before dinner, and the food is Michelin-starred, local produce, a modern

French menu with a twist.' He's joined me on the sofa and is now reading from the brochure, our heads together, pointing at things like two excited schoolchildren.

'We're both such foodies I knew you'd love it but it's difficult to get a room unless you book months – even years – in advance, but I know someone who knows someone and after much negotiation, persuasion and blood, sweat and tears we have a room for next weekend.' He is sitting next to me, still holding the brochure, flicking through the pages, smiling. My heart goes from sky high to zero in a millisecond.

'Next weekend?' I say, my mouth now dry.

'Yes, I know it's short notice, but apparently it was a cancellation – you can't get a room for another two years.' He's still smiling, then his face slowly drops. 'It's okay, isn't it? You can do next weekend?'

'Oh, Peter, I'm so, so sorry, I can't. Next Saturday is Isobel's birthday.'

'Oh no. Well, we'll only be away two nights, perhaps you could celebrate with her on the Thursday, or the following week?' I feel frustrated at the way he assumes everyone and everything can just be moved to accommodate his plans.

'No, I'm sorry, I can't move her birthday,' I say, trying not to show my irritation. 'She's forty, we've booked a restaurant for a family meal . . . it's a special birthday.'

'Well, I'm sure she'll understand if you explain ...'

'No, I don't think you understand,' I say, tersely. 'It's my daughter's fortieth birthday, all the family are going, we're having a meal, gifts, a birthday cake and it's very, very special.'

'But I've booked the meal, ordered champagne, we're having afternoon tea on the lawn, just the two of us ...'

I feel terrible – what started out as a wonderful idea, a thoughtful and beautiful gift, has now become a bone of contention between us and I honestly wish he'd never bothered. Within seconds my new, calm, Zen-like self has popped and I'm desperately scrabbling around in my brain trying to work out the Rubik's cube of dates, the tangle of relationships that I keep in my head like a huge emotional human calendar. I'm a mother, it's what we do, but I want a rest from all this, I'm fed up with trying to be everything to everyone. Peter and I have only just begun this new relationship and already I'm beginning to feel the weight of being pulled in all directions.

'You're supposed to be the one who calms me, the one who lifts me out of all the daughter drama and worries about the family and soothes me, but this time you're adding to it. Of course it was a lovely, lovely gesture, Peter, but perhaps you should have checked with me first?'

He sighs. 'I should, yes – but I had to take it straight

away or someone else would have. People book years in advance—'

'Yes, yes, you said,' I snap, now frazzled, but slowly the tangles are unfurling in my head and I know whatever happens, and however upset he is, I will be at Isobel's birthday on Saturday. The girls are grown-ups, but in the same way we are all managing Emma and Katie's feelings about their parents' divorce, I'm also minding my daughters' emotions around their deceased and very much missed father. What kind of message does it send for me to be absent from a big family birthday celebration? The girls would be so hurt, and besides, I want to be there. Yes, I also want to be sitting on a perfectly manicured lawn drinking champagne with the man I love, but in real life we don't always get what we want.

'I'm sorry, Peter, I can't do it,' I say. 'The last thing anyone needs is me announcing for the first time ever that I won't be there for Isobel's birthday because I'm off for the weekend with my lover.' I have to be strong on this, I know he doesn't get family ties, but he must know that in some things my family have to come first. I feel a sparkle of anger flicker through me – why does real life always have to come in on us and ruin everything? After our lovely weekend the splash of reality has woken us both up and all the calm I've been nurturing inside has fizzed to nothing. Is it too much to ask that my partner and my family can be in my life at the same time without conflict?

'Oh, I understand,' he says. 'A fortieth is special and it is your daughter – I was being selfish. But I wonder should I send Isobel a card? A gift?'

I thank him but say there's no need. They don't yet know about the nature of our relationship and it may seem odd to suddenly receive a gift from my friend. I point out to him that he hasn't really met them officially, only briefly at the Parker wedding, when he and I first met again.

'Yes, I've been thinking about that. Perhaps I should meet them. What do you think? I feel like I know them, and their partners and the grandchildren. If you and I are going to be spending time together it's only right we're introduced. And from what you tell me about Anna, she'll want to vet me like your mother did.'

We laugh about the day he visited and my mother 'received him' in the front room like the queen mother, serving stale Battenberg and strong tea and telling me to 'sit nicely'.

Then he says, 'I'm just thinking about Isobel's birthday . . . is it a dinner just for close family?'

My heart sinks and I try not to grimace. Oh God, I can't bring him along to Isobel's birthday just like that. Yes, it's close family, but in saying that to him I feel like

I'm telling him he isn't close to me – that he means nothing. Knowing he has no children of his own and aware this is sometimes a point of sadness for him I try to say no kindly and with tact so as not to hurt him.

'I think you meeting the girls is a great idea, but I need to talk to them first and then I think we need to prepare the best possible time and place,' I say. It seems my family are a constant reminder of him being alone and I sometimes feel like we're all on the inside and he's on the outside looking in. But I'm really not sure I'm ready for the full announcement, or the commitment.

'But they know about me. They know we were together once, that I make you happy. Why don't you want to introduce me?'

'It's not that,' I say. 'I just feel that to introduce and hope to integrate someone into a family takes time and it needs to be managed.'

'Managed? I just want to be part of your life. This is about saying hi, chatting, getting to know them ... it isn't a corporate takeover.'

'You don't understand, I'm talking about people's feelings here. We are treading on delicate ground and yes, I do need to "manage" feelings. I have been looking after other people long enough to know when some empathy is required, I don't just walk away from things when they don't work, Peter, I stick around and sort them out.'

'That was a low blow,' he says, looking at me.

'I'm sorry, but so was your comment about me being "corporate" about this. We can't approach this like some bohemian get-together where everyone just accepts each other and gets on with their lives. I'm sure that's how you see it ... but it doesn't work like that.'

'Don't tell me how I see it, Rosie – I know how I see it. I want us to be together, but I know how much your family means to you, how they are a big part of your life – and I just want to fit in. But how can I if you push me away?'

'I'm not pushing you away. I just know my girls and I know you – and bringing you in on a special occasion when everyone's thinking about Dad is not the time. You're going to have to trust me that I'll know when the time is right and everyone – including you – is ready. I want this as much as you do.'

I hear echoes from the past as I think of Peter's family, their coldness towards me, and the way my own family may or may not accept Peter now. Different times, but the same issues, the same obstacles coming back through the years to haunt us. 'I understand,' he says, and we say our goodbyes with kisses. But in the car on the way home I know he can't ever comprehend the daily pull that a parent feels for their child. From the moment they are conceived they sit in our hearts and our heads. When they are born we drop everything the minute we hear their cry – for the rest of their lives. And how can Peter ever understand how it feels to want to do one thing, but know you need to do something else? I will start living again, I will chase the light and grab what's left of life before it's too late, but I'll still be there for my family. It can't *just* be about me, it never has been – but for Peter it always was.

Chapter Nineteen

I left Peter's that day feeling crushed. This was going to be my time and I find myself once more torn between the wishes and needs of others. I want us to be together, I don't yet know the shape of this, I don't know if we'll ever marry, or even if we'll live together, but I do want us to be accepted as a couple by my family. I feel ready for this and just hope we can find a way for it to happen, without causing too much upset or conflict for any of us, but first I need to find the courage to tell them.

I keep telling myself that cancelling the hotel break with Peter was the right thing to do, but I still feel guilty about it. I can only be in one place at one time but then I think about Peter's face smiling at the brochure, the special afternoon tea on the lawn. My heart aches, knowing he'd listened when I'd talked about the gardens and he'd taken the time and the trouble to present me with something that I would love.

We keep in touch and I celebrate Isobel's fortieth with everyone and I have a wonderful time knowing it's the right thing, and I wouldn't be anywhere else. And I know it's stupid, but I miss Peter terribly and long for him to be part of these celebrations too. I realise that I could have asked him to join us but I know it was my own cowardice stopping me. I always say that Anna is resistant to change but I'm beginning to realise where she gets it from – me. I've never been tested before, because life with Mike didn't involve huge amounts of upheaval. But now I'm faced with the possibility of change and I want something new it's dawning on me I'm going to have to be the one to instigate it. And I'm daunted by this.

Anyway Isobel's fortieth was a big success and everyone was happy, so feeling like I need to make it up to him I call Peter and invite him over for lunch the following Friday. I feel guilty about rejecting his idea to come to Isobel's and stalling his suggestion about meeting my family. I don't intend to introduce him to anyone at this stage, but inviting him into my home, the place I shared with my husband, is a first step to bringing him gently into my life.

It's another watershed as he hasn't been to my home before and I want to reveal the more recent Rosie to him. I don't invite him to stay over; this is the family home and it would be inappropriate as I still haven't mentioned to the girls that Peter and I are now in a relationship. I don't need their permission, but I would like their blessing.

Before he arrives I set the small table in the kitchen and prepare a Stilton and walnut salad. I tried to call the shop first thing to tell the girls Peter is coming over for lunch so they won't keep calling or wondering where I am if I don't pick up straight away. But they must be busy as the answer machine is on. I don't leave a message.

Peter arrives in a flurry of flowers and wine and kisses and I apologise again for our weekend and he says it's fine and we sit in the kitchen as I make coffee.

'I was upset about the weekend,' he suddenly says. 'And when you left I did wonder about us now, how we fit together.' He looks up at me from where he is sitting and I feel a little stab in my heart. Not again?

'Well, I'm afraid that's the way it is, Peter, my family is part of me, it's who I am now and as Margaret used to say, "If you don't like it you can lump it".'

He reaches for my hand. 'You're quite feisty these days, aren't you? Some might even say defensive.'

'I suppose I am, but to say you don't know how we fit together makes me feel cross. You know where I stand and—'

'Stop. You didn't wait until I'd finished. What I was thinking was that when we started to meet for lunches and chat about old times and talked through the baby and everything – I just thought it would be plain sailing after that. I asked you if we could be more permanent and you agreed and I just sat back and enjoyed the view. But spending last weekend with you brought it home to me that it will require some effort and sacrifice if I want to be involved in all aspects of your life. We're still good together but I also know we may have quite a rocky road ahead – not because of us, because of everyone else. So let's just face it head on and make a start.'

'Yes – what you say makes perfect sense. And I agree we are great together – I love you and I love this ... you and me. But are we ready for me to make a big announcement to the family, try and integrate you by inviting you to all the family gatherings, then six months down the line you decide you've found another Italian vineyard?'

He looks puzzled.

'You tend to leave,' I say, gently. 'And that's okay, but if you're already worried about the road ahead, we'd better stop now, because you haven't met Anna yet.'

'Oh God, is she as feisty as you?'

'She makes me look like a pussycat.' I take a long sip of hot black coffee, wondering how she'll take it when I tell her about Peter and me.

'Look, I know I haven't got a particularly good track record, but trust me, I'm here for the duration,' he says, reaching out to me. I get up from my seat and sit on his knee, feeling young and cherished in a way I haven't for a long time.

'I don't want you to feel trapped,' I say, putting my arms around him. 'I just want us both to be sure this time before we go making any promises and announcing our love to the nation.'

'Then start the announcements, Rosie. I told you, I learned my lesson long ago and if something's worth fighting for – this time I'm going to stick around and fight!'

I smile, and take another sip, not completely comfortable with the analogy given that he wouldn't last five minutes with Anna in a fight, but I feel his commitment.

Later we eat lunch with the French windows open, a summer breeze wafts the net curtains and the sunshine trickles in like honey and I feel so happy. Everyone's okay, my family are happy, Peter's here and all is right with the world, and even thinking about Mike doesn't make me feel as bereft as it has done. One day at a time.

'I have dessert,' I say, after I've cleared away the salad plates and put more coffee on.

'Oh good, you know I have a sweet tooth,' he says.

'Yes, and guess what, it's ice cream! I couldn't decide so I bought three tubs. Pralines and cream, cookie dough and strawberry cheesecake.'

'You are really going for it, aren't you?'

'Oh yes, I am going to try every ice cream flavour in the world before I die.'

'That's some bucket list . . . let's have them all.'

'Really? But we can't open all three tubs at once.'

'Why not? Is there a local by-law that forbids the opening of ice cream tubs in multiples of three?'

I laugh and go into the kitchen, taking all three tubs from the freezer and getting two spoons.

'That's what I'm talking about,' he says as I plonk them down on the table and we open each one and taste.

'OMG, as my granddaughters say . . . the praline one is just LMFAO, or something like that.'

'I think that means laughing my f . . . arse off,' he says.

'Mmm, I'm never quite sure what they mean when they use letters like that, but this ice cream is lots of letters all rolled into one. Why have I always stuck with mint choc chip?'

'Because no one told you how big the world of ice cream is,' he says, licking his spoon.

I watch him and think how I'd like to kiss him now, here in my own living room with ice cream on the table and curtains wafting in the breeze. He's looking back at me and I think he's having exactly the same thoughts.

Then he does kiss me and my stomach feels like strawberry cheesecake ice cream, all sweet and swirly.

'I like this one,' I say, gouging out a spoonful of cookie dough and pushing it gently, but I hope seductively, into his mouth. It's a larger portion than I'd realised and he almost chokes then he laughs and we fall together on the sofa as he tries to force a large spoonful of pralines and cream into my mouth. I'm screaming for him to stop and he's laughing and tickling me and we must have been making quite a noise until I look up and see Anna in the doorway.

'Mum?' she says, looking confused and horrified.

'Oh, hello, love. You know Peter, don't you? He's here for lunch and we're ... having dessert. It's ice cream ... We're having ice cream for dessert,' I say. I'm mortified to be discovered like this by Anna of all people, but at the same time I instinctively know I have to brazen this out – if our Anna smells blood she will be worse.

'I can see that. Hello, Peter,' she says, like she's addressing primary school children. 'I hadn't heard from you,' she goes on, distracted momentarily by the ice cream carnage, 'and as I had a delivery I thought I'd pop round.'

'I did try to call you this morning.'

'We've been busy,' she says, looking from Peter to me.

I'm embarrassed for Peter more than myself, and Anna's making us both feel stupid. I suddenly feel like I'm being judged and this makes me quite angry and somehow emboldened – how dare she make me feel like this in my own home? We were just having fun and after the freedom of being at Peter's home last weekend I suddenly feel rather claustrophobic.

'Mum, I wish you'd let me know when you have someone over, I wouldn't have barged in.'

'And I wish you wouldn't barge in when I have someone over,' I say back. I don't want to embarrass her in front of Peter, but it seems she's quite happy to do the same to us.

'I'll be off then,' she says. 'Bye, Peter.'

He says goodbye and she leaves, but I follow her into the hallway.

'Anna, please don't speak to me like that in front of Peter ... in front of anyone. I am not a child and I resent you treating me like one.'

'Then stop behaving like one,' she snaps, banging the front door a little too hard as she goes.

'I'm so sorry about that,' I say to Peter, returning to the room and clearing up the tubs of ice cream. 'So much for my corporate approach, perhaps having you just turn up at a family do might have been better after all.'

'Yes, I'm not sure you and me squealing and feeding each other ice cream was quite the introduction either of us would have chosen. I'm sorry, are you upset?'

I shake my head; I want to cry, but for the first time it isn't because I've upset Anna, it's because she's upset me – and I'm angry with her.

'I think I'm beginning to understand your life,' he says with a smile, and kisses my forehead. 'I know I'm not always very wise when it comes to families, but I think I may have been right when I mentioned the rocky road ahead.'

Peter leaves about eight p.m., and I wave him off on the doorstep. We've had a lovely day but I'm still stinging from my awkward encounter with Anna earlier. And the following morning over a cup of tea and a million carnations I broach the subject with both my daughters: 'Girls, I've been meaning to tell you that Peter and I are now seeing each other,' I say. I wait for their reaction, I'm sure it will be fine, but after yesterday I'm feeling slightly awkward.

'Well, that would explain why you looked like something from an ice cream commercial when I walked in yesterday,' Anna snapped.

Isobel laughs and looks at us both, puzzled.

'Anna, I love you . . . both of you, to bits, and having

Peter in my life doesn't change a thing, but he may, at some point in the future, visit again and yesterday was embarrassing.'

'You can say that again,' Anna starts. 'I went to see if Mum was okay,' she explains to Isobel, 'and there they are, all over each other on the sofa, ice cream everywhere. Mum's laughing her head off ... I didn't know where to put myself.'

'Oh, I'm sorry if I was having fun in my own home,' I say.

'Well, I didn't know where to look ...'

'Perhaps you shouldn't have looked – perhaps you should have knocked.'

'It's my home, I was born there, I shouldn't have to knock.'

'Yes, it's your home but I would like it if you respected me enough to announce your arrival, or at least cough as you're coming down the hall. You can't just walk in when I've got company. I don't wander into your house – I don't want to find you and James in a compromising position.'

'And you wouldn't. At least not in the living room in broad daylight.'

'Well, perhaps you should, a little afternoon delight never did anyone any harm,' I say. 'Who knows what you might walk in on, storming into people's living rooms.'

'I don't believe you, Mum, you shouldn't be thinking stuff like that.'

'What, at my age?'

'At any age.'

'Oh, Anna, let go, live a little. I am.'

'Mmm, so I noticed.'

'All I'm asking is that you understand it's my space and respect my privacy. I love having you over and want you to feel at home, but sometimes you might need to knock. It's not just about me having Peter there, I might want to dance naked or do topless yoga and it's your choice, but if you don't knock I won't be responsible for the torrid scenes you may witness on the yoga mat – or the sofa.'

'Mother!' she says.

Isobel is giggling and looking at me. 'Mum, you minx,' she says, and we both laugh which causes Anna to soften.

'Like something from a bloody Häagen-Dazs ad it was, you all over him, pralines and cream splattered all over his chest,' she says, half-joking.

Isobel looks at me, shocked.

'No, it wasn't like that at all,' I laugh. 'But next time, please knock or you might see something far racier than the Häagen-Dazs commercial.'

Anna rolls her eyes. I know her and it's not about Peter, she doesn't know him well enough to dislike him, she's just uncomfortable with the idea of me having a

266

boyfriend full stop. Anna wants everything to stay as it is and I understand, I can relate to how she feels. I used to feel like that too when I was younger and less sure of myself, but these days I feel different; every day I'm feeling stronger, more capable and I'm looking forward to whatever inevitable and exciting changes are ahead ... with a little trepidation, but not enough to stop me.

We go back to our carnations and small talk. I managed to make my point without causing too much of a drama, and I'm just relieved we were able to make light of something that had the potential to become incendiary in Anna's hands. As always, Isobel helped ease the situation and defused Anna's upset with acceptance and humour, and despite her bossiness Anna usually sees the funny side. I know it isn't going to be easy bringing Peter into the family, but as long as us girls can laugh about things I reckon we can make it down that rocky road.

Chapter Twenty

I sit at Isobel's outdoor table tonight watching my family enjoy a late-summer barbecue and suddenly, in the middle of it all, I'm missing Mike. It just hits you sometimes, when you least expect it, but I suppose it's because we're all here and when we're together as a family I feel his absence more keenly. I think about how it would be if he were here now, he'd have been pouring wine, making sure the men were okay for beer, and advising Richard on their loft conversion while helping with the burgers. He'd be teasing his grandchildren, making sure Anna's partner James felt welcome, and pointing out the different stars as the summer evening drew in.

My phone beeps and I see a text from Peter. He says he loves me and can't wait to see me on Friday. I feel warm and fuzzy inside about Peter, and a yearning for Mike because I know I'll never see him again. It seems strange to be missing two men at the same time – but then I've loved two men in my life, and being with Peter again has made me realise that there really isn't one person for each of us. Our partners can be made up of many things, they can appeal to our values, sexuality, sense of humour, and they can also be right and wrong at different times in our lives. I'm still a bit wobbly and unsure, and I'm trying not to see my love for Peter as a betrayal of Mike. It will take time to be completely free from my own guilt, my own imagined infidelity, but I'm slowly working through it.

Richard arrives at the table with a plate of steaming chicken and steak and everyone drools. Isobel has filled the table with vibrant salads and huge platters of buttery garlic bread as the wine of many colours flows freely.

As I look around at my family I feel so lucky. I'm in the middle, the heart of everything, the noise, the trouble, the fun – it's not always a bed of roses but it's my life and I love being here. But Peter is on the outside, and if we're to love a second time and make the most of what we have left, I know I need to bring him in.

'It's a bunfight,' Anna yells as everyone piles in with their plates, filling their glasses, chatting. A couple of the children's friends are here and an old school friend of Isobel's, but other than that it's just us. We're quite insular, I think, we all get on well and apart from younger disagreements over 'borrowed' clothes and make-up, my girls have a good relationship.

Lily sits at my feet, salivating, as I take a bite of the juicy chicken that Richard has marinated in lime and chilli; it tingles in my mouth, a salty, savoury heat I love. I wonder at the exotic dishes Peter has enjoyed on his travels as I watch them all laughing, arguing, eating and just being – and I wonder what it would be like if Peter were here. I like the idea, but my stomach dips when I consider the bigger picture. The girls still miss their dad and the grandchildren miss their granddad and however I try to convince myself that bringing Peter into this arena won't change anything, it will. The girls are old enough to understand that I would never try to replace Mike, and why would I? But by bringing in my new partner I am changing the dynamic of this lovely family group. They will see me differently. I'm still Mum and Nana, but I'm also someone's girlfriend, and I have a relationship that is completely independent of all of them. It doesn't matter how much I love him or how wonderful I believe him to be, someone here might not like him, and someone might not approve of me having a lover.

Then again, there's mine and Peter's relationship to consider and there will have to come a point when he is included. And perhaps if he were to meet all my family he might begin to understand the strength of my commitment to them and why sometimes I'm torn, and spread myself too thinly. I watch James as he talks football and loft conversions with Richard – he's been welcomed with open arms, and he fits in so well. He gently touches Anna's arm as she stands up from the table to get more wine and the look of love between them makes me think of Mike . . . then Peter once more.

'You okay, Mum? You look sad.' Isobel is onto it immediately, like a dog with a bone.

'No. I'm fine, I'm having a lovely time.'

'Good.' She squeezes my arm. 'Glad you're happy . . . Have you got everything – garlic bread?'

'Yes, and it's all delicious – but if you were the perfect hostess you would be able to move the sun a little to the left,' I laugh.

'Is the sun in your eyes?' Anna steps in, mothering me again.

'No, darling, if it was I would move, I'm not infirm yet.'

'That reminds me, I've been thinking that in the next few years you should probably think about having the house adapted,' she says, taking a bite of garlic bread.

'Why?'

'Well, you're going to be there on your own now until . . . well, you're very old. A friend of James's is a builder, and I was thinking of asking him to come and have a look at the house, see if he can lower the steps, get a rail for the bath, have some kind of alarm put in, you know?'

'No, I don't know. What kind of alarm?' I'm horrified.

'If you fall you can press a button and the police or someone will come ... or better still it could be linked to my phone and I could come out to you.'

'Anna, I'm sixty-four, not ninety-four, and as long as I'm still doing Pilates and walking Lily round the park every day I see no need for any kind of emergency alarm. And as for a rail ... why not get a stairlift and one of those beds that sit you up and push you out and I'll buy a dozen pairs of crimplene slacks and some slippers to wear while I sit by the fire and pray for the end.'

'I knew she'd be like this,' Anna says to Isobel who looks awkward.

'We just worry about you, Mum,' Isobel says apologetically. 'And we're not talking soon, just sometime in the future.' I can see she's obviously being railroaded by Anna into suggesting this.

'Mum. Think about it. What if you fell over in the bath?' Anna asks.

'What if *you* fell over in the bath?'

She rolls her eyes, which annoys me, and I'm already deeply irritated by this conversation. 'You're on your own, Mum.'

272

'You're on your own too when the girls are with Paul and James is working away.'

'That's different.'

'Why? Anyone can fall over in a bath. I'm pretty fatalistic about these things, Anna. If I can't take a bath without risking my life I don't see the point in living. Look, I wasn't going to say anything until it was definite, but I'm thinking of moving house anyway, so there's no point in making any adaptations for my oncoming physical demise.' It's something I've vaguely considered and now, with the girls planning to turn my current home into a geriatric retreat, I'm seeing it in a more definite light.

'You want to move house?' Anna is shocked.

'Yes. I fancy a small town house. Something fresh and modern, smaller – I want to fill a wall with my canvases, pale grey walls, sexy lighting . . . you know?'

'Sexy lighting? You've been talking to Corrine again, haven't you?' She's shaking her head vigorously.

'No, the idea to move is all mine – I do have them sometimes. And I prefer *my* thoughts of sexy lighting and grey walls to yours about a bloody alarm and a stairlift.'

'I never even mentioned a stairlift, I just worry about your safety.'

'And I worry about yours, always have, always will – but I am not going to get a friend of a friend to put an emergency alarm and a stairlift in your house in case you fall out of the bath.'

'Oh, that's not what I said and you know it. I hope that Peter hasn't been filling your head with ideas about selling up and moving in with him. It's funny how you've met him and now you've got all these mad ideas about moving.'

'It's got nothing to do with Peter, and I don't feel like I want to move in with him, but, Anna, if I did I would.' I look at her and she looks at me, surprised that I am being so forthright, but I need her to know I'm making my own decisions and choosing what *I* want, not her or Isobel or Peter, or anyone else for that matter.

'If you did move in with him we would hardly see you – what about Emma and Katie? They'd miss you. And if it was his house we couldn't just come and stay, the girls would be heartbroken.'

'They'd be fine and it isn't an issue because I'm not planning to move in with him. If I were we'd have to deal with it – and when you get to know Peter you'll know that he would welcome you into his home with pleasure. I hope you'll be the same with him.'

'Anyway, it's nonsense, you can't leave our family home and sell it to a . . . stranger,' she says, continuing in the same vein, not answering me or acknowledging my comment about Peter. 'It's where Isobel and I were born, it's where we come when we need to get away ... it's home,' she's saying, her eyes now damp.

I remember the little girl of seven on the sofa, clutching her teddy, covered in a duvet, her temperature through the roof and school out of the question. 'I'm glad I'm home, Mum, I always feel better at home.'

'Oh, darling, home is about the people not the place. I can get a lovely new house and you can come over anytime and get away from it all there. I'll still have wine in the fridge and my shoulder will still be here for you to cry on.'

Anna's not convinced and I know it will take some persuading for her to come round to the idea, but I'm feeling stronger these days – it's my life and I have to reclaim it.

Later, as I get ready for bed, I think about the evening at Isobel's – the sun going down, the wine, the lovely cheesecake Anna made. I long to share summer evenings like today with Peter and despite all my conflicting thoughts and concerns I want him to meet my family. I want him to see how proud they make me and to enjoy the conviviality of us all around the table as the wine and the sun goes down. I also want to put a stop to the girls' talk about having the house adapted and let everyone know that Peter is now my lover. And I don't need a stairlift, or an alarm, I need racy underwear and cellulite cream. I *want* to do this,

I have to seize the moment with Peter, bring him in to the fold and start the next phase of my life.

It's early September but it's still warm and the forecast says it's going to stay warm well into next weekend. I could leave it until next summer, but I want to do it now and who knows how many summers we have left?

The following morning I call Isobel – she's the easy one and I need her there if I'm going to do this. 'I've been thinking – I'd like to do an afternoon here next weekend. I wonder if you and Richard are free on Saturday?'

Isobel sighs. 'Sorry, Mum, we're seeing friends Saturday.'

I'm immediately disappointed.

'On Sunday then? It's just … I wanted to invite Peter along and I thought it might be nice if …'

'Okay. Sunday sounds good, but can I get back to you? I'm busy at the moment … will check with Richard.' She giggles and I hear Richard talking to her in the background. Oh God, I'm playing up to the stereotype of the mother-in-law calling to talk about Sunday tea in a week's time while they are trying to have some time together uninterrupted. I put down the phone feeling a bit lonely and rather stupid.

'I don't want to be that mother,' I say to Peter on the telephone that evening. 'The girls think I'm turning into some lonely old soul who sits around all day bored. I'm only doing four days a week at the shop and I don't want to do more because I want to spend time with you, but they think it's because I can't cope.'

He laughs. 'Darling, they clearly don't know you. You're as strong as an ox and can cope with anything.'

'An ox? Really, dude?' I say in my granddaughter's voice, and he laughs loudly.

'I am not likening you physically to an ox, I'm saying you're as energetic as you were at seventeen.'

I smile. It's nice to have another life, a secret life to share with someone special.

'Everyone sees me as the poor widow, but I think it's time I showed them that I'm not done yet.'

'You mean you're finally going to tell your children that I wasn't just there for ice cream last week?'

'Perhaps not quite in those terms.'

'I think it's a great idea — as you know I am an optimist and I just know life has a way of working out.'

'Yes, and the stars will align,' I say, thinking of Mike and smiling. Recently I've been able to remember the holidays and the Christmases and all the lovely times we had together without collapsing in a heap of tears and tissues.

'So I thought it might be nice to do an afternoon/evening at mine next weekend. A barbecue in the garden?'

'That sounds good. I'm a dab hand at barbecues, I have a secret recipe for the best marinade . . .'

My heart sinks. I really don't think the best way to introduce Peter to the girls is for them to arrive at mine and find him in the family garden slapping steak on 'Dad's' barbecue. I also wonder how the girls will feel seeing him in Dad's home, with Mum? I make a mental note to do a seating plan. Yes, I know I can only 'manage' this so much, but if Peter sits in Mike's chair at the head of the garden table I might as well cancel my summer buffet now.

'I don't want you working on the barbecue,' I say lightly, trying to come up with a reason that won't hurt or embarrass him. 'You will be a guest, I want to show you off – I want my girls to say "He's gorgeous, Mum", and I want my granddaughters to be surprised and in awe. I want Emma to say WFT . . . or something like that.'

'I think you mean WTF.'

'Whatever. Kids have their own secret language these days – wish we'd had that. Mind you, Margaret would have banned it,' I laugh.

'Or worse, deciphered it,' he says. 'The Bletchley code-breakers would have had nothing on her.'

'I can only imagine what she'd think if she heard my granddaughter and her friends when they think no one's listening. It's like Sodom and Gomorrah,' I say, repeating my mother's well-worn phrase.

'Gone but not forgotten, Margaret will be forever with us,' he says. And I smile to think how much of her is still with me and it comforts me to know that when I go my girls will have something of me. We all just pass it down and it starts all over again with a new life, a new love, and I think about me and Peter and I think about me and Mike. I still have my moments, I always will, but Peter has helped me through this, in the same way Mike helped me when Peter left. And I stand in my kitchen holding the phone talking to the man I love, looking out at the clear, starry night and marvel at our amazing universe and how life has a way of working out.

'So, I'm not ready to sit by that fire with my knitting just yet – and I need my family to understand this. We still have the same hopes and dreams and passions as anyone else ... we're just a bit more wrinkly.'

'Good for you, Mrs Carter, now you're talking. It's got nothing to do with age, I keep telling you it's never too late.'

'Thank you for reminding me, for coming into my life and showing me who I used to be, and who I can be again.'

'It's right in front of you, I just needed to point it out. Now – shall I book a nearby hotel for your summer soirée?'

'No, you bloody well won't – you can stay the night, and I don't care who knows it.'

When Isobel confirmed she and Richard were free to come over Sunday I mentioned it to Anna while we were at work.

'I hope you can come,' I say. 'It was lovely at Isobel's and it made me appreciate how much we all mean to each other. I know it isn't the same without Dad, but I've been ... well, I feel optimistic about the future, and I've invited Peter. I'd like you all to meet him properly.'

'Oh, that'll be nice, assuming he won't be covered in ice cream this time.'

'He wasn't last time, you do exaggerate, Anna.'

She's joking, but Anna's 'jokes' can sometimes be a bit near the bone and she's a little edgy today so I don't push it.

'No, really – I'm glad you're getting your life back and you want to have us all over, and your friend Peter seems quite nice,' she sighs, clearly with other things on her mind. 'It's just that I'm a bit mithered at the moment. Our Emma won't talk to me ... I worry she's getting too close to that lad from the estate. I told you about him before, bit sullen, not exactly polite and I think he's having an influence on her. This morning I only asked her if she was okay and she was so rude to me. Ended up with her storming out and me sobbing . . . I nearly didn't come in today.'

'You shouldn't have done, darling. We're not busy – perhaps you could take some time off and pick Emma up from school, take her shopping?'

'I don't think her behaviour this morning deserves a reward, Mother.'

'No, absolutely, but I mean, just spend some time talking to her.'

'I do . . . I spoke to her last night. I told her she's too young to have a boyfriend and she shouldn't be messing about with lads from the estate anyway.'

'Oh, Anna. You can't stop her seeing a boy because he doesn't fit into *your* idea of what her boyfriend should be,' I said, remembering Peter's mother's attitude to me.

'I feel like a crap mother but I'm exhausted; I've been juggling everyone's emotions lately. There's Emma's boyfriend and I'm worried how Katie's dealing with the divorce, she keeps it all bottled up and I feel her pain.'

I nod, I understand all too well.

'I'm also trying to keep things on an even keel with James. I really like him and I want this relationship to work but I have to give him more and at the same time I need to be with the girls. I just need a break, some time for myself, you know?'

'Yes, I do know.' I smile at the irony: we're all struggling with the same things in different ways at various times in our lives. And I'm beginning to think there's no such thing as this 'me time' everyone talks about.

'Tell you what,' I say, 'why don't we close early, you go home, have a bath, relax and I'll pick the girls up and take them both out for pizza?'

'Katie's at a sleepover . . . but if you collect Emma that would be nice. Thanks, Mum. I think sometimes I get on her nerves and she might tell you stuff she won't tell me. I'm just worried she might end up having sex with this lad through peer pressure or, worse still, boyfriend pressure. You know how good her GCSE grades were, she needs to really buckle down for her A levels and I'm worried – things like this can wreck your life at this age.'

I nod. Yes, it can wreck your life. Love at sixteen can be the best thing that ever happens to you, it can be the most intense, vivid and beautiful relationship of your life. And it can also wring you dry, it can change the course of your life and shape the person you are – but that's what being alive is all about.

'Don't be too hard on Emma,' I say. 'I think you'll find these things have a way of working out.'

'I just don't want her throwing it all away thinking she's in love when she isn't. You know what lads are like … Well, you don't, but trust me the internet has turned them all into bloody sex pests.'

I smile, knowing only too well what lads are like at that age, and I doubt they are any different today than they were when I was Emma's age.

'Leave it with me. I'll collect Emma. I'll bribe her with doughballs at Pizza Express … and she'll sing like a canary.'

'Thanks, Mum … Sorry if I've been a bit short today. I had a row with James last night.'

'Oh, I thought you two seemed so – together.'

'That's what I thought, but I suggested he think about selling his flat in the next few months and move in …'

'Well, that's good, isn't it? If it feels right, there's no point in waiting, you might as well start to share a life together,' I say, having toyed with similar thoughts myself recently.

'Yeah, that's what I thought. The girls will be away at university and living their own lives soon and I don't want to be left on my own. But he says he's not sure he's ready. Honestly, Mum, I don't know where I am. I can't wait until I'm your age and I don't have to worry about men.'

I smiled. If only she knew.

Chapter Twenty-One

'Now you come to mention it, Nan, I do have a problem, a serious one,' Emma confesses over pizza and doughballs later that day. We're sitting in Pizza Express, just the two of us, and I fear she's about to reveal something cataclysmic.

'Really, darling? You know you can tell me anything,' I say, taking a deep breath and telling myself we can cope with this, whatever it is. Nana is here.

'Yeah ... I have a serious addiction ... to doughballs.' She pushes a whole one in her mouth and looks at me defiantly under crusty black eyeliner. I raise an eyebrow and start on my pizza. Emma reminds me of me when I was her age: artistic, sarcastic, skinny and blonde – she probably has my weakness for slightly dangerous boys too. She'll get hurt, but when she does I'll be there for her, and I'll be able to tell her truthfully that it's not the end of the world and everything will be wonderful with the next one.

'You know you don't have to sleep with someone just because you're going out with them,' I say, taking a bite of pizza and trying to sound nonchalant.

'No, really? I thought it was a strict rule that you have to have sex on a first date?' She looks up from her vegetarian topping. 'I know what's going on here. Mum told you to talk to me, didn't she?'

'No. I just thought it would be nice to spend time with my eldest granddaughter and check out what's goin' down, girrl,' I say in my 'cool rapper' voice to make her laugh.

She is horrified. 'Never say that again, Nan,' she monotones. 'Nothing is "goin' down", as you put it.'

'Well, tell me about this new boyfriend, is he gorgeous?'

She rolls her eyes, but I know she wants to talk about him. 'Okay, so I'm seeing this guy, he's cool, I'm cool, but Mum isn't.'

'Sounds like my love life at your age,' I laugh.

'I love him and he loves me.' She stops eating, and has that faraway look in her eyes – I recognise it, it's the one I used to have when I thought about Peter – perhaps I still do?

'So, tell me about him.'

'Okay, so his name's Greg, he is totally gorgeous, and he's in a band. They're really sick . . .'

'What?' I can barely keep up.

'Oh, that means cool . . . and as soon as they get a record deal he's going on a world tour. He says if we're together he'll take me with him and we're going to live in Japan.'

'That sounds wonderful, Emma, it's lovely to have a dream.'

'It's not a dream, it's going to happen.'

'I hope it does, I really do but . . . you're sixteen. Take my advice, don't put all your eggs in one basket, some lads at this age can be a little – fickle.'

'He's not "some lad", we're in love. I'm sixteen – it doesn't mean I can't love someone. Why does everyone think that I'm too young to love?'

'I don't. I wouldn't dream of saying that. I understand, I know how it feels to get that rush through your bones, that wonderful high when you know you're going to see him. And the way he says your name . . . it's like poetry, isn't it? No one else says "Emma" like he does.'

She looks surprised, but she nods.

What can I say? I know her like I know myself, she's me all over again. I want to high-five her and tell her to go for it, just love him now because tomorrow he might go but you'll have your memories to keep you warm, and it won't kill you but will ultimately make you stronger. I also want to tell her that it feels just the same when you're sixty-four ... except then you're considered too *old* to be in love. I want her to fly, to know real love and not be scared to embrace risk, yet at the same time I don't want her to have to suffer the pain I went through at her age and I want to protect her from this, just like Margaret wanted to protect me. And I'm reminded again of Margaret's saying: 'What goes around comes around.'

'Look. I don't want to go against your mum,' I say to Emma, 'but I believe you when you say you're in love. And I understand exactly how you feel because I fell in love for the first time at your age and it's never quite the same again. I never loved anyone so intensely, so deeply. Of course I adored your granddad – I always will, but that first time—'

'What, you mean your first love wasn't Granddad?'

I shook my head.

'But I thought in the olden days you married the first guy you went out with. You didn't actually ... sleep with this guy, did you?'

I nodded, thinking, *Yes, Emma, I was as wild and abandoned and in love as you are now ... and just like you I couldn't wait to feel his body on mine. I longed for his kisses, to hear him murmuring my name and while you dream of Japan, we dreamed of Paris*. But I just smile enigmatically while spearing rocket leaves with my fork.

'Whoa, Nan, you goer,' she giggles, taking a large drink of Diet Coke. It's always rather special when one of my granddaughters approves – and I feel a shimmer of ridiculous pride.

'I wasn't exactly a goer, but hey, I had it going on, as they say.' This causes another eye roll, but I keep talking. 'But back then, in "the olden days", as you put it, we didn't have the freedom you have today with the pill; condoms were only available at the chemist or the gents' toilets, which wasn't much use to a seventeen-year-old girl. So we took chances, which I don't recommend – it was silly.'

'Well, I'm not silly. I went on the pill six months ago, I was literally the last of my girlfriends to do it.'

'Oh. I didn't realise ... does your mum know?'

She shook her head. 'No, but I'm almost seventeen, she doesn't have to know.'

'Yes, she does ... and what's more she cares and *wants* to know.'

'She *wants* to know so she can give me the bloody lecture.'

'Oh, Emma, stop swearing ... and that's not fair.'

'Well, she isn't fair. I mean it's not like sex is illegal or anything.'

'That's not the point ...'

'Nan. Please don't tell Mum, she will literally kill me.'

'She will not "literally" kill you,' I say, vaguely amused at the way young people have appropriated the word and the images it often conjures up. 'Your mum wants only to protect you. Trust me, her mission isn't to spoil your fun or ruin your life, she just loves you,' I hear myself say, while thinking about my own mother who also tried to protect her challenging child from the big bad world. There was little mention of sex, but a vague metaphoric reference to 'men's needs', and 'men's seeds' being 'sown'. I came away from that conversation none the wiser but with some concern regarding the time my father spent sowing seeds on his allotment.

Consequently I was confused between the free, fun-loving creative, experimental art student I wanted to be and the virginal, cardigan-wearing, Bible-loving daughter Margaret wanted me to be. Until Peter, I'd never imagined anything so shameful as having sex with someone before I was married, and I marvel at how much easier and more honest Emma's life must be today.

We continue to eat our pizzas and finally I say, 'Two things, Emma.'

She looks up.

'Number one, you're on the pill, but are you also using condoms?'

'OMG, Nan, please.'

'You may be protected from pregnancy with the pill, but what about sexually transmitted—'

'Of course we use condoms, we learned about STIs and HIV when we were in Year Nine, for God's sake.'

'Okay ... well, that's ... good.'

'You said two things.'

'Yes – the second one is, I won't tell your mother you're having sex as long as you promise me it's what you want, and not just what he wants.'

'Of course! God, I'm not some kind of loser who lets dudes walk all over me.'

'I'm glad to hear it,' I say and think about offering one of those high fives, then think better of it, because knowing Emma she'd leave me hanging – as they say.

'So what happened to him, Nan?'

'My first love, you mean?'

'Yes ... What was his name?'

'His name's Peter.' I put down my fork and look at her. 'And he's still alive and well and just as good-looking as he was when he was eighteen.'

She lifts her head from her food, open-mouthed with surprise. 'Whoa, you've seen him?'

'Yes, he's coming over on Sunday and you're going to meet him.'

She covers her open mouth with her hand, unable to take the shock – and the smile – from her face. This is a good, positive response, which gives me the confidence I need to continue with my plans and gently bring Peter into the fold.

'We all have secrets, Emma, even those of us from the olden days.' I smile, and ask for the dessert menu.

When we've both ordered chocolate cake and coffee I say, 'If you're meeting my boyfriend it seems only fair that I meet yours. Why don't you suggest to your mum that you bring Greg along too – it would be fine with me.'

'Oh, that would be great. I know if Mum would bother to get to know him she'd love him. He's literally the best.'

'I'm sure he is.' I smile. 'So let's do this together. Tell Mum that Nan has invited Greg, but ONLY if she's okay with that ... and I will check.'

'High five, girl,' she says, reaching out her hand. I lift mine and we slap and I feel 'cool' and 'sick'.

'I can't believe you've got a boyfriend – I am literally LMFAO.' She's shaking her head in wonder. I think I know what she is 'literally' doing, because Peter translated for me, although I don't fully remember it, but whatever it is she's trying to express I just hope her mother has the same positive vibe on Sunday when she meets Peter again.

Chapter Twenty-Two

I have been planning this gathering for days now and decided against a barbecue because it brought up a whole raft of issues in my head. Mike always did the barbecues, and it would be too symbolic for all of us to have Peter standing behind the burgers in Mike's comedy apron. So I've made what Mary Berry would call a 'summer buffet', and combining my TV chefs I've made the old family faithful, Delia's goat's cheese and thyme tart. I've also conjured up some fresh coleslaw and dressed a piece of bright coral salmon which looks so pretty with the pastel green cucumber slices. I twist pale pink Parma ham onto a small slate and dot with slippery olives while imagining how the afternoon will go. It's going to be lovely, but I am nervous. I know everyone will be scrutinising

Peter – I just hope they're subtle and don't make him feel like he's being watched. I stand back and survey the dishes and platters laid out in the kitchen before covering them all in foil.

I'm almost ready, and I want it all to be perfect. I want Peter to think I'm a brilliant hostess, the perfect mother and the 'coolest' nana. I want him to love my food, love my family and feel at home here – and I want them to love him back and think he's perfect for me and though he'll never replace Mike they'll accept him nonetheless. And having hosted many dinner parties and summer buffets over the years, I know the food and wine will help all this come to fruition – and I just hope the chilled Sauvignon and Delia's tart come through for me.

I keep thinking about how the girls will respond to Peter, to the news that he's perhaps more than just a friend now. I know Anna walked in on us feeding each other ice cream, but she thinks being in your sixties means being infirm, so probably assumes I was feeding him because he couldn't feed himself. I smile to myself at this and make a mental note to tell him – it'll make him laugh. Since Mike went, I've missed the chance to laugh with someone my own age about how the younger world sees us. They think we're different, but we're all the same and one day they'll find out what we already know – that it doesn't matter how old you are because inside you're always twenty-five.

I am now ready, everything is prepared and I'm just waiting, which is lethal because it gives me the opportunity to overthink everything and find ridiculous things to worry about. And top of my list (after 'what happens if everyone hates him?') is will my food be too safe and boring for Peter, who talks passionately about Indian street food, Vietnamese sandwiches and French gastronomy? As my mother would often say, 'You can tell a lot from a person's table.' I often hear this in my head when I visit someone for a meal and I worry my own table may expose me in some way. Today I may be spilling my secrets over the salmon and not even realise this, and I smile just thinking of her serving stale Battenberg to Peter and enquiring about his mother and father – who she never met.

I'm cross with myself even now for the way I felt so ashamed when Peter came to meet my parents. I'd never really seen my family through anyone else's eyes and I was mortified at my mother's dodgy grammar and Dad's inability to hold a conversation about anything other than football. Mum was so impressionable and when I told her Peter's dad was a doctor she almost touched her forelock. She'd polished the front room, brought out the best china and tried so hard it still makes me want to cry because it didn't matter about the china and the polish, there were no books, no art on the walls, nothing interesting or intellectual discussed – and the cake was stale. I look around now at the bookcases and the art on the walls and realise it's okay, I landed on safe ground in the end and it was because of my mother, not in spite of her, that I survived.

I try to relax. The food will be fine, and my salmon won't give me away, but what about the different dynamics? If nothing else they will be interesting today: Anna can be a bit bossy, Isobel's a pleaser, which can make Richard appear domineering. Then there's the whole James situation and the current stalemate about him refusing to take the relationship further and move in with Anna.

And, oh God, what about Peter and me as a couple in all this? The girls met him at the wedding, when I first laid eyes on him, but they have yet to meet him in the capacity of my boyfriend. Once they realise we're together they will watch us like hawks, particularly Anna who will be ready to mark him out of ten for everything. I think about Anna's face if he puts his arm around me or dares to kiss me on the cheek and my heart sinks. I have had this vision of everyone sitting around the table outdoors and this has propelled me on, like sunshine and food will make it all okay. Then the sunny, olive oil commercial running in my mind turns into a dark reality show about a dysfunctional family. My thoughts of Peter joining us may be quite different to Anna's or Isobel's, who may view this whole scenario as Peter sitting on Dad's furniture, eating from the plates he chose, and enjoying time with Dad's family. I am overthinking again, and it's beginning to feel less like a summer buffet and more like a social experiment. I need to stop, be more philosophical, more laid-back like Peter – if they don't like him, they don't like him, there's nothing more I can do.

Whatever happens today, we have plenty of time and I can introduce him gradually. If things go well I can invite him over again for another family gathering, but the secret is the softly-softly approach. I hope that slowly but surely he'll be included in family events, that Anna will invite him to hers for lunch and Isobel will include him in barbecue invites. It would be nice to be part of a couple for those things again. It's important to me because his mother never accepted me, and my own mother never accepted him either. Now I want my family to change all that and I really believe their acceptance will help us both to move forward.

The first to arrive are Anna and James, and I'm glad to see they are holding hands and she's smiling. I ask James if he'd open the wine and Anna follows me into the kitchen with her home-made banoffee pie.

'Is all okay . . . with you two?' I ask in a low voice,

taking the plastic container holding the pie and expressing my deep lust for the contents.

'Yes,' she says excitedly. 'He's thought about it and he's moving in.'

'Oh, that's wonderful.'

She nods her head eagerly. 'We talked about it on Friday night and he said I'd sprung it on him and demanded an answer, and he wanted me to realise I wasn't in charge of everything. He said I was being bossy.'

'That's not at all like you,' I say, poker-faced, and she laughs at my sarcasm.

'Yeah, okay, I wasn't exactly subtle but he just wanted to make his point and . . . '

'And you're back to being in charge?' I smile.

'Something like that,' she giggles. 'But with James it feels right.'

'Good. I'm delighted for you, darling,' I say, putting the pie into the fridge. James is good for Anna, he may let her win the battles, but he's smart enough to win the war.

'Well, the girls are getting older, I'm no spring chicken and I'm damned if I'm going to wait around for him to decide what he wants,' she's saying. 'I told him, life's short, you have to grab it while you can.'

'So true,' I say to her, carrying a jug of iced water through the French windows and into the garden.

'Oh, Mum, it looks lovely out here,' she says, following me through and stepping out onto the patio.

'Well, I wanted it to be special ... ' And just at that moment Katie appears, followed by Emma and her boyfriend Greg. In my concern about Peter I'd almost forgotten about *that* invite and shoot a look at Anna who, to my relief, nods reluctant approval with her eyes.

'Greg, I'm so glad you could come,' I say as the teenager smiles shyly, nodding his head in my direction and Anna's.

Isobel walks in soon after, followed by Richard who's brought with him a box of wine and the plans for his loft conversion which I'm sure we will all 'enjoy' in far too much detail later. But I'm not worried about Richard boring everyone because Peter will charm them all with his stories and his adventures taking photos all over the world. And I will just bask in Sainsbury's tea lights, Delia's tart and everyone's approval.

With half an hour until Peter's arrival I decide it's time to prepare the girls, so I ask Isobel and Anna if they'd like to help me with 'the salads', a euphemism we've often used in our household. 'Help me with the salads,' has, over the years, meant anything from 'Come away from the table with that attitude,' to 'Don't eat all the strawberries, leave some for our guests' when they were younger.

I think to pre-warn the girls and ask them (Anna) to

play nicely, will avoid any problems when Peter arrives and in the unlikely event of either of them having any issues (Anna) we can deal with them before Peter turns up. I don't want some embarrassing little niggle (Anna's) in the air curdling Delia's goat's cheese and ruining all my meticulous planning and culinary expertise.

I smile as the three of us congregate in the kitchen and suddenly feel incredibly nervous about their reaction.

'I just want to say ... thank you for coming today—'

'God, Mum, it's not the queen's garden party. You don't have to give a speech.' Anna laughs and sips on her wine. I'm obviously coming over as a little formal, addressing them both from my place by the oven.

'Have you been drinking?' asks Isobel.

'No,' I say, horrified, though I'm so nervous I did consider a glass before anyone came.

'Mum, you don't have to thank us for coming, we were delighted, saves us cooking.'

'Well, it's just that—'

'Oh my God, are you ill?' Anna the worrier pipes up, reaching out to me, her brow immediately concertinaing into lines.

'No, no, it's nothing like that. Don't frown, you'll be sorry when you're my age. No, it's just ... I feel a bit foolish, I'm making a big thing out of this and it's nothing really.'

'You've got to tell us now,' Isobel sighs, putting down her glass and crunching on a breadstick.

'Okay – well, as you both know I want to introduce you to Peter, because . . . we're growing very fond of each other.'

'He's officially your boyfriend?' Isobel is smiling.

'So I was right – this is where all this "moving house" talk has come from,' Anna starts. 'I knew it. He wants you to sell the family home, doesn't he?'

'No . . . of course not. I haven't even mentioned it to Peter – it's got nothing to do with him.'

'What about Dad?'

'Well, Dad's, not . . . it doesn't mean I didn't . . . don't love Dad. It doesn't change . . . anything.'

'No, but it's a bit soon to start flogging the house and running off with other men, isn't it? How long have you known this guy?' Anna says.

'Forty-eight years . . . and I'm not running off with anyone.'

Isobel tries to intervene. She's clearly uncomfortable about Anna's reaction, but I'm afraid my eldest tends to put her mouth into gear very quickly, always has.

'Mum, he dumped you. Who's to say he won't do the same thing again?' Anna is desperately looking for the negative outcome. I can see now that my mention of selling the house has played on her mind. She can't believe

300

that I'd want to move, she sees it as a personal betrayal, a desertion, and finds it less painful to blame Peter. I'm battling Margaret all over again.

'Anna, he was eighteen, we wanted different things then . . . and he's changed. I've changed.'

'Mum, no offence,' Anna starts, which usually means there will be deep offence arriving any second now, 'but you only went out with him for a few months, you didn't really know him. And now you're selling the house, introducing him to the family—'

'We were together for almost a year and I knew him . . . know him . . . well, and as for selling the house, you must try to see it from my perspective. I know it's our family home, but both you and Isobel have your own homes and your own families. If and when I sell the house it will be my decision.'

I look to Isobel, who smiles sympathetically. 'Anna, it's okay for Mum to have a boyfriend,' she starts. 'And it's not like he's a stranger . . . ' I smile a 'thank you' smile to her.

'I am not objecting to Mum having a boyfriend – I just didn't realise it was serious. And I wish she'd told us about it so we could check him out first.'

'Anna, he's an old friend . . . and since when did we "check out" anyone's new boyfriend in this family? I never checked out any of yours, though perhaps I should, it could have saved us all some heartache.' I am being mean, because we all know I'm talking about her ex-husband who led her a merry dance for years with various dalliances. I hate myself for saying that and want to hug her, but she's not in the mood for hugs from her mother.

She is about to respond when we are saved by Emma who's obviously heard raised voices and is now marching into the kitchen, darting an accusing look at her mother.

'What's the matter? You look nice, Nan.' She puts her arm on mine protectively and looks into my face for signs of distress which makes me feel a little tearful.

'Thanks, darling, I'm just telling your mum and auntie Isobel that I have a boyfriend.'

Anna is now standing with her arms folded. Tightly.

'I just hope he doesn't move in, convince you to sell the house then when you're homeless he'll run off with the money. It happens, Mum.'

Emma is used to battling Anna and is straight in there: 'Leave her alone, it's Nan's life. Who cares if he's homeless? God, can't a girl have a man around here without everyone getting in her grill?'

If I wasn't so upset I might have laughed and even Anna can't help smiling at this. 'No, darling, he's not homeless. Peter has a home, a lovely home in Oxford ... and it's all fine.'

'I know he's got his own place, it's just that I'm only thinking of you, Mum,' Anna says, softening.

'Look, I can see where you're coming from, but I'm not stupid. Your dad and I worked hard for all this and I won't be giving it away to anyone – but for the record Peter has plenty of money of his own.'

'Okay, he's probably not after your money – but Dad was here ... what about the memories?' Anna says. This is the crux of it for Anna, she doesn't have anything against Peter but she doesn't want him to replace Mike.

'I told you, it's not about the place, it's the people. We all carry our memories inside us, they stay in here,' I say, touching my chest. 'No one can take those away. And don't think because I'm with Peter I can just move out of the house and forget Dad and everything that happened here – it doesn't work like that.'

'I don't know, it just feels like one thing after another. Dad goes, you meet someone else and then you want to sell the house. I didn't even know you were seeing Peter like that,' she sighs.

'That's why I'm doing this today. I wanted to tell you together and for you to meet Peter again. It's only in the last couple of weeks that things have moved on with us and I haven't been sure of what I want and if we fit together after all this time. But I didn't want to make a big announcement before because if things hadn't worked out I may never have felt the need to tell you.'

'Never told us?' Anna says.

'Yes. I'm sure there are things in the past, even now, that you haven't told me about your lives. You didn't tell me the first time you stayed over at James's flat ... and Isobel didn't tell me about Richard until she'd been going out with him for a month, and that's okay,' I say. 'The only difference is that I respect your privacy, and don't expect you to tell me every little thing about your personal lives. Please afford me the same respect.'

'We do ... we just ... I just worry about you and wish you'd tell us what you're doing. I thought you went to the odd garden centre with him, had the occasional lunch, fed him ice cream. I don't know – I just didn't realise it was serious. I just want to know what's going on.'

'And I will tell you what you need to know, but I won't be calling you from Peter's bedroom to say, "Hi, Anna, we just got the bulbs from the garden centre and now we're about to go to bed together",' I say, my voice raised in exasperation, causing everyone to look a little surprised.

'Nan ... ' Emma murmurs.

'No one is asking you to do anything like that, Mum.' Isobel is talking gently, trying to keep everything calm.

'Look, all I'm saying is treat me as I would treat you.

304

We've always had a good relationship, even as teenagers I gave you respect in the way my own mother never did me. And you need to know it's *my* life, girls – including my sex life.'

Anna rolls her eyes, Emma gasps.

'Yes. For your information I have slept with him, but it's not like I've been on Timber or anything.'

'Tinder, it's called Tinder, Mum, and I should bloody hope not,' Anna snaps.

'WTF? Whoa … I'm outta here,' Emma says and turns on her heels.

At this we all look at each other and I can't help it, my face breaks into a smile and Isobel catches my eye, while trying not to laugh.

'Come on, Anna, lighten up,' I say. 'You're worrying about stuff that won't happen for a long time. There are other things I want to do before moving house and I promise I won't sell up or do anything big without discussing it with you first.'

'Good.'

'And I said "discussing" with you, not "agreeing" with you or being told what to do by you – those things are quite different.'

'Yeah, Anna seems to have a few problems with that concept,' Isobel laughs. Anna shoots her a look, but I can see it's not too serious.

'Family hug?' I say, and the girls both walk towards me, their arms outstretched. I hug them to me, stroking their heads as I did when they were little girls. 'I know in an ideal world things would be as they were, your dad would be here and we'd all be the same family we were eighteen months ago. But we're not, the rug was pulled from under us, and now our life has to move on. I'll always love your dad, I'll always miss him, but he would want me to be happy and Peter makes me happy. I feel seventeen years old when I'm with him.'

'Really?' Anna pulls away slightly. 'If that's the case I think I'd like to go out with him too.'

'It's early days, girls, but I so want you to like him. I did all this so you could meet in happy circumstances. The sun's shining and you're all here and I want you all to welcome him and see how happy he makes me.'

They both smile and I have to hope Peter can convince them of just how wonderful he really is. Or am I blind because I've always been in love with him?

'Come on, let's go back to the others, he'll be here in a few minutes.' I take a breath and they follow me out through the French windows to the garden and the laughter as Greg tells a very funny joke.

'You see,' I whisper to Anna, 'you must never judge a book or a relationship by its cover. And you're never too young or too old to fall in love.'

She gives me a sidelong look, lips pursed à la Margeret. 'Yes, Mother, but I will continue to keep my eye on you. I don't know who's the teenage rebel here, our Emma or you!'

Peter arrives early. I hear the knock and immediately feel calmer. He's here – it will be okay now. My daughters will love him and the rest of the family will be charmed by him and we'll all live happily ever after, I think to myself, over and over like a mantra as I walk down the hall.

Carrying a bottle of wine and a huge bunch of blue hydrangeas, he steps into the hall and I thank him. 'You always remember ...' I say, looking deep into the flowers.

He's asking if he's parked the car in the right spot, but I don't care – wordlessly I take him by the hand and pull him into the living room. I want him all to myself for a moment, a blissful moment of calm before I unleash him on my family. I kiss him firmly on the lips, put my arms around his waist, feeling the cool linen of his shirt, and I feel guilty even thinking this, but I wish it was just him and me – and everyone else would go home.

Eventually I release him from my grip and guide him through into the garden, still carrying the hydrangeas deliberately, like the spoils of war. I'm holding them high and letting them know what he brought: *Look, he loves me – and if you don't believe it just look at the magnificent flowers he's given me.*

I stand by Peter in the garden and introduce him to each member of the family. Everyone nods and smiles in turn and says 'Hello, Peter,' even Anna, albeit awkwardly. I want him to chat to the girls, not Anna on her own. I need Isobel there so when Anna does her 'bad cop' Isobel can do her 'good cop'. But within minutes Richard is giving him the equivalent of a PowerPoint presentation on loft conversions. For a few moments my heart sinks, until I see him smile and hear him ask about Velux windows – nice one, Peter, he's done his homework, and after a while I can see he doesn't need an intervention and is coping beautifully.

'You'd think he was actually interested in lofts,' Anna whispers to me as she passes by to get more wine.

It's not easy being the hostess, cooking and serving food, and making sure everyone's happy, but it's just like being a mother and I've been doing that a while. As I bring out the first tranche of food I am disappointed to see my seating plan has already gone to pot. James sat in the wrong seat from the beginning and cocked everything up which means Anna's next to Peter (where she can intimidate him easily) and Emma's using the seating mess as an excuse to sit on Greg's knee and wind her mother up. And trust me, Anna does NOT need winding up any more than she already is. Poor Peter is now pinned next to Richard and what he doesn't know about loft conversions by the end of today won't be worth knowing. While sitting all over Greg, Emma is now telling me she's not sure about her options for sixth form and under normal circumstances I would be all ears but I'm discreetly checking around the table for clues to how Peter is being received. The only silver lining to this whole seating-plan fiasco is that Greg is the one sitting in Mike's armchair, but it's little consolation as Emma is now virtually on top of him. I see Anna listening to Peter and seeing her smile for a moment, am delighted. But my wave of joy and relief is immediately replaced with a twist in the stomach as I see she's smiling at Isobel while Peter talks. I clench inwardly – is it a bitchy sister look or is it a 'Yep, he's a keeper'? I'm in agony not knowing.

The goat's cheese tart sits in the middle of the table, warm, golden and melting, surrounded by a rainbow of salads. I watch us all and imagine how we'd look through a filmmaker's lens. The sixty-something widow presiding over a summer table, her family eating and chatting in the sunshine, while her new old love catches her eye. I love this scene and will play it over and over in my head for years to come.

The food is eaten, the tart is perfect and Anna's ban-offee is sublime. Peter even asks her for the recipe and

I'm delighted to hear her offer to email it to him, which suggests that she sees Peter in the longer term. I've never been happier. Something as apparently insignificant as this email exchange lifts me up and like a balloon I bob around the table refreshing the drinks. Everyone is sitting round chatting and I think how lovely this is and with time we could all be one big happy family. And then, without warning, it all starts to go horribly wrong.

Chapter Twenty-Three

It's about six p.m. when James gets up from the table and starts to clear the glasses away.

'Leave that,' I say. 'Relax, enjoy the last rays of warmth – it's supposed to rain tomorrow.'

'No problem, Rosie, I thought I'd make a start on the washing up,' he says kindly. 'I could at least fill the dish-washer . . . there are already loads of glasses . . . don't want to leave everything to you.'

'That's so thoughtful but you're a guest tonight. You all do so much for me, I'll wash up later – and anyway, tonight I have help.' I look at Peter, who raises his glass and winks at me. I smile back, and I nearly suggest Katie lights the new tea lights – she's always loved that job – but at twelve I think she probably feels slightly patronised.

I ask Peter instead and throw the box of matches to him. He catches easily and everyone claps. 'I was always a good fielder back in the day,' he laughs, and James sits down again and they chat a little about cricket. More bonding with my sons-in-law, I am delirious, but just as I'm about to relax into this bath of joy, I hear Anna's voice at the end of the table.

'James, you shouldn't be talking cricket now, I thought you were supposed to be helping clear the table?' she says, feigning, but not pulling off a light-hearted look, and suddenly the air is loaded. James looks at her and I can't see the love in his eyes I saw earlier, and I'm reminded of how my daughter can upset people with her brusque manner and demanding ways.

But being Anna, she can't leave it and goes in for the kill. 'Come on, James, I'll help – Peter won't want to hang around now he's eaten, he's got a long drive back to Oxford tonight, haven't you?' she says with apparent concern, but betraying her real feelings by banging plates and wearing my mother's tight lips.

My stomach is churning. 'No ...' I protest, but she leaps up and is now collecting glasses aggressively while simmering. In the awkward silence I can feel the atmosphere thick with tension – how can my own daughter be so thoughtless, so selfish as to ruin this for everyone, especially for me?

'Peter is staying *here* with me tonight,' I say, loudly and clearly. I'm now standing at the head of the table but in an effort to be assertive with Anna realise I have just announced to the assembled throng that Peter and I will be sleeping together. Tonight.

Everyone looks round at me, except Anna who continues to clank glasses and crockery and sweeps through the French windows into the house without acknowledging what I've just said. Aware I'm probably making things worse by walking out on my now ruined party, I go through into the kitchen. I'm hurt and embarrassed but determined to try and nip this in the bud.

When I walk into the kitchen, Anna's at the sink, scrubbing hard at the platter that held the antipasti, and I walk over to her.

'What the hell was all that about?' I say.

'I'm sorry, Mum, I just think it's all a bit much. You may have known him years ago but I can only go off now, and all I can see is a man you've been seeing for six months making himself very much at home in my dad's house.'

'It's also my house and your dad has nothing to do with this, so don't use his memory to manipulate me, Anna.'

She whips round and looks at me, open-mouthed.

'I know exactly what you're doing, and I understand

313

you – I've known you a long time and I know why you're upset. You don't want things to change, you lost your dad and now you think you're losing me, but you're not. And you have to get your head round this. Peter isn't a threat, and even if he could, he doesn't want to take me away from the family or come between us – the irony is that he would like to be part of it.' I put my arm around her and I see a tear fall down her cheek. 'I know you miss your dad and you feel a bit shaky about life at the moment, love, and I want you to know I'm here for you, always. But I'm not giving in on this one, so help me make it easier for all of us and accept that Peter is my future ... in the same way that I accept James is yours.'

She leans her head on my shoulder and I squeeze her like she is seven years old.

'I just didn't expect him to be staying the night ...'

'He offered to stay in a hotel, but I didn't see any reason. He's a good man, Anna. Don't make me feel bad about someone who makes me feel good.'

She finishes what she's doing, tells me she has an early start in the morning and all I see is my angry, confused little girl walk out of the kitchen. She lost Paul, then her dad, and now she thinks she's losing me, but until she's calm there's no talking to her.

I'm filling the dishwasher when Peter walks into the kitchen with an empty wine bottle.

'Anna's upset,' I say, grateful to have a confidant, a supporter just for me at last.

'Thought I sensed something, that's why I brought this bottle.'

'What, for ammunition?'

'No,' he laughs, 'so I could see if you were okay. Are you?'

'No. Oh yes, sort of . . . but it's more to do with Anna and what's been going on in her life. Really.'

'Is she okay? Should I perhaps try to talk to her?'

'No, that's kind of you, but I don't think that would help. When she's like this she needs a little time to adjust – and she will.'

James, the girls and Greg appear in the kitchen; Anna is now standing in the hall with the car keys. Emma hugs me and whispers in my ear that she's sorry it's all been a bit 'tragic', but informs me I will, at some point in the future, LOL about it. I doubt that very much but I smile and hug her back.

'Thanks, darling.'

'Nan, I'm glad your boyfriend came today. I know it was a bit tough on you, but Mum was so distracted she didn't even notice when I swore and Greg had a fag.' She giggles conspiratorially in my ear. 'I'm LMFAO.'

I hug her again, feeling a wave of comfort, a poultice on the open wound left by my daughter.

315

'It will all be fine, and so will you and Greg . . . even if you swear and he smokes, LOL,' I say under my breath, before walking them all to the door, including a rather sheepish James. 'Sorry, Rosie,' he says. 'It's not you. She just takes everything on . . .'

'I know. She always has. Look after her tonight.' I half smile, touching his arm gratefully as he nods. James has only been with Anna for a matter of months, he's only ever talked to me about superficial stuff like the weather so for him to acknowledge the issue feels big for me. I think he's giving me a signal that it's okay and Anna's just overreacting.

I stand on the step to wave them all off and Anna opens the car door and waves absently at me. I blow her a kiss and she smiles. She'll come round.

I return to the garden where Isobel and Richard are saying goodbye to Peter, and Isobel hugs me.

'Don't worry, Mum, it will all be fine,' she says in my voice. Isobel and I have always tended to gravitate towards each other, and while Anna sometimes rails against the world we think things through before saying them. People like us seem quiet and cautious next to the Annas of the world who wear their hearts on their sleeves. But I've learned that we are stronger, more flexible and accepting of what life throws at us. Isobel and I have both been through the same experience of losing

316

children – though I've never shared it with the girls Isobel knows I understand. She told me once that the four pear trees in their garden had been planted for the babies she'd lost, because she needed to see them and remember. And we cried together.

I close the front door on them all and stand in the kitchen awhile, leaning on the worktop. All the planning, the expectation, even the bloody tea lights and the goat's cheese tart. I never realised until tonight – I hate goat's cheese. It's like the mint choc chip ice cream, I was doing this for everyone else. Peter's right, it's time to start doing things for me. And if one of my kids doesn't approve then that's up to her, but I will never be able to put my arms around them all at once, be in two places at the same time, or please everyone.

Apart from a short spell of rebellion somewhere around 1968, I spent a lifetime trying to please my mother and now I'm trying to please my daughter. I look through the window and see Peter at the table alone. I feel like I lost him in the emotional chaos of the evening and seeing him lifts me. I desperately wanted this evening to work, for Peter to be welcomed into the family, but it wasn't that easy after all. I wonder what this means for our future. I will have to keep trying and hope one day we can all be together, but I worry that day may be far away and neither of us are getting any younger.

He's pulling a sprig of hydrangea from the jug, gazing at it, lost in thought, and I feel a surge of life flowing back into me. I run from the kitchen into the dusk, surprising him with a flurry of kisses.

His face lights up when he sees me and he puts one arm around my waist, places the hydrangea in my hair and we look into each other's eyes.

'I feel bad. Have I caused problems for you?'

'No, Anna will be fine, we've been here before over much bigger and much smaller stuff than this. Anna has always liked everything in its place, people in their pigeonholes and the doors locked from strangers. But it's time for me to open the doors and windows, and let life back in.'

'I'm sure in the end it will be okay. Life has a way of working out,' he murmurs into my hair. 'Look how you came back to me. That was fate … magic.' Then he pulls away slightly to look at me. Our eyes meet, and they are the same eyes that gazed on each other almost fifty years ago.

I slip off my sandals as we lean on each other, slowly merging into a lazy dance. There's a warm breeze blowing through the trees, the sky is unusually clear and the stars are out in their millions. I think of Mike and wonder if it's a sign that he's looking down tonight and giving us his blessing.

We sway for ages as early evening turns to black and in the thick silence I look up again into the night sky. Here in the garden there is just eternity and us, and like a string of fairy lights in the dark, we are all tangled together by the stars, the years and the beating of our hearts.

Chapter Twenty-Four

The night of the party Peter stays over and we sleep in the spare room. I couldn't sleep in the bed I'd shared with Mike, that was ours. But I know that Mike would understand, he'd known all about my love for Peter, he'd known more about my feelings probably than Peter himself. Mike would know this is right and that Peter is good for me, and makes me happy – and ultimately that's all Mike ever wanted.

Thinking about him as I lie in Peter's arms in the family home, I feel the familiar wave of guilt for the hurt Mike must have secretly endured over the years, for the knowledge that he wasn't the love of my life. Mike was the man I married and he was the best husband and father I could have chosen. While Peter was off round the world treading on grapes and girls' hearts, Mike was the one who stayed up with the children when they couldn't sleep, held my hand and mopped my brow during two tough pregnancies. He was the only other person in the world who looked at our girls the same way I did, with unconditional, parental love – and no one can ever take that away.

The following morning it seems strange to wake up in bed at home with Peter and as soon as I open my eyes I remember the night before. He is a wonderful, gentle lover, and only Peter could take me to bed and make me almost forget.

'I must phone Anna . . . ' I say out loud, causing Peter to stir.

'Yes, phone Anna. You'll be miserable until you do.' He reaches out and touches my hand.

I try Anna at the shop, but there's no answer, not even the answerphone. I know she's probably trying to avoid speaking to me, so I just keep calling again and again until she picks up.

'Anna, are you okay?' I say, relief flooding over me.

'I'm fine. But extremely busy, which is why the phone was left to ring – in fact we could do with you here.'

Monday mornings are always quiet in the shop, so I know she's just being mean – and it is no excuse to leave the answer machine off.

'I will be in tomorrow and the rest of the week, and if this is just a ruse to make me feel guilty about being with Peter, I'm not having it,' I say.

'I'm sorry, I will get used to the idea. I just need time.'

'I know, and I understand all you've been through and know what your concerns are. But I think it might be time for you to look at this through my eyes and see how happy he makes me. I love him, but I'm not being stupid or naive, and you have to trust me that I know what I'm doing and I'm doing it for all the right reasons. He came back at a time in my life when I never expected to feel like this again, so try and support me and enjoy this journey with me because it will be so much better with you there.' I tell her I love her and put the phone down.

In the past I've given in to Anna too much. Often it was little things like where we buy our sandwiches from at work, or which lamp would look best in my living room, but when Mike died the little things became bigger. I wanted to keep his ashes until I knew where to scatter them, but Anna said we should scatter them at the crematorium, so we did. Now I might like the option to move house and Anna's saying I can't leave the family home. Having done everything for my kids all my life, I feel it's finally about what I want. It's my life and I have to love it and when I'm rattling around in the family home Anna will be happily in hers. And it's the same with Peter – he's such a wonderful part of my life so why should I give him up because Anna doesn't feel comfortable that I have a boyfriend? I wasn't comfortable about her having a boyfriend at fourteen, but I didn't try to stop her.

As I reach the bedroom door I hear his voice and I'm about to ask what he's saying, because I think he is talking to me, but I realise he's on the phone.

'Yes . . . okay, if you want me I'll be there, no worries. No, I'm really happy you called. I just wish you'd told me sooner . . . Actually, I'm with someone.'

I stay outside the room on the landing, slowly walk over to the window and open the curtains. The morning sun floods my face and my organs feel like they are being moved around my body. His voice sounds gentle, intimate, like it does when he speaks to me – my whole foundations are shaken.

'Okay, okay, I can be there tomorrow. Oh, sooner? Really? I suppose . . . if you insist.'

He puts down his phone and I walk in, pretending I haven't heard, and make like I'm preoccupied fluffing pillows. I climb back into bed and he looks at me.

'Camille,' he sighs.

'Oh . . . you were on the phone? I didn't realise. Is she okay?'

'Mmmm, I'm not sure. She's desperate.'

'To see you? I thought she was happily married? She can't just walk back into your life and—'

'No, no, when I said desperate, I didn't mean like that, you haven't met Camille, have you. She really is done with me.' He reaches his arms out. 'You are so sweet. No one's walking back into my life and I'm not walking out.'

'I'm sorry, but I just sometimes feel like this is all too good to be true.' I lie on the bed in his arms and he strokes my forehead.

'She rang because she's doing a piece for a French magazine about concrete architecture and she wants me to go over and do the photos. I haven't done a magazine shoot for a while, but she knows I can't resist a challenge. She wants something a little more avant-garde, you know?'

I had never considered concrete to be avant-garde, but I nod.

'Thing is, she's booked a flight already, she says the magazine will pay all expenses. I'm torn, Rosie. I want to stay here with you but I'd love the chance to do a big shoot like this. Have I still got it in me?'

'Of course you have, you're the one always telling me to take chances and let go, it's later than you think and life's too short.'

'Oh, do I really speak in clichés?' he asks.

324

'I'm afraid so. Get your bag packed.'

'Would you mind? I feel bad just going off and leaving you, but I think I may be having a renaissance, both in my personal and professional life.'

'Of course you *must* take up this chance – who knows how many chances like this you'll have.'

'I love you. I'll be back by the weekend. You could come to my place. I'll spoil you to make up for my sudden departure.' He's getting dressed, already eyeing up that concrete in his head. 'Camille says there's a lot of interest in my type of photography at the moment – it's fashionable again and this job could bring me to a newer, younger audience,' he says excitedly, pulling on his shoes. 'She says we could show in a gallery again ... wouldn't that be amazing?'

'Amazing,' I sigh. 'Will you have breakfast?' I'd bought croissants from the local French patisserie – I'd planned for us to sit on the patio and pretend we were on a pavement in Paris.

'Sorry, darling, no time, the flight's this afternoon from Heathrow. I need to swing by Oxford and grab some more camera stuff on my way. Not sure which lenses I'll need to take ...' He's in another world, lost in light and apertures and bloody concrete. 'Camille says the editor loves moody black and white pictures with meaning and when she mentioned me he said "No way, he's too famous," so she said, "It's okay, I was married to him once, I'll pull some strings".' He's smiling and shaking his head and for a millisecond I feel almost jealous of Camille because she was his wife.

'Let's just hope she didn't have your best years,' I say, and he stops and reaches out to me.

'Ah no, trust me – the best is yet to come.'

And so he heads off for another country. It's another echo from our past, but this time it's different: I'm older and wiser, and though I love him, I'm not emotionally dependent on him as I once was. I'm my own person, I've had a lifetime of being loved and it's given me the confidence to be secure in myself. I love him and I'll miss him, but this time he isn't everything to me. I have a family, I have a life and I have my own future, with or without Peter Moreton.

After Peter has left, I put croissants in the oven and grind some French coffee beans. And just as I'm pouring hot water into the cafetière and the kitchen is filled with the scent of strong coffee and sweet croissants, I see a parcel on the table with my name on.

I sit down and, ripping off the pretty wrapping paper, I open it. There is a box of soft pencils and a pad of paper. I hold it to my chest and my eyes fill with tears. He gets me, he always did.

Later, after Lily and I have shared croissants on the patio and pretended we were on a pavement in Paris, I take out my new pencils and begin to draw a fat cluster of roses. I love that he bought me pencils, he's the only one who knows I can sketch – and I want him to see that the artist is still here, she's just been asleep for a while.

Chapter Twenty-Five

I'm missing Peter while he's in France, but I'm enjoying some time alone too. I'm working in the shop during the day and in the evenings I sit in the garden and draw. I love my new box of pencils and the pad of thick, white drawing paper. Holding the pencil between my fingers feels good, natural after all this time, like an old friend I've missed. I wrap up warm as the evenings can be a little chilly. But whatever the weather, my best friend Lily joins me, sleeping contentedly at my feet while I sketch. The sun is weak and low, but it dapples light through the foliage, bringing such intensity to the colours it makes me want to bring my sketches alive with colour, shades of green and all the different tints of the oncoming oranges, browns and faded yellows of a new season. I resolve to buy some paints and start painting again – I'd forgotten how comforting it is to draw and become involved in the picture. And for a little while, nothing else matters.

I've never really allowed myself time alone, just to think and look at my life objectively. Peter texts and phones me every day, often several times, and it's good to hear him. But I realise he has another big life somewhere else that doesn't include me – and it strikes me that he always has. I expected Peter to fall into line, to do just what I wanted and make me his everything – but the reason I find him so attractive, so enigmatic, is because he isn't part of my small world, he comes from a bigger place and he brings all the excitement and colour and strangeness with him. The way he could just fly off to France on Monday was at first difficult for me, then strangely liberating. It explained a lot about the dynamics of our relationship.

If Peter had stayed with me and we'd married all those years ago it wouldn't have worked, and I know that with conviction. His dreams of a shabby workshop in Paris or a life on the beaches of St-Tropez would have conflicted with everything I needed at that time. In the same way, I wasn't what he needed back then either. But after all these years, perhaps now is our time.

Being with Peter again I can still see just what it is about him that captured me all those years ago. There's all the obvious stuff like his charm and looks – but it was much more than this. Recently I've thought about my life and the people I've known, some vague and distant, others make me smile or cry or just feel something. In my experience, we meet lots of people along the way and most of us are unremarkable, we are all on the same journey heading in the same direction and we may share a lunch, a love affair, a lifetime, but when we're gone, we're gone. But every now and then someone comes along who makes an indelible mark on us, changing the way we think, the way we live, the way we love. And these special people have made such an impression that even when they leave, a sparkle of their gold dust stays with us. For me, Peter is one of those people; he changed me by making me see the world as so much bigger, by showing me anything was possible. And forty-odd years later, he still takes each day as it comes, still sees the beauty in the unlikeliest things and has a passion for life that's never dimmed. And as other people our age are looking at winding down, he's talking of photographic exhibitions and going with me to Paris. Peter hasn't allowed his age to dictate to him, the way he never let anything tie him down – and even now he won't give up on his dreams; if he did he wouldn't be Peter and I think he would die. Despite feeling sad when he went to France recently I watched him dressing, talking ten to the dozen, the light in his eyes and so many ideas in his head – and I finally got him. He still loves to embrace new challenges, discover new things, and find those flowers in the rubble of life – he's still chasing the light.

Now he's swept back into my life and brought even more gold dust with him. Like an elixir of youth his presence has reinvigorated my ideas, my plans – my future. And having been empty and sad about my little world, I'm really excited about the next chapter.

I spent my life feeling resentful of the way he treated me when we were kids, but being with him now has erased all the hurt and I can see things from an older and wiser perspective. Peter isn't a hero, he isn't a perfect, wonderful guy – and now I see his flaws. He's a thinker not a doer. He's had an easy life and he's taken what he wants and needs from the overflowing fruit bowl fate handed him when he was born. He had the looks, the charm and the artistic talent and his parents had the money for him to pursue every glittery object he saw. Back then I was too young to appreciate who he was, and though I still believe he was wrong to reject our baby, I understand him better now. This time I wanted him to go to France and enjoy the avant-garde concrete, grab at the opportunity to be published and artistically challenged and fulfilled. It's what he needs, it's what he's always needed, but what gave me the emotional security to let him go was because I feel loved and I know I can do it too. He's made me realise that I can do all the things I've ever wanted to do. My family are fine, they have their own lives and the only thing that's stopping me is me.

Chapter Twenty-Six

Things have been a little strained between Anna and me since she stormed out of my house, but I am not giving in on this. I think she feels if she makes me uncomfortable enough about Peter I'll just give him up, but she's being selfish. It's late afternoon and Isobel's at the doctor's so there's just Anna and me working at the shop and I feel sad that there's an atmosphere. At the moment everything is good in my life, I'm feeling good about Peter and I'm also adjusting to not having Mike around and I can see a clear path forming. But this stuff with Anna is a blot on the horizon. I tried to explain this to Peter. 'They say you're as happy as your saddest child,' I said. It took him a while to work this out, but I explained that they fill my

333

heart and there's room for him, but they will always be with me. I can't be happy with him unless both my girls are happy with me.

I don't want her to see this as me capitulating on any level, but I steel myself to try and talk to Anna as I need to take next weekend off. I work four days a week, usually when I'm needed, which is often weekends – so it's perfectly reasonable for me to take the odd weekend off, but I know Anna won't like it. I wander to the back of the shop where she's doing the paperwork, a small lamp on the counter to help her see.

'I told you to get some glasses, you'll ruin your eyes doing close work like that in this light,' I say. We look at each other over a mountain of tiny daisies.

'Have you heard from Isobel?' I ask.

'No, her appointment wasn't until four p.m., so she'll still be at the hospital.'

'I thought she was going to the doctor's?'

'Yes – that's what I meant.' She's short and a little stressed, this is going to be a delightful encounter.

'Anna, I know it's short notice, but I won't be in next weekend. I asked Mrs Jackson and she can cover.'

'Oh God, she's a waste of time.'

'Well, let's start considering some new staff. I've been thinking that I'd like to consider the idea of retiring. Dad and I always thought we'd be retired by now, sitting on a deck on some cruise somewhere, being waited on ... going to that place in New Zealand, you know, the one where the stars are amazing?'

She nods and smiles. 'Shame he never got to go.'

It's my biggest regret that I couldn't get Mike to the Dark Sky Reserve in New Zealand. When he was first diagnosed we toyed with the idea, I even looked into the insurance, the flights – but he deteriorated so rapidly we would never have made it.

'So you're thinking of retiring? Oh, Mum, it feels so soon.'

'No, it feels like the time is right. It will be good for all of us to have a change. You and Isobel will be great together running this place. Do you know why she's at the doctor's? She told me it was just a routine thing – a forty-plus MOT, she called it.'

'Yeah, I had one when I was forty. You should have a sixty-something one, Mum.'

'Let's not start down that road again, you'll be having me measured up for a wheelchair.'

She laughs. 'Mum, you're paranoid.'

'Perhaps I am,' I laugh.

'And about the house – Isobel has convinced me it would be good for you to find a place of your own, somewhere a bit smaller ... You know, a bungalow, somewhere for your wheelchair?'

We're both giggling now. 'I was thinking more pent-house apartment with a hot tub,' I joke.

'If you're getting a trendy penthouse apartment I'm leaving home and coming with you.'

Our amusement grows, and then she says, 'Are you okay?'

I nod. 'I'm fine, as long as you are ...'

'I'm good.'

'I don't expect you to understand. But as we get older we often lose focus on the passions in our life. It's too easy to forget about the things that make us who we are. I like what Peter sees in me, he makes me feel young again, and sometimes I want to remember the young girl who painted and sketched and danced ...'

'But, Mum, you don't paint or sketch and you and Dad never danced ...'

'I used to paint and sketch all the time when I was at college and I've started again recently. As for dancing, well, Dad didn't dance, but that shouldn't have stopped me from dancing ... and being without Peter shouldn't have stopped me from sketching and painting ... or dreaming of Paris, but it did.'

'You wanted to go to Paris?'

'Yes, and I shouldn't have seen marriage and children as a reason to stop dreaming, stop dancing ...'

'No, you shouldn't. We should go dancing together ...

336

I've always fancied salsa classes. Let's do it! I'll ask Isobel too.'

I am yet to convince Anna about Peter, but I'm delighted at the prospect of going to a dance class. It makes me feel like one of them, rather than 'Mother' who needs super-vising and patronising. What a turnaround – perhaps even Anna is seeing a bit of the old Rosie now too?

Later, Anna calls me at home. 'Mum, James and I were planning to go out on Saturday and I wondered if you fancied a night in with your granddaughters? There will be popcorn and chocolate.'

'Ah, in that case, count me in, but I thought it was their weekend with Paul?'

'Well, it was, but he's got his girlfriend now, hasn't he, and she wants him to take her to Girl Guides or something.'

I have to smile, Anna is so unforgiving. 'Perhaps now you've got James and everything is good you can start to move on? Stop chipping away at Paul and his much younger girlfriend. That way madness lies,' I laugh.

'Well, you keep talking about fresh starts and how life is to be lived so I thought why not treat James to a nice meal at that new wine bar you and Peter went to.'

I like the way she includes him in the conversation, and I like the way 'you and Peter' sounds, like she's finally coming to terms with us.

Chapter Twenty-Seven

It's the beginning of *Strictly Come Dancing*, my favourite, and I watch with Emma and Katie, lost in the swirl of the foxtrot and the fiery passion of the Argentine tango. Katie swirls around the room while Emma laughs and I see Peter and me, our bodies touching on the dance floor, his hand in my hair, his arms around me. Then, just as the programme finishes and we decide to watch a DVD, my mobile rings. I hunt for my phone in my handbag – the girls have secretly changed the call tune and all I can hear is Rihanna offering to lick something off someone.

'Girls, you're outrageous!' I'm saying, giggling as I try to put on my glasses and answer the phone at the same time while they roll around the floor laughing. I must remember to take that off before the next Ladies Luncheon, or Rihanna could cause quite a stir.

Then I stop and see his name flash up on the small screen. 'Hello, sweetie,' I say, and I can't hide the smile on my face.

I'm flushed with the pleasure – and also feeling rather awkward in front of my two granddaughters now staring openly at me.

'I missed you,' he says, simply.

'Yes, me too. I'm with Emma and Katie,' I add, in an attempt to explain why I may sound a little monosyllabic. He's been away for a few days now and I want to say so much, but I stay on the surface, asking about the magazine project in France and he seems exhilarated by the whole experience.

'I haven't been out in the field for a while,' he's saying. 'I've had years of being very cosy with the wine- and canapé-fuelled exhibitions and PR jobs, but this was a challenge and I needed it. I did it for fun, but the editor called and said he's delighted and asked if I'd do some more photos . . . Iceland next.'

'Great . . . that's great news,' I say, happy for him.

'Of course you'll come with me?'

'I'm not sure. I'm going to be quite busy myself,' I reply. 'But we can talk about it when you get back.'

Neither of us speak for a few seconds – I hope that he

understands that my granddaughters are both listening avidly, and that's why I'm not being very talkative. We will always be two people with so much to say, our past, present and future are entwined – and yet here we are, speechless again.

'Anyway, I'm back tomorrow and I can't wait to see you. I'm lonely in my hotel room and just wanted to hear your voice.'

'Me too,' I say again, as Katie sits open-mouthed, waiting to hear what I'll say next.

'I'm just going through them, but in a little while I'll send you some of the photos so you can see them.'

'Oh, photos of the concrete architecture?'

'No, I did those, but while I was there I just had this massive moment of inspiration. I just couldn't stop shooting. I've never felt so creative – I think that's what being in love does for a person.'

'That's lovely.' I smile, wanting to say so much more.

'Anyway it's a sort of "cycle of life" piece, the idea that people and places change, die, get left behind, but the spirit lives on.'

'I love that – it's profound.'

'Yes, I just kept thinking about us, and how we've come full circle – we're different but the same, like something inside us kept going in our absence. And something you said also inspired me. You talked about

340

Anna being like your mother and Emma being like you. It made me think about how the past is tied up in the present and the future. It doesn't matter if you were born now or a hundred years ago, we're all human and despite amazing technology and scientific discoveries we stay the same and the life-force carries on. And as buildings go up and are pulled down, roads are built, churches demolished, human beings will continue to love, hate, go to war, and make the same mistakes over and over again.'

And as he speaks I think about the past and the way my own life has reflected my mother's and my daughters' lives have reflected mine. And I remember the night I told Margaret I was pregnant and expected her to scream and shout and tell me I was shameful, but she didn't. My mother held my hand and cried and told me it wasn't my fault. 'People make mistakes,' she said. 'Sometimes the same mistakes generation after generation. I used to be just like you, Rosie – saying I'd never end up in the same life as *my* mother, but I got pregnant with your brother and I had to get married. I had big dreams once too, you know, but I never was that secretary in the big office in Manchester with my own typewriter and a key to the stationery cupboard.

'So when I had you I said, "This girl's going to do everything I didn't do. She's going to do things with her

341

life, not spend it stuck in a little terraced house with a baby at her breast every few years.'"

I was my mother's future, I was going to redeem her, but I let her down. It all makes sense to me now. The way she scolded me for love bites and short skirts and boyfriends was just her way of trying to prevent the same thing happening to me that had happened to her. And as I railed against her domestic jurisdiction, vowing never to live the same life she had – she didn't want me to either. Margaret and I were on the same team all along, but our class, sex and time conspired against us and any aspirations we had were strangled before birth. Then again, it might just have been fate because I do believe some things are written in the stars.

Later, Peter calls me back to say he's sent me the photos on email.

'Great. I don't have my computer here – I'll have to look at them later,' I say.

'No, you don't have to wait, they are on your email now,' he explains gently. 'You can open the email on your phone and see them.'

'Oh, really? How does that happen?' I ask. It's all a bit technical for me, bordering on magic really.

'Oh dear,' he says. I can almost see him smiling, he always laughs at my lack of technological know-how.

'Hang on, I have a teenager here . . .' I say now, before it becomes complicated and he misconstrues my computer illiteracy for lack of interest in his work. 'I need you to help me see Peter's photos on a big screen,' I say, making a large square shape with my index figure, pointlessly and rather helplessly.

Emma rolls her eyes with a smile. She is also highly amused by my computer illiteracy.

'I can do it . . .' Katie pleads. Oh God, I'd forgotten about sibling rivalry.

'Nan, give me the phone.' Emma is authoritative, ignoring her little sister. I hand it over. The little baby I used to rock to sleep now has her mother's (and my mother's) assertiveness – which is good for her, if a little scary for me.

'Hi, Peter, it's Emma here,' she says.

'I'm here too, Peter,' calls Katie.

'He says hi, now shut up, Katie.' Emma is listening to him and suddenly starts laughing. 'Yep, you're right. She has no clue,' she says, looking over at me with a knowing smile.

'Hey, I hope you two aren't talking about me?' I'm delighted at this unexpected rapport between the two of them. He hasn't yet had a chance to really get to know my granddaughters and it's my dearest wish for them to love him too.

343

'Let me give you my email address. You can send the jpegs to me and I'll get them up on my laptop,' Emma is saying to Peter. 'They'll be lost in Nan's email. And even if she ever finds them, she'll end up posting them on Facebook or Snapchat by mistake and before you know it they'll have gone viral.' She laughs as she twiddles one of the buttons on my phone so I can hear Peter's voice too. Teenagers are so clever these days, aren't they?

After some more good-natured teasing we say goodbye and Emma puts down the phone.

'Peter was saying that once he gave you his camera and you ended up taking pictures of pavements.'

'Yes, I did. Nothing wrong with that – I was going through my pavement period,' I say and they both laugh. I suggest we have hot chocolate and look at Peter's photos and to my delight the girls agree. But then Emma gets up and leaves the room saying, 'BRB.'

I wonder if she's annoyed and look questioningly at Katie, who's gazing at the TV screen. 'What does BRB mean?' I say, wanting to know.

'It means I'll be right back,' Katie monotones.

I make the chocolate and when I return with three mugs on a tray Emma has settled on the sofa with the laptop. Then she does what teenagers do and uses her magic to get Peter's pictures from the email.

'It's weird to think you can take pictures and develop

them within minutes and send them anywhere in the world,' I say, marvelling at the way life has moved on. I remember how Peter used to spend hours in the dark-room at college – it was a long, laborious process just for one photo. Neither of the girls marvel along with me at this – they are used to life being instant, all there at the click of a mouse. They never lived through the endless wait for holiday snaps to turn up at the local pharmacy, arriving weeks after the holiday was over, and at least half the photos flooded with light. My generation has lived through such enormous change, it makes me think about what Peter said earlier – the human spirit survives it all and carries on, just like the stars.

We all sit together on the sofa, Emma in the middle, with the laptop on her knees, and Katie and me on either side. Watching the black and white moody shapes and structures swiping across the screen fills me with awe and reminds me how talented Peter is. I would have known his work anywhere – the process is smoother, the pic-tures more accomplished, but the essence remains. Sharp structures splashed with shapes of light, brickwork so beautiful and detailed, texture so real you think you can reach out and touch it. Ordinary people walking, stand-ing, chatting – but he somehow elevates them into the extraordinary with his angles and compositions, his use of natural and artificial light. I feel I know these people, and glimpse their dreams as they wander anonymously along city streets alone and in human clusters. Peter could always get inside people's heads, their hearts – seducing them into being photographed, and reproducing so much more than just a face or a shadowy figure. He tells such stories with his pictures, his ideas are brilliant and exciting and just looking through these photos I feel such pride.

The pictures move seamlessly from France then and now, to Salford then and now. Little kids play hopscotch on grey pavements, a woman pegs out washing, letting it blow in the dirty, sunny breeze, then a recent shot of a busy dual carriageway knifing through the city, an old church juxtaposed next to a new concrete block of housing – old values and new lives. All these elements are special, and in Peter's hands so much more than the sum of their parts. In these latest pictures he's also discovered his signature flower pushing through rubble, a reminder of nature's indestructible force among the concrete jungle of new and exciting structures.

'Peter's cool, isn't he, Nan?' says Katie, nodding like a confident art critic as the pictures pass by us.

'Yes, he's very cool.' I smile.

'Look at her – she's gorgeous, is she a model?' Emma asks.

I lean closer to see the face of a pretty blonde girl

346

standing among rubble, the caption underneath reading: *Even in his earliest work, Moreton found his flower in the Manchester slums.*

I blush. 'That's his girlfriend.' I smile.

Both girls look at each other, then they look at me, touchingly hurt on my behalf, but I don't torture them for long.

'It's me, the girl is me – I was seventeen when that picture was taken.'

'Oh wow. How cool is Nan?' Katie says, and even Emma seems impressed.

'OMFG. You could have been a model. That is way cool.'

I look to Katie for translation. 'OMFG?'

'It means oh my fuc—' starts Katie.

'Oh, okay, thanks, darling, I just got it,' I say in time.

I peer at the photo and see my reflection in the screen, an old lady wearing glasses looking at her younger self staring back. And I see the Rosie Peter loved before – the one with dreams and ambitions and the lopsided smile. The camera is almost beneath me and I'm smiling into the lens, bare arms outstretched in abandon – happy, crazy and in love. The cameraman clearly loves me in these photos and I him – and for the millionth time in my life I wonder just what might have been. I was the flower, the life and hope springing out of despair and my

347

eyes water. I now know the future wasn't the one she dreamed of, but that lovely girl with the long blonde hair had a good life. And now she's getting a second chance at those first dreams. My throat constricts with a kind of sadness for the past, for what we once were, and knowing Peter was right, and life did have a way of working things out after all. But that was yesterday, and now I'm excited to see what those tomorrows will bring.

Later, at home, I sit for a long time looking at Peter's photos. Emma showed me how to download them from my email – she seems to understand that I want them (him?) with me until I see him again. I think it's because Emma and I are both in love, and she understands that we may be almost fifty years apart, but in essence we're the same.

I gaze for hours imagining his trip, wanting to share his journey and look through these photos together when he returns. I want to know his thoughts, ideas, the stories behind these wonderful pictures, and I think about where he's flying off to next in search of the light. Seeing the girl with the long blonde hair, the tiny flower in the rubble, reminded me once more of who I used to be.

I dig deep into the memories, reliving the day he took the photos of me. It was the day of the storm and I can feel the weight of air, bloated with smog and pressure, leading to the moments just before when you know the world can't take any more and it will soon explode. Then the lightning and the passion, thunder rolling along as we made love in the lashing rain, gripping each other so tight, holding on to each other so we didn't fall. Wet hair and clothes, rain on our kisses, exposed to the elements and each other. It was a time of taking what was ours, carefree abandon and a sheer lust for life – and I may not be as skinny, young, or beautiful, but I'm just as blonde, and I'm even more feisty. And I'm damn well going to be that girl again.

Chapter Twenty-Eight

Peter and I are having lunch in Oxford. It's a chilly day and on my arrival at the train station he's brought me to a lovely traditional old English pub. A fire is glowing in the grate and we're eating good steak and kidney pudding which is going down well with the full-bodied red wine and delicious company.

We talk about his marriage and he says he never really felt 'right' with Camille.

'We had everything,' he sighs. 'And I remember once sitting at Heathrow in the VIP lounge waiting to go to some exotic location . . . I think it was Bermuda. All the pieces were there, she was lovely, the food was wonderful, the prospect of a comfortable first class flight to a five-star destination was pleasant. But that was all – pleasant.'

'Wow, I'd have been doing star jumps all over the VIP lounge,' I laugh.

'Exactly. And you know me, I'm enthusiastic, I see the best in most situations, but looking back, I was about to have the most wonderful holiday ... and I've never been more sad in my life. Just this inexplicable sadness. I never said anything to Camille, but I went to the toilets and cried, I just cried and cried quietly so no one would hear.'

'What was it? Why do you think you felt so wretched?' I ask.

'Everything in place, except the one thing that mattered – I was with the wrong person. And the fact that all the other elements of the trip were perfect made me realise it would never work for me.'

'So you knew then that your marriage was over?'

'Yes, and a few months after that I introduced my wife to my rich banker friend who she's now married to. I didn't actually do this consciously, but I knew she had to have someone because I could never leave her. After you I could never leave anyone ever again.'

I ask how they met and he says she turned up one night at his student house in Clapham, looking for somewhere to stay. The daughter of a shipping magnate, Camille had abandoned the academic life at Oxford for that of an artist. Apparently she stayed that night and never left.

'How very bohemian,' I laugh. 'And how very you.

351

A beautiful, rich, intelligent girl lands on your doorstep looking for a bed – it's the stuff that young men's dreams are made of. You never did have to try, did you, Peter?'

'I suppose not. But that's the problem, isn't it? When you don't have to give anything in return you just take and take and it doesn't make for a happy life.'

He puts down his knife and fork, peruses the dessert menu as I sip my wine.

'We were in our late twenties when we married, having lived together for a few years,' he continues, after we discuss then abandon the idea of dessert. 'As you rightly say, fate has been kind to me – and everything in life has been handed to me on a plate. And so we started to think about children, assuming a baby was our right, as two spoiled brats might. Well why not? We were successful, fairly happy, been married a few years, money not a problem – a baby is what happens next, isn't it?'

'So you both . . . wanted children?'

'Desperately.'

'Really?' Am I detecting a chink of darkness in the life of St Camille of the Renovated Farmhouse? I think rather unkindly.

'Oh, I assumed you had such busy lives you'd *chosen* not to have children.' Peter has told me all about his travels, his photographs, but his marriage is still a mystery to me; he's never really opened up about it.

352

'No. We had busy lives *because* we had no children. We tried IVF for years, but never hit the jackpot.'

'I'm so sorry, it must have been such an unhappy time for her, well, for you both.'

'She eventually came to accept it, but I struggled for a long time. I still wonder if it's my punishment for rejecting you and our ... baby, and even though we've talked and we've grieved I don't know if I can ever forgive myself.'

Neither of us say anything, but his words weigh heavily in the air between us, and I can't help but think about Isobel and her own desire to have a baby and my heart hurts. And Peter's heart will probably always hurt too. What happened will always be with him, but I think for both of us the pain has faded now we've shared our loss.

'All that time I never realised. I imagined you living your big life and never giving me – us – a second thought. I didn't even know if you'd remember me.' In a strange way it comforts me all over again to know he always cared, it means I'm right to love this man now.

'How could I ever forget you? I know I was your first and I'd been with other girls, but I really loved you – I was just too young to handle the big feelings that came with that. But later, I thought about what we'd had and what we could have had and my life became meaningless – what was the point? My friends were taking their sons to football, worrying about their daughters' boy-friends, the clothes they wore, driving them here and there. I envied them, teaching their kids to swim, ride a bike, play cricket – I even envied their trips to the dentist.' He shakes his head. 'I wanted it all. What do I have to show for my life? A few photos? Money in the bank? It's all meaningless. Whole generations of happy, painful, beautiful life were being lived while Camille and I kept an immaculately decorated empty house,' he says, running his fingers through thick, steely hair.

I eventually reach out and touch his hand. I always thought he had everything, but it was me who had everything after all.

'You never told me any of this, Peter.' At the beginning I asked him about Camille, but he only ever wanted to talk about the art, the beautiful home; he never really revealed what their life was about.

'I'm a photographer,' he shrugs. 'I observe and document other people's lives, not my own.'

'But that doesn't mean you can't open up to people.'

'Perhaps I'm good at what I do because I don't share my feelings and aspects of my own life too much. After I left you I never really felt comfortable talking about myself, my life – I was ashamed about what I did and I continued to keep things to myself until now, with you. Camille always said that I never opened up to her and

354

that's how I wanted my relationship to be, but with you it's different – I can finally begin to look at my life and the choices I made.'

I'm moved that he feels able to talk to me. Everyone needs to talk, and however confident they may seem, or perfect their lives may appear to be, we all live with shadows.

Later, we walk back to his house in the crisp autumn sunshine. I put my arm through his and he smiles as I tell him something outrageous Emma said. Back at his house he pours us both a large whisky; the afternoon is closing in and he lights a fire while I read a newspaper. Later we go to bed and an hour later we get up and have cheese on toast at his kitchen table and Albert purrs around our legs as Peter tells me funny stories about his trip. Then we light candles and sit on the sofa and he talks me through his photos and it just feels so good to be back again.

The following morning Peter wakes me with a tray of toasted soda bread and home-made marmalade.

'Stay in bed, darling, I've started the fire but as this place is so big it takes a while to warm up.'

I sit up, still sleepy, still naked and not a bit self-conscious, save pulling the sheet up over my breasts. He puts the tray on my lap and kisses me deeply.

We finish the toast and coffee and he takes away the

355

tray and I ask him to wait a minute while I pop down-stairs. I wrap the sheet around me, grab my pencil case and run back upstairs, and start to set up his easel which stands in the corner of the room.

'Oh, you're going to sketch?' he says, smiling.

'No, you are. You're going to draw me.'

He smiles, he remembers.

'You're going to draw an old lady with nothing on before it's too late.'

'You'll never be an old lady to me.' He grins. 'You're Rosie Draper from Nightingale Road, the girl with the long blonde hair and the crooked smile. And I always said that one day I would capture you naked.'

He gets off the bed and I drape myself across it as he adjusts the easel, checks his perspective by holding out the charcoal pencil.

'I want to do everything we talked about back then, Peter,' I sigh. 'Starting with this.'

'Me too,' he says, walking towards the bed and kissing me, adjusting the sheet around me until it falls right.

He stands behind his easel and I lie on the rumpled sheets, feeling like the artist's model we all had a crush on in those far-off college days. I lean on one elbow, trying to cover my tummy with the sheets and he walks from behind the easel and gently pulls them away.

'I want all of you,' he says, walking back to his easel.

And for the next couple of hours he scrutinises me, rubbing his fingers into the charcoal like he's caressing my flesh. His eyes dance over my nakedness. And when the drawing is almost complete he climbs on to the bed and runs his charcoaled fingers all over my body. His lips kiss the charcoal bruises on my thighs and breasts and within seconds we're making love.

'I loved you then and I love you now, and that's all there is,' he says between kisses.

Later I look at his drawing and wonder if he's been kind. The woman in the picture is beautiful, strong and healthy, she has stretch marks around her tummy and her breasts are small and slightly flatter than she'd like, but I love Peter's vision of me.

'I actually like myself,' I say.

'At last. My flower in the rubble is finally appreciating her own beauty.'

Chapter Twenty-Nine

After an idyllic weekend with Peter I feel happier than I have for a long time and return to the shop on Monday morning in a positive frame of mind.

I've noticed that Anna doesn't really ask me about Peter much. She knows I went to his home this weekend, but whereas Isobel would ask questions and engage with me as I recount my stay, Anna stays silent. But Isobel's on holiday, so I don't have the opportunity to talk to anyone about it. Normally Anna just listens and it must kill her not to ask questions or contribute her own thoughts to mine and Peter's relationship. I know this is her unspoken protest at my other life, a life she isn't part of and therefore can't control, and I fear Margaret's ghost haunts me still.

Everyone else in the family seems to be welcoming and accepting of Peter, and it's my dearest wish one day to bring him into the family fold. But while Anna is still rather closed to the idea there's no point in me pushing him down her throat and attempting more social gatherings. If she's not happy she will make it clear, she may even say something to me or make a comment to Peter and perhaps ultimately cause a bigger rift. Consequently I only drop his name into the conversation every now and then, a warning shot across her bows that I'm still with him, and whatever her views are on the matter, we are together and happy. It's an invisible mother–daughter stand-off, where to anyone on the outside of the relationship everything seems fine, but it's a huge chasm between us and I know we both feel it.

I've lived with this for a few weeks now and it's okay if Anna and I just talk about work and the children, anything but Peter and where we've been together. There's been much excitement in Anna's world recently as Katie is performing in a dance recital at the school she attends and we're all really looking forward to it. The performance is on Saturday, I've kept the evening free, and this morning I ask Anna what time it starts.

'Would you like me to drive?' I say, knowing James is away working in Wales so Anna and I could go together.

She suddenly goes quiet, and I immediately think there may be problems with her and James.

'Oh, Mum . . . I don't know how to tell you . . .'

'Is everything okay?' I ask, holding my breath, worrying what she's going to say.

'It's James . . . he's back early on Saturday and he'd like to see Katie dance.'

'Well, that's okay as long as you two don't mind me playing gooseberry – I'll come along with you.'

'That's the thing . . . I only bought two tickets, I wasn't sure if you were free . . .'

'I kept it free, I always go to the girls' events,' I say.

'I just thought you might be having a weekend with Peter.'

She knew damn well I wasn't seeing Peter, I'd made a point of telling her that I was keeping Saturday free – I'd told Katie the same.

'Anna, you know I wouldn't arrange to see Peter when Katie is dancing.' I'm hurt to think she'd even suggest this. 'Can I get another ticket?'

'No, there aren't any left. I'm really sorry, Mum. I'll call round some of the mums and see if they have any spare . . .'

'Okay, thanks, I really would like to be there,' I say, stinging, but trying not to show how hurt I am.

'I feel really bad. But the thing is James needs to start

360

doing stuff like this with us – as a family, you know?'

This is a low blow from Anna, who is only too aware of my own desire to bring Peter into the family.

'Yes, I do know, Anna. I know exactly how it feels to want to bring your partner into your life and your family.'

'It's not the same, Mum—'

'STOP telling me it's not the same. Just because I'm older, it doesn't mean I can't *feel*. It doesn't mean that I don't hurt every time we have a family gathering and he isn't included, or there's a conversation about James or Richard being your partners, deliberately leaving out the fact that Peter is mine. And now you're punishing me for having a partner by making it impossible for me to go to Katie's dance evening, something you know I love to do. Please don't use my granddaughters to get at me, it's a cheap shot and I'm disappointed in you. I know you're bossy and controlling, but I really thought you were kinder than that.' I storm out in tears of hurt and rage and when I finally pull myself together, I do what I've been doing a lot recently: I turn to Peter.

'I know it's only right that James goes,' I say on the phone, 'and I understand that she wants him to be part of the girls' lives, but I can't help but feel upset and angry about the way she's excluded me deliberately.'

361

Peter suggests gently that perhaps I'm being a little oversensitive which makes me feel better because I don't want to think that Anna is being mean. I'd rather believe she's being thoughtless and I'm being silly.

'Look, why don't I come over and cheer you up on Saturday instead?' he says. 'We'll do something special together and then you can see Katie on Sunday. Perhaps you could ask Anna to take pictures? She could video the whole thing?'

It wouldn't be the same. I can't explain to him that I want Katie to know I'm in the audience. It's about seeing her dance, but more than that it's about being there for her.

'Anna can even borrow one of my cameras! I've got a great little Leica that would do the job,' he's saying. I have to smile, it isn't about the camera, but I doubt he'd understand, to him it's just my granddaughter's dancing show and he probably wonders what all the fuss is about. It's at times like this I miss Mike.

I call Katie to wish her good luck for Saturday and she says it won't be the same without me there, which brings a lump to my throat. 'Yes, but your mum and James will be there and James hasn't seen you dance, so I reckon it's his turn,' I say, trying to sound happy about it. But I just feel wretched.

*

362

When Peter arrives on Saturday I'm so glad to see him I hug him before he's even halfway down the drive – I can't wait to fall into his arms, and feel the world fall away.

'As you were so upset I've booked theatre tickets and a meal at our favourite restaurant this evening to take your mind off everything and cheer you up,' he says as we walk arm in arm into the house. I'm delighted, it's a lovely gesture, and the fact he's gone out of his way to get last-minute tickets and wants to make it special makes me feel loved, which is just what I need right now.

'It won't be quite the same as seeing Katie on stage,' he sighs, 'but almost.' I am touched at his thoughtfulness.

'I've been keeping this wine for a special occasion,' he says, taking it out of his bag and putting it on the kitchen worktop. 'But then I thought, define a special occasion. It's been in my cellar for over thirty years ... and an occasion doesn't get more special than being here with you. I've also booked a taxi to the restaurant and home from the theatre and before we go out we will enjoy a glass of this together.'

When it comes to lovely things, he thinks of everything. He's also brought with him some croissants, and a pale pink box of pastel macarons.

'You are such a hedonist, Peter,' I smile. 'And I love it. This is just what I need right now: a little TLC laced with wild abandon and expensive wine and these macarons . . . '

'Just a little reminder of Paris,' he says fondly as I gaze at the pastel-coloured discs.

'My favourite, and they look very special.'

'They are. Pamela brought them back for us from Paris – she says hello, by the way, and wants us to go over there for dinner as soon as we're free.' He rolls his eyes. He always rolls his eyes when he talks about Pamela, but I know it's done with affection and he loves her dearly. He says her dinner parties are extravagant and I will need to starve for at least a week before we go. I reckon there's a genetic streak of pleasure-seeking and high-living running through Moreton blood.

'Lovely, I haven't seen her since the wedding,' I say. 'I'll look forward to it.'

I'm delighted she's invited us, especially as I'm feeling rather rejected by my daughter. Here's someone from Peter's family who wants to celebrate our relationship and is happy to welcome us as a couple. I know it sounds silly after all these years, but for me Pamela's overture is extra special having never been welcomed by his parents. Finally I feel accepted by Peter's family, which is bittersweet, because Peter hasn't yet been accepted by mine.

When Peter met my parents I remember being

ashamed and hating myself for it, but he told me it was okay. 'So you don't want to live your parents' life, who does?' he said.

'Yes, but your parents read books and talk politics, they have interesting friends . . . you must want to be like them?'

'So why did I call myself Pierre and wish I lived in another country?' he said. 'I don't feel comfortable at home, my parents are bourgeois, they pretend to be liberal but it's all just an act. They'd be as horrified as the other snobby neighbours if a black family moved into our street – and I hate them for it. At least your parents are honest, working-class folk who don't put on any airs and graces.'

I remember thinking then that we were both lost, like two children searching for a home, a life. We both went off in different directions searching for the same thing and it makes me wonder if any of us ever really find what we're looking for. I was one of the lucky ones: I found it with Mike and now I really believe I've found what I've been looking for again, with Peter, my first love, my second chance.

I put the lovely pale pink box of macarons to the side, admiring the delicate pastel palette of shades, like watercolours. I resist taking one until later – I want to enjoy

365

them on our return with a cup of coffee when we can lie in bed and talk about the play we've seen. It's those times together afterwards that I enjoy when we can dissect the evening, discuss the food, the gallery we visited and just enjoy being alone. I'm still sad about missing Katie, but I tell myself there will be other times.

At about five o'clock I leave Peter downstairs tinkering with his new camera (the one I'm not allowed to touch) and I go upstairs to get ready. I'm just applying my lipstick when the phone rings and I almost fall downstairs to grab it before Peter does because I think it might be Anna calling to see how I am. I can't imagine anything worse than Anna ringing up contrite about me not being able to go tonight and Peter picking up the phone. Then in the few seconds it takes me to get down the stairs I think of something much worse: what if this is Anna to tell me she's got me a ticket for tonight after all, and Peter's booked the theatre, the table, the taxi – what on earth would I say? Who would I have to hurt? I hear Peter on the phone.

'Hey, hey, calm down,' he's saying. I am now walking slowly down the stairs, trying to work out who is on the phone.

'Anna ... it's okay ... Anna, listen to me ...' he's saying.

My heart thuds and bounces down the hall. NO. Anna

is probably furious that he's now answering the phone in my house, and just as I'm about to ask him to hand me the phone so I can tell her off he says something that stops me in my tracks.

'Which hospital is he in?'

Peter's now nodding and I'm desperate to know what's going on, but he seems to have this and when I look at him and gesture for him to give me the phone he just mouths, *It's okay.*

'Anna, it's fine, you go now. Don't worry about anything, your mum and I can go and watch Katie. Yes, we'll do that ... tickets from school reception, yes. Oh, don't cry – I'm sure everything will be fine ... yes, we'll pick up Emma. Does your mum have her friend's address? Don't worry, just go – call your mum on her mobile as soon as you know. And Anna ... life has a way of working things out, you know.' He puts down the phone and I'm just standing in the hallway, almost unable to speak for fear of what he's going to tell me.

'It's James, he's fallen from a roof he's working on in Wales. He's been taken to a hospital in Cardiff and Anna's going to be with him. They won't tell her anything over the phone as she isn't his next of kin, but his friend is going to drive her there.'

'Oh God ... I bet she's devastated.'

'Yes, she's upset but she's also worried about the girls,

and I knew if we could look after that side of things it would free her up to just be on her own and get to James. Whatever happens when she gets there is another issue ... if he's in a bad way ... but I said we would have it all covered here.'

I look at him in disbelief. In this moment of terrible anguish with everything suddenly thrown up in the air, Peter has stepped up. The man who lives alone and by his own admission can be selfishly living a life where he thinks only of himself has just cancelled his plans and taken on this huge family responsibility without question.

'Peter, I'm so touched ... you bought theatre tickets and booked a restaurant and—'

'Yes, but who cares about that when something like this happens? I'll take my camera and try and film some of it for Anna ... she won't want to miss it. Now hurry up and get ready – I told Anna we'd get to Katie's dance event early.'

The old laid-back Peter is cool about this. I love him.

So as I finish getting ready, he calls and cancels everything then puts the cork back in the wine, packs a couple of cameras and we head out for an unexpected evening of dance. But tonight is about so much more than seeing my lovely granddaughter shine on stage;

this is about Peter discovering that he can be the man he always wanted to be. And who knows, these might be his first steps on the rocky road to becoming part of our family.

Chapter Thirty

We arrive early and Peter asks for permission to film the performance. I positively glow when he explains that he's Katie's grandmother's partner and a professional photographer. We take our seats just as the curtain goes up, and as soon as Katie appears on stage I can tell she's scanning the crowd for her mum. Her eyes are darting everywhere and she eventually sees me. I give a little smile and it's good to see the relief on her face – it's not her mum but I am the next best thing. I'm so glad we're able to be here and grateful to Peter for being so understanding. To see a child looking round from the stage for family who isn't there is one of the most heartbreaking sights.

The children give a wonderful performance in a way only kids can: they are energetic, funny, talented and they are ours, so we're totally biased. I did wonder if Peter would be bored; after all, it is amateur in its purest sense to someone who isn't watching their own child on stage. But Peter genuinely seems to enjoy it, he's videoing while tapping his hand to the music, and sharing this special evening with him is wonderful. I'm showing off my lovely, talented granddaughter and when she takes her bow and Peter shouts 'Bravo' and stands up to film a close-up, my eyes fill with tears.

'We should have bought her flowers,' he whispers to me as they bring the curtain down.

'She's a twelve-year-old at a dance school recital, not Darcey Bussell,' I laugh.

Later, as we wait outside in the cold for the girls to come out, Peter goes back to his car to pack away the camera. I see him wandering back down the road to where I'm standing waiting with some of the mums and suddenly notice him climbing over a garden fence. It's dark and he's gone into someone's front garden, which concerns me. A lot. What the hell is he doing? I am quite disturbed by this until a few minutes later he emerges, carrying a bunch of flowers, clearly stolen.

'What are you doing?' I ask quietly so as not to alert the other parents.

'I got them for Katie. I used to steal flowers from people's gardens for you and you never seemed to mind.'

'That's because I didn't know,' I say. 'All those blue hydrangea?'

He nods. 'Yes, the woman three doors down had a lovely garden.'

I giggle at this, remembering the reckless, daring Peter I once knew, and watching him arranging the stolen flowers I see the spark there still.

Eventually Katie comes running out to meet us. She's on a high and dying to talk about the evening and as Peter hands the flowers to her she stops talking and looks at him with genuine gratitude.

'Ah, thank you, Peter!' she says, the sheer delight on her face saying it all, and then she hugs him and I think I might just burst with happiness. She clutches her 'bouquet' to her chest like an old film star as we walk back to the car and she tells me all about the gossip and the drama of the evening. I gently explain where her mum is and at that moment Anna texts and says James is going to be okay, to our great relief.

As we collect Emma, she is at first a little confused about the strange car waiting outside for her.

'Oh, it's Peter … Peter's here,' she says in a sing-song voice, climbing into the back. 'Thank God, you can help me with the project I'm doing for photography this weekend ...'

He seems pleased with this and as we drive off I touch his knee and he winks at me.

As soon as we get home, Anna rings me on my mobile. She says all is fine, James is under observation and should be out tomorrow. She asks about the dance recital and I put Katie on who's talking nineteen to the dozen.

'And Peter videoed it for you, Mum, so you can see it all – isn't that cool? He's got the most amazing camera and he says he got everything – me and Em are going to watch it now, and you can see it tomorrow.'

Eventually, when they've finished chatting, Katie hands the phone to me.

'Hi ... Mum. Thanks for everything, I don't know what I'd have done without you tonight.'

'It's my job,' I say with a smile, appreciating her thanks. 'Now you go and get some sleep and we'll see you tomorrow. The girls are safe and happy, James is fine, so you need to look after yourself now.'

I'm about to put the phone down when I hear her say something.

'Mum?'

'Yes, sweetie?'

'Did Peter really video the dancing?'

'Yes, he knew you wouldn't want to miss it.'

'I didn't ... I ... Will you say thank you to him?'

'Yes, of course, he was happy to do it.'

This isn't praise, it isn't acceptance, that will take time – but for Anna this is huge.

I put down the phone, glowing with something like happiness. For once all is right in our world, James is well, Anna's okay and Isobel is oblivious and enjoying a much-needed holiday with Richard. But best of all my granddaughters are happy and here ... and so is Peter.

I wander into the living room where he is now setting up the video so we can watch the performance again. I'm just about to go back into the kitchen when I see Emma playing with his expensive new camera and for a moment I feel rather on the spot. If she messes up his settings he'll be upset, but I don't want him to be put in the position of having to ask her to put it down – that will embarrass them both.

'It's Peter's new one, very special,' I say lightly, hoping she'll get the hint and perhaps put it down before he realises. But she doesn't flinch, so I laughingly add, 'I was told off when I picked it up. I'm not allowed to play with that camera.'

'No, you're not allowed anywhere near it,' he says from behind the TV set. 'But Emma is because she knows what she's doing.' I am so relieved, I stick my tongue out at him and Emma laughs and continues to twiddle with all the buttons.

I go into the kitchen, make sandwiches and hot chocolate and bring it all back out on a tray.

'Come on, Rosie, we are about to have the Royal Command Performance in here,' Peter's saying.

'I'm just the usherette serving refreshments,' I laugh, settling the tray down on the coffee table.

'Shall we have some wine too?' he asks.

'The expensive one, for special occasions?'

'Yes, this is a special occasion,' he agrees, smiling. 'It's Katie's film debut, so bring four glasses.' The girls, particularly Katie, are delighted at this (I expect Emma prefers something stronger) and I pour two small glasses for them and hand them over. Peter is talking light metres with Emma as she sips her wine and I realise he doesn't know how to be around children – so he simply treats them like adults. And they love it.

After we've watched Peter's film, the girls are tired and head off to bed hugging both of us goodnight, which clearly touches him.

'Thank you for tonight,' I say, snuggling up to him on the sofa, finally alone. 'The wine that probably cost a month's salary has been quaffed, and I know it hasn't been the most romantic evening.'

'No, romance was definitely off the cards tonight,' he

says, pouring the last dregs of the wine into our glasses. 'I'll admit I brought this wine along with romance in mind. But . . .' he turns to look at me, 'tonight has been one of the best nights of my life.'

I laugh. I think he's joking until I look up to see his eyes are red-rimmed.

'Peter . . . really? One of the best?' I put my arm around him.

He nods. 'All the stuff kids do, the way they are – joking and being kids and Katie being thrilled with the film and Emma wanting to know about photography. It probably happens all the time for you, but I've never known it. I felt appreciated, like I was needed, I'm helping Emma with her project and Katie says she's put a photo of the flowers I gave her on Facebook. They are just so kind and funny and bright. I love the energy kids have and tonight I realised children don't have to be your blood for you to pass on your ideas, your photos . . . your immortality.'

I look into his eyes and know if I want this I could have it all – he is not only accepting, but embracing, and will, in time, be accepted in turn. We kiss and I'm just about to suggest we go to bed when Emma appears in her dressing gown.

'Hey, I've just been looking through these, Peter,' she says, holding her iPhone. 'I was wondering what you thought about them. Are they strong enough for my project?'

Peter looks tired and I wouldn't blame him if he suggests they look at the photos tomorrow, but he puts down his glass and taking the phone from her says, 'Talk me through them.'

'Budge up, Nan,' she says, and plonks herself between us, scrolling through the photos which I have to say are brilliant (I know, I know I'm biased). Peter seems genuinely impressed and as they talk about the light and the composition and the structure I join in and Emma seems quite surprised at my contribution.

'Your nana was the best artist at college,' Peter says. 'That's where you get it from.'

'I know, she's almost as cool as you,' she says, and winks at me. She then takes my glass of wine with the few precious dregs left and knocks it back.

'Hey, Peter, that's some good shit,' she says.

'It sure is.' He smiles.

Later, in bed, we talk about Emma's photos and Peter says he thinks she has a real talent.

'Is that why you let her play with your camera?' I say, giggling.

'I nearly died when she picked it up,' he sighs. 'I was worried she'd change the settings or drop it, but as it happens she discovered a few things about it that I didn't know. So it just shows you.'

377

I'm amazed, he must have really struggled with that yet never gave anything away.

'That was kind of you, to hold your breath and let a sixteen-year-old mess with your favourite, profanely expensive camera.'

'Yes, but you made me think about the way I am when you came to stay in Oxford the first time. You said that I wasn't used to people messing with my things and if I had a family I wouldn't be able to be so precious. And I thought if I'm going to be with Rosie and be part of her family life I'd better damn well get used to people messing with my stuff.'

The following morning I wake later than usual to the smell of something cooking downstairs and at first I'm alarmed. Who the hell is in my kitchen? Then I remember that Peter's here and so are the girls, which fills me with joy and I leap out of bed, put on my dressing gown and rush downstairs. I walk in the kitchen to be greeted by Peter at the stove wearing my pink apron.

'Good morning, darling, we're having pancakes,' he says. 'The girls requested it.'

I go into the living room where both girls are lying across a sofa each on their phone and I return to the kitchen smiling.

'The great Peter Moreton, famous photographer, world traveller, light-chaser, is in the kitchen cooking breakfast for my grandchildren,' I say, going up to him and putting my arms around him, my cheek resting on his back.

'And I'd rather be here than anywhere else on earth,' he sighs.

I set the table as he makes pancake after pancake, piling them on a plate, and I think about how much he always wanted children and how he'd told me he even envied his friends taking their children to the dentist. And as I pour the orange juice I realise that it's *not* having children that changed Peter. When he was married he wanted children, but they were one of the few things he couldn't have in life, and that's why he appreciates what he might have had – and what he lost. But it's only now that he's ready – he has the time, the commitment and a new-found selflessness for kids in his life.

'A tower of pancakes awaits,' he calls, and the girls squeal and come running into the kitchen.

We all sit round the table and Peter tells the girls about his time selling doughnuts on the beaches of St-Tropez, working on yachts at Cannes, and his dream to paint in Paris.

The girls sit transfixed, listening to his stories and tucking into their food.

'Nan told me that you guys used to talk about going to Paris together. So why don't you go now?'

'That's an idea.' Peter smiles and looks at me.

I smile back. 'Yeah, that's not a bad idea, Em.'

Chapter Thirty-One

When Anna arrives late on Sunday evening the girls are permanently glued to their phones in the living room, so I make a pot of tea and we sit at the kitchen table together.

Peter drove back to Oxford late afternoon, offering email support to Emma for her project and promising to come back soon to work with her on it. Meanwhile, Anna had returned to her house with James to find his parents waiting anxiously on the doorstep. They are apparently now fussing round him which has irritated Anna.

'I was glad of an excuse to get out of the house and come for the girls. I hate people in my house,' she says.

'Oh, Anna, you're terrible, they're his parents. Just

think how you'd feel if it were Emma or Katie, you'd want to be with them,' I say. 'I've told you before, you need to try and put yourself in other people's shoes ... it will make you a more tolerant, and dare I say more pleasant person?'

'I wouldn't go as far as that,' she says, self-mocking. Anna's always been able to laugh at herself – it's her redeeming feature.

Everyone's relieved that James is going to be okay and Anna has a little weep – she's tired and I just sit and listen while she tells me all about it.

'Well, you'll be glad to know everything's been fine here,' I say as I pour the tea into two cups. 'The girls are great and we had a lovely evening watching Katie dance ... Peter enjoyed it too,' I add, looking at her. I am determined to mention him, he was wonderful with me and the girls and turned a potentially awful, worrying time into a fun one.

She looks back at me and I can see she's uncomfortable. 'I was really scared yesterday,' she says. 'I just thought how awful it would be to lose James. I love him, you see?'

I nod, reaching out to touch her hand across the table.

'I've been confused. I wanted James to come and live with us because I was scared of losing him and then yesterday I just thought, Oh God I could lose him anyway. And I couldn't bear to think about it, but the thing that upset me after the prospect of his death was the idea that I'd be alone. And I thought about you and how lonely you must have been when Dad died.'

I nod. 'Yes, but I had you and Isobel and the rest of the family.'

'I know, and I'd have the girls, but could I really spend the rest of my life with no one for myself? I thought a lot about it while I was waiting in the hospital and I kept thinking about you ... and Peter. I don't want you to be lonely, Mum.'

'I was prepared to be alone for ever, you know. I didn't go out and look for someone when your dad died, Anna ... Peter just kind of turned up in my life and it feels like fate.'

'I know, I just think it's worried me because I always felt that you and Dad were soulmates, you two were so good together. It scared me to think that you found the one for you and now you're with someone else. And if even you can love someone else, then I have to question true love. Does "the right one" even exist?'

'No, there's no such thing as "the one". There are probably lots of "the ones" for everybody. I loved your dad, but he wasn't the *only* love of my life.'

I think back to Mike, in our sitting room, who'd turned out to be as solid and reliable as my mother had predicted: *If I was with you and we found out we were having*

383

a baby the first thing I'd do is ask you to marry me, he'd said. And it was at that moment I began to feel something for Mike. He was saying what I'd wanted Peter to say. The right words, the right time, the wrong man. And the autumn sunshine sank lower into a crisp blue sky as my summer with Peter faded, and lovely Mike with his kind eyes, steady job and reliable love offered me everything I needed.

'So do you love Peter?' Anna is saying, bringing me back to the present with a jolt.

'Yes, I do. And he feels like "the one" now, at this time in my life, in the same way your dad was "the one" back then. I've told you before, I still love your dad, being with Peter doesn't change that, but I'm not ready yet to give up on the idea of another love in my life.'

'Mum, I'm sorry. I know I can be a bit full on ... I just blurt out stuff I think without really considering it from someone else's point of view. It breaks my heart when you talk about "second chances", and I want you to love again. No one wants to think their life's over or their legs are going to give up any minute.'

'Because they are not,' I say in a mock stern voice.

She laughs. 'And I think Peter's good for you ...'

'Do you?'

'Yes. I think he genuinely cares, and he makes you happy, what else is there?'

'You're right, it's no more complicated than that ... and thank you, darling, that means a lot.'

I am so happy; dare I say it seems that Anna is finally beginning to accept my relationship? I know there will be dark and shade along the way, but I'm positive and it feels good. I hope that seeing me move forward and living for today will help her to move on with her own life, and ultimately feel more independent and at peace within her own relationships, too.

Chapter Thirty-Two

I've decided to take the bull by the horns and for Christmas I'm planning a Boxing Day gathering with all the family, including Peter.

I told Anna she can like it or lump it but Peter's here to stay and she said 'good,' which both stunned and delighted me. We're in her kitchen – I've just dropped Katie and Emma off from school and we are sorting out our plans for the festive season. James is on the mend now – his injuries weren't as bad as initially feared. He had some broken bones and was shaken up, as was Anna.

'James's injuries scared me to death, Mum, and I still feel like everything's falling from my grasp. I can't keep all my plates spinning,' she says.

'I know, sweetie, it's called being a mum. You're trying to keep everyone and everything safe – even your own mother! But there are times when those plates just have to fall, don't beat yourself up about it.'

She smiles. 'I saw Peter's picture, the one he did of you. Emma got it up on screen for me to see.'

I almost died. 'Oh no, not the one of me on the bed . . . he hasn't put *that* on the internet, has he?'

'What? No, the one when you were seventeen in the slums in Hulme. God, Mum, what do you mean the one of you on the bed? What the bloody hell have you been doing with him now?'

'Nothing . . . I was going to say, if there *are* any pictures of me on a bed on the internet – it's not . . . me.'

At this point Emma walks in. 'Nan, WTF? You're not posting bedroom pics of yourself on the net?'

'No, I'm not. Honestly, your mum misunderstood what I was saying.' I smile at Emma, ignoring Anna's look that says *Oh no I didn't*.

'Anyway, I just wanted to ask if you'll come over on Boxing Day?'

Anna nods. 'Lovely, yes.'

'I'm also inviting Peter and I want you to play nice,' I say, looking straight at her.

'Okay, okay, I'll be lovely and kind and make everyone feel at home.'

'Don't, that would be weird, just be yourself,' I say, and she giggles.

'Peter's cool,' Emma's saying. 'I told our photography teacher about the photo of you, Nan, and he was well impressed. He says Peter's a really famous photographer and he's asked if he might come and do a talk. You can come too, Nan.'

'Looks like Nan might be famous too with her bedroom pics. I'd get her to check her showbiz diary, Hugh Hefner's booked her for January,' Anna says under her breath.

Emma pulls a horrified face and leaves the room and as Anna puts the kettle on Isobel arrives.

'You look good, Mum,' she says, giving me a hug. 'I haven't seen you for a few days, are you enjoying your time off? Do you want to come back to work yet?'

'Oh no, I'll come in if you need me, but I've been busy.'

'Doing what?'

'Oh, exploring possibilities . . . new ideas.'

'Really? Ooh, get her exploring her possibilities,' Anna laughs, putting tea bags into three mugs.

'Yes, get me! I'm not too old for possibilities. One day you'll be my age and you will wonder what might have been . . . and if you're lucky, you'll be excited about what's going to be.'

She puts the mugs on the counter top.

'Yeah . . . I like that. Let's drink to what's going to be.' We all clink our mugs and sip our tea and I reach out my hands and hold theirs across the kitchen counter.

'For the first time I'm actually thinking about next year and the one after that in a positive way . . . I'm happy, and that's okay. I don't feel guilty about feeling happy. Your dad would want that for all of us.'

They both nod and Isobel squeezes my arm. 'It's all good, Mum.'

'So you and Richard will come over on Boxing Day too?'

'Of course, if only to keep an eye on Anna and make sure she behaves. But don't worry, she's got nothing against Peter, she told me she'd have been just as vile, bitter and resentful about *anyone* you went out with.'

'Ah, that's sweet,' I say sarcastically, my head on one side, smiling at Anna.

They both laugh as we finish our tea and make final arrangements for Boxing Day.

'So I want you all to come at two p.m. prompt,' I say as I leave. 'Oh, and I'll have an announcement to make.'

'What?' Isobel calls after me.

'You'll have to wait until everyone's together and I can tell you all at once,' I say, taking my coat from the hook in the hall. I wander back towards the kitchen where they are both still at the counter and pop my head round the door. 'And FYI, as Emma would say, if you don't approve of what I have to tell you – then LFOL!'

It's been a lovely Christmas so far. Isobel and Richard joined us for lunch at Anna's yesterday and Peter called me on my mobile in the afternoon to say Happy Christmas. I'm aware I still need to take this gently, for him as much as the girls, and for me too, because Christmas is about memories and family and Mike's chair is empty. It will get easier, but I know he's with me. I see him when I look up into the night sky and he tells me I must decide what I want next. I think I've finally worked it out. I'm excited and in the words of my granddaughters, I'm 'going for it'.

Peter has arrived and everyone's in the living room with drinks and nibbles and Corrine's turned up with a bottle of bubbly. I'm wearing red lipstick for the first time in for ever and Katie's just told me I look 'hot'. I'm feeling like a supermodel. I think I'll find some high heels in the New Year sales and start strutting my stuff – I always said heels aren't me, but I'm discovering a new me and I think she'd look hot in heels. I sit on the arm of Peter's chair as he chats with Greg. I can see the teenager is impressed – Peter's attained a certain 'cool' celebrity status with the younger ones since the last family gathering. Emma is going round with her tablet showing everyone the photo of me when I was seventeen and Peter is beaming. He's bought gifts for everyone, but as I was busy getting the drinks and nibbles I'm not sure what he's bought for whom until Anna grabs me when I'm alone in the kitchen chopping cucumber.

'Mum, did you tell Peter we're United fans?'

She almost shouts this in my face and I see her neck is mottled, which is a red flag to me. My heart sinks: oh God, what now?

'Er, I may have told him, why?'

'Because he's only gone and booked a box at Old Trafford for all of us – and you and him too.'

'Oh – is that good?'

'Yes! I've never been in a box before . . . James and the girls are so excited.'

'Good, good, when is the match?' I ask.

'February.'

'Oh, I might not be able to make it, but you'll still go with him, won't you?'

'Why, you're not ill, are you?'

'No . . . and stop asking me if I'm ill. Just because I'm in my sixties don't assume everything I do revolves around some oncoming ailment. I'm not dead yet.'

'Sorry, I've just been a bit stressed recently, worrying about James, then Isobel, and now you're behaving weirdly.'

'What do you mean "worrying about Isobel"?' My radar is alerted.

'Oh ... I just mean the way she left the teaching job and now she doesn't know if she wants to work in the shop or not.'

I see a flicker and wonder whether that's really what she meant. I make a mental note to talk to Isobel later.

'Well, that's up to Isobel. I've said it before, but I really think we should be taking on new staff now.'

'Can't you come in a couple of days a week? I know you're trying to leave, but ... Oh. Has Peter asked you to marry him?'

I don't answer her question. 'You know, Peter only ever wanted to belong. He never had a family. He wanted children, but he and his wife couldn't have kids,' I say.

Anna's face softens. 'I didn't realise.'

'He gets on so well with the girls and I know he's not Dad, but he'd be there for you and Isobel too.'

She half-smiles, which is a big result.

'I think Peter will be around quite a bit, and I know he'd appreciate some support from everyone,' I say, taking a platter from the cupboard and laying thick slices of Christmas ham onto a large plate. The ham is laced with zingy orange and aromatic cloves and the fragrance reminds me of my home as a child at Christmas. And I think of Margaret presiding over the turkey, queen of bloody everything, her life swallowed up by disappointment. She wasn't happy with my father, and she didn't want her life for me, and I know she only kept Peter's visit and his letters from me out of love to keep me safe from any more hurt. As mothers we do our best to put our arms around our kids, determined to keep them warm, happy and safe. It's our job and we all do it in the ways we think best. And sometimes we make flawed decisions, but that's okay, because those choices are made with love and as long as there's love everything will work out in the end.

Chapter Thirty-Three

Later, when everyone has almost finished eating, I go into the lounge and find Isobel to interrogate her. I tell her Anna mentioned something about being worried about her and I ask if she's okay.

'I'm fine. You know our Anna, she worries about everyone and everything.' Then she leans in and whispers, 'Anyway, Mum, is the announcement that you and Peter are getting married?'

'Ah, you're about to find out.' I wink and step out into the middle of the room. 'Hello, hello, I want to talk to you all,' I say loudly, addressing everyone around me. I've retouched my lipstick and I'm clanging my knife on my glass as they sit around with crammed buffet plates.

'Okay ... well, I have some news, but first I just want

to say I was married to a wonderful man for forty-six years and I was very, very happy. Dad will always be with us and no one's ever going to take that away or try to replace him, but recently I met Peter again, and I believe that Peter too will make me very happy.' I hear a collective gasp, and Anna smiles; she thinks she knows what I'm going to say next.

'But before I live with another man, I want to live with me first.'

'You go, girl,' shouts Emma with a whoop and a tear springs to my eye. She gets me, my granddaughter, she always has.

I smile at her and she raises her glass. I look away before my chin trembles and I start to cry.

'So, as of next week I'm formally handing the business over to you girls as Dad and I always planned. I'll some- times be available to help out if you're busy, but now it's time for you to fly and for me to fly too. I'm going to do the things I've always wanted to do but thought I'd left too late – like paint and draw and travel.

'Then I may, at some point in the future, sell the house, and buy something smaller. I might live on a houseboat, erect a tepee in someone's back garden, live in a hippie commune in Cornwall and call myself Sunflower – who knows? I'm just going to see what happens, because I want to test Peter's theory that life just has a way of working out.' I smile again at Peter and he winks at me.

'So, on Christmas Eve, on Dad's advice, I booked a world trip. I'm starting in New Zealand then flying to Thailand, on to Vietnam, India and the Middle East. After that I'll probably go by boat to Italy and then take a train to Paris, where six or seven months into my adventure, I hope to meet up with Peter.'

I hear some gasps and Corrine, always the drama queen, screams.

'How long will you be away?' Isobel asks.

I take a large glug of my wine and continue. 'A few months, perhaps as long as a year, depending on how long my money . . . and my back last,' I laugh.

Emma's second whoop is followed swiftly by Katie's and everyone seems smiley and positive. Even Anna isn't actually scowling at this, but she looks surprised.

'I want you all to know that though this trip is the most selfish, stupid, inconsiderate and foolhardy thing I've ever done, I have to do it – because if I don't do it now, I never will. I also want you all to know that the only reason I can be so pigheaded and ridiculous at my age is because I have a wonderful, supportive family who I love very much. Oh, and because Peter's agreed to look after Lily for me!'

'See you in Paris,' Peter says, raising his glass. He's been behind me all the way with my crazy 'Grey Gap

Year' plan. He understands it's my time and I need to do all the things I wanted to back when we were teenagers. Peter also understands that I can't accept his proposal of marriage – not yet, anyway.

I love him and I'm certainly not ruling marriage out, but before I consider sharing my life with another person again I need to find out about me. I want to know what side of the bed I like to sleep on, whether I prefer planes or trains, boutique hotels or hostels? Champagne or beer? I don't know because I've always lived with other people, from my parents' home to a life with Mike and the girls. Now I want to see how I fit in the world through my own eyes in my own time.

'Woohoo! YOLO, Nan!' Emma is shouting and clapping her hands at my news. I'm not quite sure what YOLO means, but I think it's good.

Peter is smiling proudly at the side of me. I think I may be a little tipsy but I don't care, I can't stop beaming and I look over to see Anna who's looking at me and saying a silent 'love you'.

When everyone's gone home and Peter and I are alone in the aftermath of discarded wrapping paper and goodbye kisses, he pours us both a glass of champagne.

'That went surprisingly well,' I say, clinking glasses. This time there was no drama, Anna not only accepted that Peter would be staying the night, she asked us both round for brunch tomorrow. She also suggested they keep in touch while I'm away. 'You know what she's like,' I heard her say. 'She'll be sending weird messages with predictive text like "I've been taken" when what she meant to say was "I've been to the Taj Mahal". You'll be calling the Embassy and I'll be having kittens.'

Peter then told her he was setting up some computer tracking thingy that will follow where I am and if she wanted he would link it to her computer too so she would also know where I was.

'Our Anna must have LOVED the idea of her computer tracking me all over the world,' I laugh.

'Yes, it seemed to bond us even more than the box at United,' he laughs. He's doing this for me and I know in his way he's trying to make it up to me for the past.

We sit together on the sofa, toasting the future while looking through old photos. Our past is never far from our present.

I show him photos of the kids when they were little, and more recent ones of the grandchildren as babies. Every time one of us says 'ah', Lily, who's sitting between us, wags her tail slowly, assuming naturally that we're talking about her.

'Me and Lily are going to be best pals,' he says, tickling her neck. 'And I'll keep an eye on everyone else for you while you're away,' he adds, gazing at photos of little Anna and Isobel making snowmen.

'I know you will, and it's you being here that's given me the courage to go. I know you feel you let me down, but we were just kids caught up in emotions we didn't understand and both too young to cope when the grown-up stuff came along. I feel like you waited for your cue and turned up in my life when I needed you – and you were all grown up and helped me find my way back in the dark.' I sip on my champagne, it's cold and tingly, and I feel blissfully happy. For the first time in a very long time there are no shadows. We put away the photos and finish our glasses of champagne, both exhausted, invigorated and looking forward to what happens next. My life is opening out onto new horizons, and who knows where they will lead. Peter may not be for ever, but he's shown me a new happy ending – made me realise that I am capable of anything, regardless of my age.

Finally, Peter and I exchange our Christmas gifts. We chose to save this for when we are alone and I'm glad we did as, along with a beautiful silver necklace that says 'Bon Voyage' on a tiny gold heart, Peter gives me the framed picture he drew of me. I love it. If you'd told me that Peter Moreton would finally get to draw me naked one day, I would never have believed it. And if you'd told me I was

the one who asked him to do it I'd think you were crazy.
I hold the picture on my lap and gaze at it, tracing the
lines over the glass frame, seeing myself reflected back, the
older Rosie seeing the younger Rosie both finally in sync.

'This makes me feel so special,' I say, contemplating
the soft, undulating curves, the strong, straight back, the
eyes filled with fresh hope and sparkle. 'I'll put it on my
bedroom wall and when I wake up in the morning with
aches and pains and think about how old I am, I'll only
have to look at this and see how *beautiful* I am.'

My gift to Peter is the Paris map we once pored over
together – it's covered in sticky tape and wrapped in old
newspapers from 1968 which Emma searched out on the
internet for me.

'It's a piece of you and me,' he says, running his beautiful long, slender fingers slowly from the Arc de Triomphe
all the way down to the Gare de Lyon.

He looks up. 'You know I'd come with you on the
whole journey if you wanted me to?'

'I know, but I have to do this alone. It's my journey,
I have to lay some ghosts, see some stars, sleep under a
faraway moon and see a foreign sunset through my own
eyes.'

He hugs me and I feel warm and safe and I wonder
for a moment if I'm doing the right thing leaving it all
behind, even if it is only for six months.

'Peter – I'm excited, but a bit scared.'

'Scared is good. There'd be something wrong with you if you weren't. You're spending a long time on the other side of the world. You won't see your family for months ...'

'When you put it like that I want to cancel it all – where's the phone?' I half joke.

'You won't cancel,' he says, leaning back to look at me, his fingers forming the square, mentally photographing me. 'My Rosie's back, the one with fire in her belly and excitement in her eyes ... Chase the light, draw everything you see and see everything you possibly can.' He stops a moment, his eyes are damp, red-rimmed. It will be hell to be apart again. But how can I stay and carry on as I was? Peter has sprinkled his magic again and life is slowly opening out onto new horizons.

He kisses me and I can already see those stars twinkling in that dark sky in New Zealand, the sunset melting over India and a dream coming true in Paris. We're still in love with the people we once were before life came between us and now it's time to discover who we are now.

'Fly away, Rosie,' Peter says, stroking my face. 'Go out there and do what you have to do and see what you have to see, and know I'll be waiting for you in Place Saint-Germain-des-Pres, at our little Parisian coffee shop.'

We'll visit the Paris we used to dream about long ago

as we stood in wet bus stops or in fields looking up at the stars. We'll sail down the Seine, visit Mona Lisa at her home in the Louvre and hit the top of the Eiffel Tower, then we'll look down on our city and just take her in. Some days we'll spend like teenagers staying in bed until noon in our artist's garret in Montmartre, then Peter will take photos and I'll sketch on the Parisian streets. We'll spend the afternoons lying on the grass in the sunshine eating French pastries until we're fat. Together we'll have new adventures, make new pictures and new memories. The past is what brought us here – but it won't hold us back.

Epilogue

Peter and I are enjoying coffee and croissants on a park bench in the sunshine.

The sky is incredibly blue for late autumn and though we're both wearing woolly jumpers the sun is warm on my face. The croissants are soft and buttery, still warm from the French bakery near the park and I tear mine apart, eating mouth-size morsels, the flakes so light they are melting on my tongue.

'These are the best I ever tasted,' Peter says.

'Me too, that's because they are made by a Frenchman,' I say, sipping my coffee.

It's wonderful to finally be together again. In the past few months I've been to places I'd only read about and seen things I thought I'd never see. I relished it all and appreciate the world far more than I did as a younger woman because on this trip I took nothing for granted. Every moment was a gift.

'Your emails from New Zealand were quite beautiful,' Peter says. 'I hope you did Mike proud?'

I smile. 'I hope so. The vast blackness of the night sky took my breath away.' I stayed in a hotel with windows in the roof and lay in bed under an infinite black canopy alive with shimmering stars. I felt like Mike was with me and helping me put everything into perspective. We live these lives with such big emotions, oceans of love and turmoil go into our existence and yet we're so small. We are such a minuscule part of the bigger picture and it could all be over in a moment, so we have to keep going, we must never stop chasing the light or gazing at the stars. 'I just felt this awe, a powerlessness in the presence of what looked like eternity. And I suddenly thought, it's all going to be okay, nature's got this, and I let go. You can't fight it – whatever will be, will be,' I say.

He nods, listening intently as I relive every second.

Then I tell him about a Sunday afternoon, on a train trundling past Goan beaches, children splashing in the sea, the smoke from late-afternoon cooking floating through the carriages. I share with him my memory of Phang Nga Bay at sunset, water the colour of burnt orange pooling into dense turquoise as the day dipped.

And I describe the bliss of cold beer on a hot day on the café terrace of the Uffizi art gallery, looking out over the Florence skyline.

'Sorry we didn't get to meet in Paris, darling,' I say, leaning against him, my head on his shoulder.

'Not this time, but we could hardly have missed the birth of your new grandson.' At the very mention of baby Michael my heart fills with something like warm strawberry jam.

Given her history it was a lovely but scary surprise learning about Isobel's pregnancy. I had a feeling there was something the girls weren't telling me when Anna slipped up about Isobel's 'appointment', despite Isobel saying all was fine. Anyway, Isobel and Richard had decided to try one last time for a baby and the appointments were Isobel visiting the hospital for treatment.

They didn't tell me because Isobel didn't want me to hold off going away on my trip of a lifetime and she didn't want me to go through the trauma if things didn't work out. We always protect each other, us Carter girls.

Not long after I left the UK Isobel and Richard told Peter the news and he was sworn to secrecy. Isobel was right, I would have been a mess for the whole nine months but I was blissfully travelling the world unaware. Meanwhile, back home Peter was there for everyone, taking Isobel to and from the hospital, ferrying

405

grandchildren, helping Anna in the shop and holding Richard's ladders during a particularly tense period with the famous loft conversion, now a nursery. I think perhaps, in my absence the others have learned to trust and rely on Peter, creating a new family dynamic involving him in their everyday lives. And when Anna called the other day to ask if she could talk to Peter I smiled from ear to ear – as I passed him the phone. Life does have a way of working stuff out after all.

Peter and I look out onto rolling fields and a feeling of pure happiness rushes through my bones. You know those rare and lovely moments when you want time to stand still, everything is right, from children, to partners to dogs, everyone's happy and healthy and the world's a wonderful place? That.

'So, Rosie, now you've seen the world – are you ready to come home to me?' Peter asks.

My heart swells then dips. I cast my eyes down, not sure how to say what I want to say. We sit for a while longer while I try to work out how to answer him.

'Peter, I love you, but ... '

'Ah, there's a but?'

'Just a little one. I want to be with you, and I have no doubts. But recently I rediscovered the flower in the rubble and I need to get to know her, just a little longer. I want to find out who she is ... '

'And her favourite flavour of ice cream?' he says, touching my cheek.

I nod, my eyes filling with tears. Peter gets me, he always has.

He runs his hands through his hair. 'Okay, I understand . . . you need to know some things before you settle down again. Perhaps I could share some ice cream tastings along the way?'

'I'd like that.'

'So, I know we have the grandchildren to think of, but – let's run away to Paris, just for a little while?'

'Yes. We owe it to those teenagers who wanted it so badly – and we're only forty-eight years too late.'

'I told you, Rosie, it's never too late,' he smiles and kisses me.

Then he takes my hand and we walk back through the park, Lily at our feet, the sun in our eyes, and Paris, as always, in our hearts.

Join us at

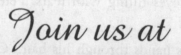

For competitions galore,
exclusive interviews with our lovely
Sphere authors, chat about
all the latest books
and much, much more.

Follow us on Twitter at
🐦 @littlebookcafe

Subscribe to our newsletter and
Like us at ⓕ/thelittlebookcafe

Read. Love. Share.
Bruce County Public Library
1243 Mackenzie Rd.
Port Elgin ON N0H 2C6